A NEW
Hope

A NEW
Hope

James Burgess

STRONG TOWER
PRESS

Strong Tower Press, PO Box 293632, Sacramento, CA 95829
http://strongtowerpress.com

Cover Art by: Whetstone Designs
Images: Kevin Carden, and Denis Ismagilov / 123RF Stock Photo
Fonts: Apostrophic Labs, and Gatis Vilaks and Evita Vilaka / DaFont.com
Interior swirl: https://www.123rf.com/profile_seamartini'>seamartini / 123RF Stock Photo

ISBN-978-1-942320-33-3

DEDICATED TO MY BELOVED, BEVERLY
You have been my inspiration and encouragement
for over fifty years.
Thank you for being there for when I cried
and for sharing the laughs.
Who can find a virtuous wife? For her worth is far above rubies.
The heart of her husband safely trusts her;
So he will have no lack of gain.
She does him good and not evil All the days of her life.
Proverbs 31:10-12

A New Hope Acknowledgements

Quite often we come across individuals throughout our journey that have a vital impact on our lives. Their separate paths cross ours as we zig-zag through time on this earthly terrain. Positive and negative events impress us in a manner that imprints and brings about value to our existence. They, in turn, guide us to either passively accept or become proactive in our behavior. It was considering this when I partook on the excursion which led to this story.

First and foremost, I must acknowledge the main individual responsible for the writing of *A New Hope*. This person became the most important individual to ever enter my life. I remember that day vividly, June 1, 1975. It was the day I came face-to-face with my own personal shortcomings and my only hope of personal recovery. It was the day I met Jesus Christ and He has become my closest friend.

Of course, a near second must be my beloved Beverly who introduced Him to me. She and our grandson, Reese, have put up with my nose being stuck in my laptop and what a joy to live with Reese's artistic musical influence that has challenged grandpa's writing. Thank you also must go to Micah and Caleb who always encourage their daddy. Also, a quick call out to our friend, Pam, who always challenges me with the scriptures.

I shared with a church friend, Bill Hannold, who directed me to Paula Bicknell, a fellow author who encouraged me to go to a writer's conference. I want to also thank Inspire Christian Writers who pointed me to my critique group. I have learned so much from them: Dana, John, Ruth, Ricky, Frieda, Cecille, Beth, Florentine, Erin, Larry, and a few others who briefly entered my life. Dana Sudboro, Ruth, and Erin encouraged me to submit a short-story to the Inspire Press Anthology from there I met Michelle Janene Murray, also an editor and a publisher (Strong Tower Press). Michelle introduced me to her sister, Danielle Whetstone, the artistic cover artwork, and to my wonderful editor, Susan.

There have been many more too numerous to name who the Lord has placed into my writing journey down a path to give our Lord Jesus Christ glory.

Without clear research, a fiction writer will only tell fables made up in his head. It is with this in mind I want to give a nod to my own pastor, Doug Smith, who shared with our congregation his opportunity to minister at the mission in Kansas City. A special thanks to Springfield, MO, Victory Mission director, Jason Hynson, for the hour and a half he took out of his busy schedule to speak with me over the phone. Jason shared his heart and vision.

Thank you, Pastor Michael Overton of First Baptist Church of Springfield for allowing me to speak of the unique church and its outreach to the community. I know firsthand about that and the wonders found downstairs. And, lastly, thank you Ms Darlene Smith from the General Service Office of Alcoholics Anonymous and A.A.W.S. Inc. for allowing me to quote a few of the Twelve Steps that have saved thousands of lives and gave so many *A New Hope*. May we all find a new hope in the Lord.

CHAPTER ONE

Late April 2011, Kansas City

A single ray of sunlight blazed through the window and struck Hope in the eye. She squinted, pulled her hand up to shield its glare, and raised her head off the dingy pillow. With slow movements, she pushed off the bedcover, sat up, and looked at her discarded pile of clothes on the floor. Then rubbed her temples. The clothes and the jackhammering between her ears had become the norm. She groaned, "I really tied one on last night and my mouth tastes like a sewer."

Hope braced her hands on the edge of the bed to steady herself before standing as the scene in front of her tilted. She ran for the bathroom and made it in time to lunge for the toilet. After several moments of hanging over the bowl, she lifted her head, brushed her tangled, shoulder-length, strawberry blond hair out of her face, and looked around the facilities.

The acrid odor of decay attacked her nose. Black mold ran around the base of the bathtub and a rancid stench hung in the air. Her knees stuck to an indeterminate sticky substance on the floor. She looked around, and her insides roiled one more time. Again, she leaned over the commode. This time she offered up nothing but bile to the hang-over gods, as the gagging and dry-heaves commenced.

Though familiar with this situation, Hope had never experienced it in a place this shabby. Why hadn't she gone to a nicer hotel? After all, she could afford it since she owned a lucrative business, and had closed a major deal last night. So how did she get here? A memory played at the edge of her mind. A celebration. But, could you call it celebrating if you're alone?

Treachery. Sedition. Loss of trust. Now a solitary existence. A shudder ran across her. That's how she got here. If only Kenny and Janie had not…

A sheen of perspiration formed on her forehead as Hope tamped down her bitterness. Resentment always put her into messes like this one.

She grabbed a folded towel from the chrome shelf and dabbed her brow. "At least this is somewhat clean." Wrapping it around herself, she stepped over to the sink. Water-rusted stains pointed to the drain. A face in the mirror returned a stare. Hope didn't recognize the woman who looked back at her. Her blood-shot, caramel eyes told the story.

Hope grabbed a wad of toilet paper from the dispenser. With deliberate movements, she removed all the smudged lipstick and smeared mascara and then stepped back into the bedroom.

She gasped at the chaos of the room—several Styrofoam cups scattered about, a tipped over whiskey bottle on the nightstand, and clothes strewn about. Why was her blouse draped over the lamp shade? What happened last night?

If she only had one of her large bath sheets from home instead of this excuse for a towel. Still, she held the cotton sheet to herself. After retrieving her pile of clothes, she hurried to the bathroom where she slipped on her undergarments and shimmied into her wrinkled red cocktail dress. The retching threatened again when the odors invaded her nasal passages.

"I swear to God. I'll never drink this much again." Hope rubbed her temples and smirked at herself in the mirror. "Yeah, until next time."

After picking up her high heels, she eased open the bathroom door and walked to the exit. She seized the knob and then spotted her knee-length suede coat crumpled at the foot of the door. Hope bent to pick it up.

Tink.

The hard-plastic case of her cell phone clicked against the flask in her jacket's side pocket. She gritted her teeth.

Hope slid through the opening, and out into the dark hallway hoping to not disturb the neighboring hotel guests. With her fingertips grazing the walls, she worked her way to the stairs and down two flights to the glassed-in front entrance. One last step brought her to the sidewalk where she leaned against the graffitied wall, and closed her eyes. She released the breath she'd held and lowered her shoulders.

The heat from the afternoon bathed her face. She sensed the sun's brightness through her closed eyelids. In an unhurried manner, Hope opened them and gaped at the spectacle before her. Broken down vehicles and glass bottles cluttered the parking lot.

"Where am I?"

She scanned the surrounding lot. Did someone steal the Mercedes? Another memory flitted across her mind of her car with a flat tire under the overpass. Why did she agree with William Scranton to meet him and his wife at the little café in *that* part of Kansas City to celebrate the closing of their deal?

Realization dawned on Hope. Scranton wanted to meet close to his plant. Hope fumbled for her cell phone and brought it out of her jacket. She switched it on. A light flickered across the screen and then went blank. She harrumphed and shoved it back into her pocket and walked without direction.

After about two blocks, she stopped. She looked up at the street sign. "I really have no idea where I am." Without her cell phone she had no clue.

High heels clacking, Hope ignored the blight while continuing up the street. Nerves on edge, she examined the neighborhood. Another shudder raced over her. How could a woman of her caliber end up in a place like this? After another block, she stopped again and looked up the street between the buildings. Hope stared at the skyline of Kansas City. Her shoulders sagged with the weight of upcoming dread. "Who knows how far I'll have to walk until I find my car."

A gurgle rumbled in her stomach as it began to rebel again, and she hurried to the alley, then heaved several times. She reached to her pocket for a handkerchief and came up empty, then patted her sides. Where was her purse? She glanced down. Could she have left it in her car? How stupid. Another glance down and she scrunched up her face, brought her arm up, and wiped her sleeve across her mouth. She would pay the price to dry clean her favorite coat.

Her gut rumbled its emptiness and the heat bore down on her scalp. "I could sure use some food and a great cup of coffee. She shaded her eyes and smiled. Too bad Loriann couldn't bring her a latté and scone right now. A cynical laugh burst from her at her predicament. Her stomach grumbled again.

Hope marched forward trying to formulate a plan to get to her car. How could she keep allowing herself to get so drunk she lost all sense of the situation? Her commemoration of every big transaction needed to stop.

Her feet ached from the three-inch heels. Hope stopped—placed a hand against the building—and yanked the shoes off. "Ah, much better." The warm concrete beneath her feet soothed them as she continued down the street. Queasy again and light-headed, her empty stomach protested once more.

Hope looked down the sidewalk where a large group of filthy, shady characters milled around in front of a building impeding her way. She would have to maneuver past them to get by. Her dry throat hindered her ability to swallow. She trudged forward. Her ears picked up the unmistakable sound of someone speaking into a microphone.

She checked both directions and stepped off the curb to cross to the other side, then darted her eyes to the crowd. Would anyone she knew see her? Once close enough, she heard the harangue…preaching? Here?

Hope watched as a long line moved through the open front doors to what looked like a cafeteria. A file of unkept and filthy people shuffled forward. Homeless? Likely. A food line? Probably. Hope's stomach announced its emptiness. Free food? Why not.

She drew in a deep breath and inhaled the fragrance of sausage gravy. Her belly cried out again. The thought of food carried her a step closer. Could she sneak in dressed like this? She gazed down at her cocktail dress. As her nose came close to her coat, she pulled back. Alcohol and body odor. Could she fit in with the others in line? How ironic. After slipping her heels back on, she made her decision. "Why not? I'm hungry."

CHAPTER TWO

Hope found herself wedged between two older gentlemen in a crowd of around fifty homeless men and women who meandered toward the open door of the well-organized lunchroom. The room resembled a school cafeteria with the tables set for diners.

One of the men bumped her. She crossed one arm over her midsection and brought her other hand to cover her nose.

And yet, knowing her own plight, she fit right in. She hoped this wouldn't take long because her stomach couldn't handle the odor much longer.

The line crept forward until she stepped just inside the front door. Her rancid breath joined that of others around her, and she mumbled, "Why couldn't I be in line at Gardelo's Restaurant?"

Close enough now to smell the hot delicacies, she saw the tables lining the wall of the long room. At the end, an open kitchen door revealed a large cooking area full of stainless-steel stoves, carts filled with full plates of scrambled eggs, and strips of bacon. Next to it, more baskets of mouth-watering, flaky biscuits laid alongside a platter of crumpets.

The old man behind her expressed his opinion to no one in particular. "Man, that looks filling. It sure does smell good."

Hope glanced back at her fellow, soon-to-be, diner. "It makes me think of E. Sunshine Street Café in Springfield and its filling, morning cuisine. All we need now is a big pot of coffee." She craned her neck and sighted the two containers set on another rolling cart. Hopefully they held coffee and not hot tea. The paper cups already sat on the tables.

She looked back over her shoulder and saw the sun and sparse clouds. "It's nice they're still serving breakfast." A chuckle followed. "After all, it's the most important meal of the day."

"I'm glad they still have some left. Sometimes if you get here this late, they run out of food." The old man rubbed his ungroomed beard.

When it was Hope's turn to find a seat, she picked a corner near a side door in case she needed an escape. She settled in, straightened the plastic utensils, and waited for the attendant.

The server pulled the cart to the edge of the table and set a plate with eggs, bacon, and a biscuit in front of her.

"Do you want gravy on your biscuit?" The scruffy-faced attendant smiled a toothless grin.

Hope extended her plate out to the server. He slopped a ladle-full of congealed, white sauce with sausage bits mixed in.

"Thanks."

The man nodded.

Another attendant wheeled a second cart over. Hope seized the paper cup from in front of her plate and poured herself a boiling cup of liquid wake-me-up. To continue her illusion and distance herself from the depression of her day's situation, she pressed her shoulder against the wall, and leaned as far from the rabble as she could while still in her chair.

Her eyes roamed across the throng. Another whisper escaped before she could stop herself. "What a useless mass of humanity. Don't these people want to better themselves? You will never see me end up in this sad state."

Hope heard wheezing and then a hard croup-like cough. She turned and looked over her other shoulder at a man also slumped against the wall at the next table. He wore a filthy, dark-blue peacoat and thick spectacles. He hacked again and tried to cover his mouth with a grimy hand.

"Sorry, miss. I'll try not to cough in your direction."

Covering her food, she moved into protect mode. Was he contagious? Visions of germs floating through the air brought a shiver across her body. How could people fall into this lifestyle? She wanted to sympathize, but couldn't come close. *It just takes a little effort on their part to clean up and get a job.*

Movement to her left drew her attention. A man who appeared around five-foot-nine or ten, knelt to speak with a lady who clutched her belongings to her chest. Hope watched him reach out and let his hand rest on the woman's shoulder, then he kissed her on the forehead. *Why would he be so gentle with someone who looked like her?*

The dirty woman smiled and patted his hand.

Hope grimaced but followed his progression around the room.

He moved to the next person, grinned, grabbed the man's hand, and shook it with vigor. He gave the man a fist bump like she had seen men sometimes do, while they carried on a conversation.

Hope continued to watch him. He engaged the people—a simple smile one minute—a frown or a nod in the next. She focused on his face. Heat washed over her when she noted his light brown hair and his muscular arms, and the way his shirt rested across his chest. He looked to be near her age. "Nice." She released a long, deep sigh.

"He is a kind man," the man sitting behind her spoke.

Startled by the remark, Hope spun around and gaped at the older gentleman.

"I guess he is attractive for a man." The frail man's brows raised as he grinned.

With her teeth clamped shut, Hope turned back around. She stared down at her plate, grasped her plastic fork, and shoveled food into her mouth. Besides the desire to crawl into a hole, she wanted to be able to slip out of this situation and find her car.

But when she heard footfalls approaching, she twisted on the chair enough to follow the progress of the younger, attractive man. From the angle where she now sat, and though she tried to focus on her plate, she could still see the greeter wore a nice pair of Dockers Overton men's shoes and well-creased Dickies khakis. She turned enough to see him standing in front of the man who sat behind her. The greeter's actions appeared quite relaxed and natural despite the environment.

"Good afternoon, Gus. Is everything okay today?"

"Doin' the best I can under the circumstances, Pastor Steve," Gus said.

Pastor Steve squatted and stared at Gus. "Are you taking your meds like you're supposed to?"

"Yes, but it's getting harder. I need to work."

How could this younger man be a minister? Hope regarded the pastor's profile and what appeared to be a genuine smile. A man so attractive and not wearing a ring had to have a girlfriend already. It didn't matter. Not my type. Obviously religious like Mom.

For a moment, she glanced at Gus and watched a crinkled look of merriment pass over Gus's eyes. Her stomach dropped. She glared as she shook her head. Would Gus get the message?

But he didn't. "Pastor Steve, this is my new neighbor, Ms…?" He finished with a coughing fit. He covered his mouth and turned his face away.

The pastor turned to her and extended his hand. "Hello, new neighbor. I'm Steve Burrow." His smile matched the sparkle in his sky-blue eyes, which danced around and then rested on her.

Hope gulped and stammered. "H-Hope Sparks, pleased to meet you, Pastor Steve." After clearing her throat, she continued. "I don't really belong here. I was just passing by and was hungry."

"You're welcome anytime, Ms. Sparks. And I love your name. We welcome hope. We will always want a spark of hope." Steve grinned.

She crinkled her nose, bared her teeth, and groaned.

The man raised his hands palms up, shrugged his shoulders, then turned back to Gus who continued to hack. "It's getting worse isn't it, buddy?"

"Yeah, I don't think it will be much longer." Gus looked over at Hope. "I contracted the HIV virus from a needle during my addiction to heroin. Recreational drugs took me down this path. I was an investor for a large corporation and lost my job. I guess I was good at it though since they sometimes get in touch with me for consulting. It helps out at least a bit."

"Oh Gus, I forgot to tell you." Pastor Steve touched the man's filthy jacket. "Turk called me and wants you to drop in at the office. He needs you to help answer why this current trend is jumping all around. He also said you forgot to pick up your last check."

"God bless that man. He has been such a good friend despite my downfall. I didn't forget my check." Another coughing spell hit him. "You know as well as I do. He is trying to slip me some extra bankroll, and it's mostly from his own pocket." Tears ran down Gus's unshaven, gray cheeks. "Pastor Steve, you once told me, if I turned everything over to Jesus, He would carry the burden when needed." Gus looked over at Hope. "And that is what happened when this addict gave himself to God."

"You're still consulting? If you're as good as I'm hearing, I wonder if I could pillage your vault of knowledge about the direction of certain stock-futures, sometime." Was he a reflection of the direction she was headed if she continued to celebrate every little success with a glass of wine…or two…or more?

A question by the pastor brought her back from her contemplation.

"Ms. Sparks, is there a reason why you have chosen to grace us with this visit? You look over-dressed for the rescue kitchen."

"My car had a flat last night, and I accidentally locked my purse in the trunk. I also dropped my keys in the car when I grabbed my coat, then I shut my door." Hope ducked her head. Her face and neck generated warmth. "I had closed a major deal with a client nearby. They couldn't stay after the meeting. They had an emergency involving their son. Have you heard of Scranton Corp?"

"Actually, I have. William Scranton owns it." Pastor Steve's brows creased. "An emergency with Billy? It must have not been too bad, or they would have called." He looked back at Hope. "I'm their pastor at Hope Harvest Community Church nearby in North Kansas City. William told me about a big deal that could increase their revenue. That was with you?"

A light snore drew her gaze to Gus.

Hope stared at the old man, then back at the pastor. "How bad?"

"Bad. Maybe a few more months. Sad isn't it, what addiction can do to a once productive life such as Gus's." He reached across the table and pulled the older man's jacket closed. "Now, how can I help you? Where did you leave your car?"

"It's under an overpass near a biker bar I wandered into to fill my flask." Hope scrunched up her face. "The Dusty Trail, I think."

"That's a pretty rough place and a long way in that direction." He pointed north. "You walked all this way from downtown?"

"I shouldn't have gone in the bar." Hope clenched her teeth and curled her lips. "I came about ten blocks from that way." She pointed east. "I only walked from there. I think someone gave me a ride last night. I don't remember too much. And my cell phone died."

Pastor Steve raised an eyebrow. "I will be finished here in about a half hour, and if you want to wait, I can help you find your car. Do you think you can get in once there?"

"Yes, I forgot last night about a key I have hidden away." Relieved with the offer, Hope relaxed. "I can wait."

CHAPTER THREE

Hope's eyes wandered across the bench seat to the stick shift on the floor as she climbed into the cab of Pastor Steve's truck. She couldn't remember the last time she rode in a pickup this old. Its coziness took her thoughts back to riding with Gramps out on his ranch. A peppermint scented candy-cane shaped air freshener hung from the mirror and permeated the cab. More emotional memories of Gramps and his pickup cascaded over Hope.

"This is beautiful. Is this a 1969 or '70?"

"It's a 1970. I didn't want to only restore it to its original condition. I wanted to make it who I am. So, I customized it." He rubbed his hand across the shiny wood steering wheel.

"This is beautiful. You must have paid a lot to have someone rebuild this for you." Hope ran her hand across the soft gray fabric of the interior.

"I did most of the work myself, except the upholstery." Pastor Steve smiled. "It took a couple of years to find the right chrome, baby moon rims, but I saved a lot of money by searching for used parts. Some I found at wrecking yards."

"You should be proud of what you've accomplished. I took an auto-mechanic elective in high school one year at my dad's encouragement. It helped me appreciate Baby. That's my car." She reached for the shoulder harness and not finding one, she grasped the lap belt and clinked it into place.

Hope continued, "I'm impressed. You have some abilities, similar to my brother, Josh and my ex, Kenny. They could take apart almost anything and put it back together, blindfolded. Like they did my marriage, but they couldn't piece it back the way it had been."

A tightness in her chest made it hard to breathe as the hurt returned. She hadn't spoken to her older brother in almost two years. Why did he have to take part in the betrayal? And Kenny? —she'd trusted with her heart until he shattered it. Both had called her cold and heartless. Did they think she was a quick-change artist? No. Nor were they capable of altering her personality. Was it her fault she was always the smartest in the room?

"Are you okay?" Pastor Steve broke in. "You don't look well. Let me know ahead of time if you're going to be sick, so I can pull over."

She smirked. Was he worried she'd soil his spotless truck?

The betrayal came into her mind every time she got sober after a heavy night. She used the carousing to make the pain go away. Once again, Hope tried to shake off her past. "No, I'm fine. Just some bitterness from former times."

"I'm a good listener, if you want to talk about it." He turned the ignition switch. The engine sprang to life. The sound of headers and straight tailpipes amplified the roar of the engine.

Hope could feel the vibration of the motor at her feet and against her tailbone. "Nice. My brother's first car had loud headers like these. He's also a mechanic."

They pulled out into light traffic and continued to discuss the pickup, along with his mechanical prowess.

Pastor Steve tried to maneuver the conversation back to the previous night.

"I don't care to discuss it." Besides the embarrassment of having to eat at the homeless rescue mission, she couldn't give him answers to his questions. She remembered little after entering the biker bar.

"Sorry, I thought you might want to get it out of your system." He shifted to the next gear. "You know sometimes it helps to unload to someone who doesn't have a personal investment in the circumstances."

"Thanks, but no thanks. I don't need a confessional or to unburden myself. I know what I am doing." She hoped so anyway. Lately, her carelessness had magnified. The drinking had been excessive. "So, did you start the soup kitchen?"

"Miss Rosa started it a couple of years ago. Did you see the elderly lady in the green pantsuit? She stood by the coffee cart. She still comes down, but her health isn't what it used to be."

They talked for a short bit about the feeding of the homeless and then he asked about the deal she and William Scranton had pieced together.

"Yes, it seems to be a good mesh. We have things Scranton needs and they have what Sparks System Logistics requires." Hope squirmed as she recounted the overhaul of her company. "I've had to restructure the main corporate office due to some personnel issues, remove some of the upper management team, and retrain assistants to replace top of the line leaders. I have begun to integrate some ideas from my college thesis for my PhD in Economic Law and Management."

"Why would you replace good management?" But he checked himself by lifting his palm to her. "Wait, it's none of my business." He glanced down toward the dashboard and wagged his head with slow, deliberate movements. "Wow. You have a doctorate in Economic Law and Management? I would have never thought."

Hope leaned away from him toward the side window and glared at him. She curled her lip and gave an undignified sneer. "Why? Because I'm a woman? Are you that shallow?"

"No. It's just you're so pretty and seem to dress classy," he nodded at her dress, "but seem to be—well, to be honest, you present yourself as uncaring and kind of superficial." He sighed. "I don't buy it though. There is more behind the mask."

Hope wouldn't respond. Why did he have to fish for more information? Was his compassionate picture a false front? He got paid to show interest to the down and out, like Mom's preacher.

"I'm sorry if I offended you. I was out of line. I stuck my nose where it didn't belong. Please forgive me. I won't pry into your private life again unless you ask me."

She sensed the shadow, which usually took her away from stressful moments like this one, start to swallow her as she withdrew to her secret thinking place. She wouldn't allow him to see into her refuge. This was her space.

"When the number of people producing goods and services goes up, often due to a population increase, an uptick in production will follow. Yes. Makes sense." Hope's mind circled around to try to regain control. "The cost index, no that's not it." Things fogged and she struggled to stay focused. "How could Janie and Susan do that to me? My own sister and my supposed best friend."

Words bounced around and echoed through the cab. Pastor Steve's voice carried though she couldn't understand. She grabbed at the sound like a lifeline. It pulled her away from the brink of a long tunnel her mind threatened to tumble down as her body swayed on the bench seat.

The truck swung to the side of the street and came to an abrupt halt at the curb.

Hope jerked when a light pressure landed on her arm.

"Hey, are you okay?"

Her foggy mind slowly cleared.

"You're not making any sense. You were mumbling something about marketing trends like Gus talks about. You went off on a tangent and talked about some women named Janie and Susan."

She crinkled one eye and gritted her teeth. *What did he hear?* "I'm sorry. When I'm stressed, I go into mathematical equations or run through some economic theories I used in my doctoral thesis presentation." She wiped the moisture from her forehead.

"Do I need to take you to the hospital?" Steve laid his hand on the bench seat halfway to her as his forehead creased.

She rotated away from him. "No. Not long ago, I just went through a bad breakup of my marriage after some major betrayals. I really don't want to talk about it, if you don't mind." Hope looked out the side window while she tried to gather her wits. Her emotions teetered on the edge of running wild. "How much farther to the Dusty Trail?"

"Not far." The pastor pulled the vehicle back into traffic. Silence reigned for the remainder of the ride.

Ten minutes later, the bar came into view. Off to the left, under the overpass sat Baby, her Mercedes, with a flat, rear tire and now a broken windshield with a shattered beer bottle resting on the wiper blade.

"Your car is—wow."

Steve stopped the truck, parked, and they both stepped out.

She ran her fingers inside the back bumper and found the hidden key. She unlocked the door and slid a hand between the seat and console. Relief flooded her as her fingertips pressed to the ridges of her other key. Now to return the hidden key to its rightful place and retrieve her purse from the trunk.

Pastor Steve finished changing the tire and walked around the car. He whistled. "It's a 2009 slk 300, 3.0 liter V6 228 horsepower, six speed manual transmission. I love the color, Capri Blue Metallic. The beige interior is perfect."

She smiled. "The man knows his cars." Hope stared at the broken windscreen and leaned over the hood to take a closer look at the splintered, laminated glass. "That's going to cost. It serves me right."

"In this neighborhood, it's good that it's still here." He pointed to the car's fractured, bug smasher. "I would consider this minor damage. A car like this would set you back forty thousand?"

"I bought it used last year with fifteen thousand miles on it. I only paid twenty-eight thousand."

"You're ready to go, except that." He nodded at the windshield. He reached into his back pocket, pulled out a handkerchief, and wiped his hands of the black tire smudges.

"I can't thank you enough. You are a life saver. You seem a genuine advocate for the down and out." Her eyes misted. She swabbed the wetness with her fingertip. "I had better go. If you see William Scranton tomorrow at church greet him for me and tell him I will be calling in a couple of days to go over a few things we might need to adjust." She tapped the top of Baby. "Forget it. You're not my personal messenger service. I'll email him later."

She opened the car door, but lingered, unwilling to let him go. He made her comfortable. "I know it's such a cliché but sometimes true, you're a knight in shining armor." A sigh of resignation crept from her as she realized she didn't feel threatened by him. He wasn't bothered by her intellect either. He did say she was pretty and dressed classy. But he also said she appeared superficial. She knew one thing about him for sure, he seemed honest and straightforward. The odds of ever seeing him again, much less starting a relationship with him, fell to near zero. She picked off the few stray pieces of broken glass from the seat, slid in behind the steering wheel, and shut the door. After she rolled down the window, she raised her hand to wave good-bye. "Tell old Gus thanks for the conversation. I hope he gets better."

"Hope, before you leave, I want to give you an opportunity to see things in a different light." He pushed his hands in his pockets, stepped back, and tilted his head while his gaze held hers. "Jesus Christ can help you get through some of these issues, if you will give Him a chance."

"Yeah, my mom keeps telling me the same thing." She smiled. "See you around, Pastor Steve. Have a good life." Hope pulled Baby into the street and drove off.

CHAPTER FOUR

Early May, Springfield

The harried call came in at five-thirty in the morning. This fiasco could create an issue capable of shutting down the whole process.

Hope's operations manager, Tommy, as wonderful as he was, didn't seem up to the job and looked bewildered.

Tommy had been Josh's number-two man before the firings of all her top management team. He always deferred to her brother, the master mechanic.

She figured Tommy snuck behind her back and called Josh for advice, even against her orders not to contact him with company business. She couldn't blame Tommy. He, Josh, and Kenny had been best buds since kindergarten.

Besides, with a major mechanical problem like this one, she wasn't so sure Tommy could pull it off. The machinist told them the calibration on the robotic arm was off. Once D-Sub connector parts were made, the male and female contacts could not align properly. If not set right, the arm wouldn't be able to place the connectors in the precise location and had the prospect to short-out the device the connector was placed in. Tommy tried everything he could to fix it, to no avail. This disaster could well be catastrophic to the company if not fixed quickly.

Hope spent her day trying to figure out where the mechanical problem started and where it would lead. Now, almost thirteen hours later, her head throbbed. She finally forced Tommy and the bedraggled crew to go home to rest. When had the work become so exhausting and unsatisfying? She arrived at her Springfield condo depleted and kicked off her shoes.

Hope uncorked the lid to the wine bottle and poured it into the glass. She stared into the blush-colored liquid hoping an answer to their dilemma would materialize.

Flopping onto the couch, she pulled an afghan off the back and wrapped it over her legs. As she tipped the glass up, the familiar liquid burn rushed down her throat and into her stomach. On her third drink, her head tilted back against a cushion behind her.

Blinking through her blurry vision, Hope's focus on the smoke detector helped clear her head. She glanced around her bedroom and watched the morning light cast a gray pallor on the walls through her white window sheers. How did she get to the bedroom?

Her eyes drifted down and settled on the empty wine bottle on the floor. She turned her head away from the unsightly object but her gaze landed on the partially filled wine glass sitting on the nightstand accusing her of another night of drinking. She still didn't have a solution to the problem.

They needed Josh's help. She needed his help. But, how could she cross the barrier? Tempted to make the call, her pride wouldn't allow it. She knew Josh hadn't been involved in the betrayal of Kenny and Janie in a direct manner, but he knew about it and hadn't tried to stop it, nor had Susan. They hurt her by their omission. In a fit of rage, she had fired all four of them. Josh had tried to explain. Her anger shut him out. He chose his best friend and older sister over his little sister and employer.

The memory of the moment she disowned Janie swept across her mind. Who wanted a traitor for a personal assistant? She could always find someone new. Then, why hadn't she? Could it be she didn't want anyone close to her? Her receptionist, Loriann would suffice for now.

Hope grabbed the covers, flipped them off her legs, and sat on the edge of the bed.

But she knew what she saw. She'd never forget them in the apartment claiming it wasn't what it looked like. Her teeth clenched as she grasped the glass on the nightstand and slung it.

Crash!

Hope ran her fingers through her hair and glared at the broken shards.

Janie had always seemed to resent Hope's abilities. It was Janie's nature to use people. Before Kenny, she had decimated the previous man who showed love to her.

Hope glanced at the mirror across the room and saw her sister's image. "Janie and I are like identical strangers. She uses her looks to get what she wants." Janie ruined Hope's marriage, and it still affected the business. She glared at the wine as it dripped down the wall. It'd be a mess to clean up. It would be best to do it soon or a toothbrush would be needed to get into the crevices of the base boards.

Even as she recalled how Janie used her looks to get things, Hope acknowledged her own attractiveness helped to disarm clients and the company benefitted from it. Her looks just made it easier. So, why not use it?

"I can't help it. This is how I'm wired." She brushed her tangled hair out of her face. "Great! Now the crazy lady is talking to herself, again."

Hope turned her attention back to the problem of the robotic arm. Why couldn't she figure this problem out? No mystery…she was a theorist with the ability to apply her hypothesis, not a mechanically inclined person.

She placed her hands on her knees and stared at the ceiling. Was she expecting the answer to float down?

As a little girl, Hope's favorite spot was on the porch at their family home in Farmington, dangling her feet off the edge through the slats with her head pressed to the rails, thinking. Sometimes an idea would come.

Even at eleven-years-old, Kenny first caught her attention as more than Josh's best friend. Though she had seen him before, this time something different piqued her interest.

Kenny Sparks directed the job of the rebuilding of a lawn mower.

Josh, wrenches in hand, did most of the work.

Tommy handed Josh tools as needed.

Each one performed the job most suited to them. Kenny, far enough away so he didn't get dirty, managed the activity. He pointed at this and suggested that. Josh, the hands-on guy, always had grease to his elbows, and Tommy, the gofer for Josh, ran back and forth to the toolbox. They made quite the team.

That morning, so long ago, also placed these three in an important role of her life. Even at thirteen, Kenny appeared to be the CEO of the group. Her future business model had formulated in her mind. But watching them work, Hope never could have imagined she and Kenny would marry years later.

Back then, Janie had eyes for him. As the boys finished up their project, Janie, age fourteen, and her two friends wandered in through the gate. She sauntered up to Kenny, threw her arms around him, and kissed him on the cheek.

"Get a room," Josh said. He laughed at his buddy's red face, while Janie giggled.

One of Janie's friends scooted over close to Tommy and kissed his cheek.

All of them laughed at Tommy's pale face.

Disgusted by the whole display of affection at the time, Hope wondered how it would influence further interaction within the group. Why not shake hands? It was the traditional greeting and made more sense.

Her mind swung back to the present and her reaction to the simple handshake two weeks ago with Pastor Steve when they first met. The action was no different from when she shook hands with William Scranton, and yet, quite different. There was no interest in the older, married Scranton other than business. The handshake with Pastor Steve had sent a tingle up her arm.

"It doesn't matter anyway. I have no chance with Pastor Steve, nor do I think I want it. And according to Mom's religion, divorce stands in the way." Her thoughts continued to tumble. Was Kenny still living with Janie? Hope looked out the window at the blustery sky. "I don't want to know. I didn't file for divorce, he did." She watched as the wind pushed the treetops to the north.

She had other issues to deal with, like the mechanical malfunction. Hope sighed and reached across the bed to pick up the schematics of the robotic arm. No matter how hard she stared at the diagram, the answer still escaped her.

Should she call someone in? It would cost and still might not get fixed as needed. She groaned and looked over at the other nightstand where her phone sat. Josh knew both the chip's function and the mechanics of the arm. Could she overcome the hurt and anger from the deception and call Josh?

She picked up the phone to make the call. Tommy would be the contact. "I wonder if I could bring Josh back as an outside consultant. I hated letting Josh and Susan go, but like her husband, she kept it from me." Somehow her voice sounded as hollow as the hole in her heart. The photograph of her and Susan, the strawberry blonde and the pure redhead at the lake both wearing goofy hats, sat on the nightstand. She reached over and touched the glass. How she wanted her best friend back. Hope missed Susan's common sense. Had Josh and Susan wanted to protect her from the truth because it would destroy the family? Didn't they realize it would affect them also?

Susan shielded Hope from the pain. But, at what cost? "I guess Kenny and Josh are right to some extent. Maybe I have no heart."

Hope dialed.

Ring, ring.

"Hello?" Tommy's morning cough followed.

She smiled to herself. She heard the same froggy voice for years when he spent the night with Josh as they were growing up.

"Hello, Tommy. It's Hope. Sorry to wake you."

"It's okay. I was getting up anyway. Did you figure it out?"

"Who is it, honey?" His wife's soft voice in the background.

"It's Hope."

"Tell Annie I am sorry for waking her. No, I didn't solve it. But I think I have a possible way to resolve the problem." Hope gulped down her bitterness. There was no other option if a chance existed. "Call Josh and ask him in for a consultation, if he's willing. If he has any questions of my feelings about it, tell him to call me directly." She missed her brother's genius with machinery. An ache crept into her chest.

"Are you sure, Hope?"

"We don't have much choice, do we?" Hope stared at the shattered glass by the baseboard. "I may regret this decision. But we need his expertise." She missed the smoothness the operation had when everyone worked together for a specific purpose. A drink would go down good right now. But she couldn't. Work now became her priority.

CHAPTER FIVE

"Thanks for changing our meeting, William. To verify, we've rescheduled to the Monday fourteen days from today, is that correct?" Hope sighed with relief as she spoke to her business associate up in Kansas City. "I'm glad it works better for you too. I believe the time will be beneficial to both of us. We'll talk again later."

After she hung up from the call, Hope twisted her back and stretched one arm straight up and repeated the motion with the other. Her shoulder tension released. Next, she flexed her knees, then pushed the chair back and raised her adjustable worktable.

The broken robotic arm for the D-sub connectors created too much strife around the plant. She hoped it would be fixed today. Hope sucked her bottom lip between her teeth. Could the problem remain unresolved? What about Josh? Would their paths cross today? Agitation crept up all morning. Distraction threatened to create more mistakes. How would she react when confronted by his presence? She leaned her elbows on her acrylic desk and stared across the room at the door. If she could just approach it from a business perspective and not a family issue it might be easier. Her brows furrowed in thought. That kind of separation would not be possible.

With all emotions invested in what was about to happen, her body protested what her mind told her. An involuntary tremor reached Hope's hand as she tried to write a revision to strengthen their weak company policy on internal romantic relationships, which had brought on the past trouble. There would be no romantic contact on company property and would become grounds for immediate dismissal.

Tap…tap.

Tommy stuck his head around the door. "Are you busy?"

"No, please come in." Hope watched as he stepped through the entrance. He didn't shut the door, so she figured whatever he wanted should be brief. "How are things going down there?"

"Actually, they are great. Josh pinpointed the problem, and we tried the solution he suggested. It worked." The tension on Tommy's face from the day before had faded. "Todd and Beth are concluding a third running of the operations to be sure everything is working proper."

"So, what was the problem?"

"Josh can describe it better than I." Tommy turned toward the door.

Hope watched Josh take a tentative step inside with his head lowered like he was counting the clay tiles. His hands folded in front of him.

"Josh, explain what happened." Tommy motioned for him to come forward. "Hope, no way would I have looked at it like he did. I never could. This man has talent way beyond me. Thank you for calling him in." Then as an apparent afterthought, he blurted, "I wish he still ran the show."

Josh still hadn't moved. *What if he hated me? Could I carry such a burden?*

"Ms. Sparks, I appreciate you allowing me to help you." Josh shuffled his feet. "If you ever need my assistance again, I would be willing to pitch in any way I can, at no charge."

"Tommy, could you excuse us, please." Hope pushed down her worktable, sat, and spun her chair toward her main desk.

Tommy turned to the door. As he stepped past his friend, he patted Josh on the shoulder. "Thanks again, buddy." The door closed behind him.

"Take a seat, Josh."

With slow, steady steps, Josh walked toward the clear, acrylic-glass desk. His head still had not risen.

"So, what was the problem with the arm?" *He despises me…I know he does.* Her emotions flew helter-skelter. She crossed her arms over her stomach and leaned back. What should she do? He was her brother and not a stranger or business associate. Should she yell and scream at him or run around the desk and hug him for dear life? If given a choice, she preferred the latter.

Hope could see his hands shaking as he milked them, and yet, he refused to look at her.

"Well, there was an error in the schematics." Josh shifted closer to the desk. "They read seventy micrometers when it was supposed to be ten micrometers. Whoever copied the digits made a small mark on the top of the one, so they calibrated it incorrectly."

He raised his eyes up to her and droplets trickled off his eyelashes. "Hope, I am so sorry for my part in what happened to your marriage, and I want to ask for your forgiveness. You wouldn't answer my calls. I have been sick about it ever since." His head dropped again, and his shoulders shuddered.

Hope's chest constricted and tears pressed the ramparts ready to spill over. She wanted control back. Her body double-crossed her, and her knees bounced.

"I understand that you and Susan hid it from me to save my feelings." She tried to restrain her sentimentality, but she heard the slight quiver in her own voice. "You should have recognized it could affect not only the family but cause embarrassment for the company. It would have been better if the two of you had told me. Your jobs might have been salvaged. I didn't know how to react to the betrayal, Josh. In the spur-of-the-moment, I lashed out."

She motioned him to sit.

"Susan and I don't blame you." Josh moved to one of the light-green, Henson accent wingback chairs in front of her desk. "She misses you like crazy. You know, she hasn't been able to land a corporate job.

Everyone says she is over-qualified with her Doctor of Jurisprudence and Master of Laws. Her specialization in business law narrows the job market."

"Couldn't she obtain a position with one of the local law firms? They could use her expertise."

"She says she would rather stay home with the children than work in a law office." He ran his fingers through his chocolate-brown hair. "Hope, she begged me to let her tell you, but I was concerned with what would happen to the company. It wasn't her fault. She still cries quite often at her loss. Not of the job loss, but of your friendship. She loves you and, Sissy, so do I. Please forgive us. Hope, that is all we ask."

"I don't understand why she didn't file a lawsuit to get her job back. With her expertise, she knew I couldn't legally fire her." The hair on the back of her neck rose as she anticipated his answer.

"Well, we talked about that and concluded that we had been instrumental in compromising the company and publicly shaming you." He glanced down at the floor, shifted in the chair, raised his head and looked at her. "You could have lost the confidence of your clients when you fired us. A lawsuit could have killed the company and put many people out of work. But more than anything, it would have destroyed what you built. We weren't about to do that."

Hope gulped, reached for the glass of water on her desk, and took a drink. *They showed their love for me by not filing a wrongful termination suit.* She wiped her forehead.

"Janie wanted to sue you at first, including doing a hostile takeover. She felt Kenny could run the company himself. Kenny flat out refused because you were the company, and he was only part of your support team. Without you the business couldn't survive, and we had done enough damage." He bit the inside of his lower lip, a family trait inherited from their dad when he had to say something unpleasant.

"I don't think you knew this, but all through high school those two couldn't keep their hands off each other. Kenny stopped seeing her and I don't know why. He wouldn't tell me. Then, you and he began dating in college. But until you started traveling so often for business, Kenny had never strayed. He doesn't seem the same even though they are together still."

"Yes, I saw him a while back and he has lost weight." Hope gave a quick swipe at her nose. "How are Mom and Daddy? I hate that they are in the middle of this."

"They don't talk to either Janie or Kenny often. It took them a long time to accept us again." He gave a snorted chuckle. "They took Susan back before me, but she convinced them we were a package deal. I think they missed the grandchildren." His face turned serious again. "Dad is not polite to Janie at all, and he won't even look in Kenny's direction. Mom's more forgiving." He stared at her and crinkled his nose. "Why don't you ever call Mom and Dad or visit them? Mom says that she prays for your well-being all the time."

"I don't want them to have to take sides. Anyway, I am busy, and I have so much to do by myself now. Janie wasn't much help as a personal assistant. She spent most of her time flirting with the help," Hope hung her head, "and my husband."

"Speaking of him, why haven't you changed the name of the company? I figured with all this mess you would change your name back to Hart and come up with a new name for the company."

"At the time I wanted to, but with the drastic change in management I feared I could lose customers. I needed the stability that our name had built over the years. Not changing my name from Sparks and the direct contact with the customers seemed to brace the awkwardness of new managmet without me having to explain the collapse of the marriage. I may still make a name change once our clients are again comfortable with me running the company and Kenny not in the picture."

He nodded. "Hope, can you forgive Susan? You don't have to accept me. I will learn to live with that. It is tearing me apart to watch what it is doing to her." Josh's eyes brimmed with moisture.

The sadness in Josh's eyes, along with his plea of forgiveness overwhelmed Hope and her emotional dam broke. "Oh Josh, I miss both of you. Of course, I forgive you." She stood and ran around her desk with arms extended wide.

Josh sprang out of his seat and encased her in a crushing hug as both wept in each other's arms.

Hope pulled away, berating herself for her outward display of affection within the office environment. She scrambled to recapture her composure. "Josh, I have a question that maybe you can answer." She motioned for him to sit again. "Tommy said something before he left and I would like your input."

"I'll try if I can." His forehead crinkled like she remembered it did when he prepared to solve a tough puzzle. He readjusted himself and leaned forward ready to jump right into business.

"Tommy made the comment, 'I wish he still ran the show.' Will you be honest with me right now?" She wanted her stare down to be so intense that his answer would either reinforce or obliterate the newly formed ideas skittering around inside her brain.

"No way will I ever be deceitful to you again on purpose. I give you my word."

She'd watch to see if he could keep that promise.

"Is Tommy up to the job as maintenance manager? Right now, I can't afford to have critical errors. I have just made a major deal with Scranton Corp. I can't have any mistakes like what happened with the robotic arm."

Josh whistled. "That's a big contract."

"It's not a contract per se. We have decided to merge some of our operations, like our parts and maintenance, while keeping our companies autonomous." She scratched the side of her nose. "But, back to

Tommy."

Josh gripped the arms of his chair. "Tommy told me that he didn't think he could do the job justice, but that he'd die trying. The guy is a good man and a great friend to you and me. Maintenance isn't Tommy's strong point. He's good at following directions and getting the job done. He's more of a delegator. He'd make a great plant manager. Of course, you already have one of those." He glanced to the floor between his feet and took a deep breath. "By the way, he had no knowledge of Kenny and Janie's dalliance and was shocked."

Hope reached for her phone and punched the inter-office line. "Loriann, could you call Tom back up here, please?"

Five minutes later, a knock sounded at the door and Tommy stuck his head in. "You wanted me?"

"Thanks for responding so quickly. I know you're busy, but I need a few minutes with you." She glanced over to her brother. "Josh, are you off work for the morning?"

"I took the day off to respond to your request." Josh's smile was sad. "It was important to me. And Carl knew of our troubles, so he suggested I take as long as needed. How can I help? Are there other issues I need to look at?"

"No. Could you do me a favor?" Hope placed her hands on the desk to quiet her shiver. "Is Susan available for lunch?"

CHAPTER SIX

Hope watched Josh's face. Would he go along with the request she wanted—no needed, to make?

"I'm sure Susan would be available, especially for you." Though Josh's lips lifted, the smile didn't reach his eyes.

"Why don't you call her and tell her to get ready. You're going to take her to Al's Pancake Griddle for lunch. Don't tell her it is with me or on me." Hope leaned forward on her elbow and placed her chin into her palm. "I might have a business proposition for you. It's ten o'clock now. Do you think she can get a sitter for the children on short notice?"

"Mrs. Higgins, next door, is always ready to watch them on the spur of the moment. Let me call Susan to set it up." Josh's smile spread across his face, and this time, the skin around his eyes crinkled.

"How about one-thirty? Let me know if there is a problem, and then I'll call ahead for a table."

"Hope, before I go, I want to tell you that I will try to never disrespect you again. I'm sorry about this whole mess. I love you." He walked around the desk and gave her another hug.

She melted into it.

After the door closed behind Josh, Hope looked over to Tommy. His cheeks rose, his eyes sparkled, and his lips parted.

"What?" She forced on a scowl to keep from breaking out in her happy dance.

"You two obviously made-up." Tommy's body relaxed into the chair.

"I guess so. But that has some implications for you." Her lips pressed together as her angst built. "You and I need to talk."

Tommy straightened and leaned forward, then rested his elbows on his knees while maintaining eye contact. "Hope, I have a confession to make and I hope it doesn't cost me my job, but I need to be up-front with you. I call Josh a lot about machine issues. What I said earlier about having him back, I would step down to be his assistant if you were of a mind to hire him back, and I'd even be willing to take a pay reduction."

"You would do that?" What Tommy lacked in ability, he more than made up for in loyalty.

"Annie and I have discussed this and even though she didn't know the driving force within our group before, she knows we were all close. She also knows of Josh's abilities, including, how things went down. And, she would love to have the old Tommy back without the stress because she told me so. We believe there would be less over-time if Josh were here since he could figure things out quicker."

Hope smiled. This was going easier than expected, and now the solution might be within her grasp. Her long-term goals could go forward sooner than she planned.

"Tommy, a demotion is not in the cards for you. You are going to stay right where you are at the same pay. Could you please go back down and recheck to make sure the robotic arm is still working?" She rose from her chair to walk over to the file cabinet. "Take care of what you need to do and clear your schedule for a business lunch at Al's Pancake Griddle." Hope watched Tommy get up and walk out the door. She pulled out a manila envelope full of her accumulated notes from college and another file of employment contracts for management positions.

Josh had been right. It had been too long since Hope had seen Mom and Daddy. Could she leave the office after clearing work issues early Friday morning and head that way? Yes it might be possible. But Kenny and Janie lived in Farmington also. The thought of any contact with them made her stomach clench. Perhaps she could check out the rumors about Broderick Dynamics while in Farmington.

Would it be possible to bring back Susan to the company? Hope grabbed her spiral notebook and researched the recesses of her mind. With a mechanical pencil in hand, she scrawled a quick outline.

First on the list came the pros and cons of having Susan back as the legal advisor. The second thing caused her pause. Should she have her as her personal assistant or her legal advisor? If only as the lawyer, what would be her other tasks? Would she insist upon working part-time to care for the children?

Hope dropped the pencil on the notepad and flopped back into the cushioned, leather chair. "Man, I forgot about Heather and Ginny. What if Susan decides it's not worth it to return?" She leaned forward to place her elbows on the desk and dropped her chin into her palms.

As she scanned her notes, she bit down on the inside of her bottom lip with a force harder than she thought. "Ouch!" She reached up to her mouth and ran the back of her hand across the corner. Blood traced her skin. Hope shrugged. Though it would hurt the payroll, Susan was worth it. It was a win-win. Make a few changes on the contract and pray she would sign. "I need her professionally…and personally." Hope jotted down a few more notes to organize her presentation to Susan.

"Now for Josh." She flipped the page and started again with pros and cons to having not one family member working for her but two. Not just two, but a married couple. What about her new iron-clad inner-office romance policy between workers? Hope reached over to the policy manual she had been working on and scribbled out the line. She'd rewrite it in a way to allow for married couples. What could she offer Josh to pull him back in while not scaring him off? Would she be able to snag him away from Carl without hurting Carl's business? How vital was Josh's position to Carl's future?

Hope shrugged. She wasn't worried about Carl's business. How would her company benefit with Josh's return? Could she trust him again? She leaned back and considered the emotional strain from earlier and what could happen at Al's Pancake Griddle. Her stomach fluttered and her heartbeat hitched. Emotions made her uncomfortable and the feelings of others confused her.

"*Humph*. I may not worry about Carl's business, but Josh will." Maybe she could bring Josh back in small increments. First, as a consultant and then in a position to run the overall plant while she did her thing. Then Carl could find someone to replace Josh. She grabbed her notebook and scribbled down her bullet points, then paused for a moment to double check her facts as they related to her future goals.

Too bad this particular restaurant wasn't known for their alcoholic treats. A drink might be the only way she could make it through the difficult conversation she needed to have with her, once and hopefully soon to be renewed, best friend. Hope shook her head. She had to be fully present for whatever happened as she met with Josh, Susan, and eventually, Tommy.

Hope's constant glances at the café clock over the entranceway didn't ease her sky-rocketing apprehension even when Josh and Susan swept through the door engaged in conversation. How would her and Susan's first meeting go? Could they ever get back what they once had?

Josh closed the glass door.

Susan turned to the dining area. Her eyes seemed to search for a spot to sit.

Hope watched her former friend's face.

Susan's body stiffened—hand to mouth—eyes widened. She spun around, grabbed Josh's arm, and whispered into his ear.

Josh nodded and looked in Hope's direction. He placed his hands upon his wife's shoulders and rotated her so she faced his sister. He leaned over and spoke, then led her forward.

As they crossed the room, Hope's heart pounded and fought to jump out of her chest.

The closer they came, the lower Susan's head tucked.

As they drew near, Hope slid out of the booth to greet them.

Susan's hands shook.

Hope's own stomach did somersaults as she struggled to breathe.

Josh gave his wife a little bump forward. "It's okay, honey. Say what you need to say. Hope and I made our peace earlier this morning." He stepped around Susan and kissed his sister on the cheek. "Hey sis, be gentle with her." He dropped into the booth beside Tommy and left the two women to face one another.

"Hope, I can't apologize enough for what was done to you," Susan quavered. "I wanted to tell you about Kenny and Janie, but Josh said to hold off." She looked away, then back. Wrinkles replaced smile lines. Tears formed in her eyes. "We began to worry about the repercussions to the company and all the families involved. We justified it. I rationalized that you were into your own zone, and it wouldn't have computed in your mind right then."

Hope brought her finger up close toward Susan's lips. "Shh. It is not necessary to explain. I know you had my interests at heart. You know me better—"

"No! That wasn't why at all." Susan's tone became ragged. "I felt I could fix things for you later like I always have. My thinking at the time was Hope's a big girl. She'll survive this. We need to save the families and the company. Your reaction stunned me. It hurt. I realized I couldn't put it back together. I had never seen you so angry."

"I did what I thought needed to be done," Hope said. "I lashed out. I couldn't think of anything but the pain and you were part of that wound. I couldn't believe that you of all people would turn on me." This wasn't how it was supposed to go. How could she fix this? Her breathing became labored. The floor became her focus. She clenched her hands ready to defend what she had done. What she would give for a drink.

Her fingers tightened around the imaginary glass of scotch. Could she survive this?

Hope looked up and watched Susan's lower lip quiver as the tears spilled over. She wanted more than anything to pull her friend into a hug, but forced out a huff instead. The strain eased. "You were thinking of the big picture. You are not to blame for Janie's and Kenny's actions. As usual, I missed your intentions." She gave her best rendition of a pouting puppy that always made Susan laugh. "Sor-ry."

She thrust her arms around Hope and bawled.

Hope wrapped her own arms across Susan's back and gripped her as the waterworks flowed. She glanced around the crowded diner and saw eyes that shined with moisture. Not wanting to make a spectacle of herself in front of strangers, she forced herself away and pulled Susan into the booth beside her.

For over half an hour, the two whispered their apologies and talked about past times while Tommy and Josh discussed different issues about the equipment.

When the tension had drifted away, Hope pulled a stenographer's pad out of her purse and pushed it over to Susan. "Take notes."

Susan scrunched her freckled nose. "What's this?"

"I can't do a business meeting without notes taken by my new personal assistant. I have to get a legal tax write-off for the lunch, right?" She raised her brows as she handed Susan a pen along with a four-page document. "After you read it, we will sign your contract dated today."

"Are you saying what I think you are saying?"

"If you'll accept the position. Of course, it would be at higher pay than you had before since I still need your input on business law. There will always be contracts and memorandums to write. There is only one clause in it that I insist on."

Before her next sentence, Susan's hand shot up. Could anything get worse than a rejection to the offer? Hope swallowed down the developing lump in her throat.

Susan took the pen and laid it on the pad. She faced Hope, eyes boring in.

"There is one condition, and that is that I will always be honest with you even if it hurts your feelings. I give you the information as soon as I analyze it and am able to present it in a manner so you can breakdown its relevance to you." She brought her hand to her mouth, spit on it, then stuck it out to shake like they had for years.

Dizziness rushed in as the endorphins released their pressure. Before Susan could take her hand back, Hope hawked an un-lady-like big one into her own palm. She slapped a squishy hand against Susan's. All four of them laughed at the gesture.

During the next hour Hope laid out her plans for the company with her soon-to-be new management team. And, she made it through the reconciliatory meeting without alcohol. Would wonders never cease?

CHAPTER SEVEN

Late-May, Farmington

Hope left work before noon on Friday. With the top down on her Mercedes and hair whipping about her face, joy and freedom breezed through for the first time in months. Time flew with the light traffic, but the two-lane highway between St. James and Farmington would soon be packed.

As she drove, her recent accomplishments raced through her thoughts; her merged operations with Scranton topped the list. Next, SSL dodged the robotic arm fiasco, with the help of Josh's brilliance. Her relationship was on the mend with her brother and his wife, Susan, and their friendship appeared on the mend as well. There were not enough words to express how glad she was to have her best friend and confidant back. She had even shared with Susan about the gorgeous minister she met in Kansas City without coming clean on the details. Overall, a good couple of weeks.

When Hope stopped the umpteenth apology, she jumped into her spiel about a possible romance between her and the pastor. She almost let slip she had a hangover when she and Pastor Steve met.

Hope pulled into the outskirts of her hometown of Farmington and took a gander at Broderick Dynamics. After she parked her car, she stepped out, pulled out her notepad, and jotted down some thoughts.

She turned to the convertible and with a smirk, patted the fender.

"Baby, it might pan out for us." She hopped back into the driver's seat and cruised past all the access streets, including the highway to see different approaches to the business.

After an hour of perusal, Hope drove to the familiar neighborhood and pulled up to the house of her memories. She gazed at the freshly painted two-story, four-bedroom house that had been her childhood sanctuary. Every five years her father painted the place. White. The fresh charcoal-gray on the trim and shutters seemed to give new life to the aging home.

Hope popped the trunk and grabbed her bag. "Dad, I hope you had someone else paint it this time. You're getting too old to be climbing ladders." Once again she was glad she told her mom that she wasn't sure of the time of her arrival. It gave her the opportunity to scope out the town and ease to the house without the usual fanfare Mom craved.

As she stepped to the sidewalk, Hope ran her fingers over the sharp points on the gate and noted the new slate pathway that matched the trim of the house. *You don't miss a trick, do you Dad? You can whitewash it or, in this case, gray wash it, but where it has worn down will never change.*

Her sight drifted up to the porch, one of her favorite thinking places. Many a great idea flourished right there. A warmth of memories draped over her. She released her breath. *Nice to be home.*

Halfway up the walkway, she saw the door curtains move.

The edges of her mouth lifted. Mom always stood watch when her kids were coming home.

The heavy oak door swept open and her favorite people stood at the entrance with huge smiles on their faces. In a split second, Mom's arms flung open. Even with a waving dishtowel in her hand, she quick-stepped toward her daughter.

Hope watched her mother descend the steps, then dropped her bag and rushed to her mother. She had been told by her grandparents and aunts that other than her eye color, she could have been Mom's twin when her mother was young. Both flooded the other with tears of joy. "I missed you so much."

Her mother espoused the deep theological litany she adopted when in such situations. "My God, my God, my God. You're here. You're here. You're here."

They danced around the walkway and swayed from side to side as they went through what had become their own choreographed welcome routine since the first day she returned from kindergarten. Hope loved this woman more than life itself, despite the woman's strong religious beliefs.

Now with the ritual ended, she turned to her father.

Hope focused her sight on the man who had inspired her. All five-foot-ten of debonair and distinguished gentleman smiled his perfect teeth at her. Her heart melted when she looked at his handsome face outlined by the graying temples mingled with impeccably groomed brown hair. Never unshaven and always wearing his standard mocha-colored loafers.

He leaned toward her.

Hope bounded up the porch steps and threw herself into her daddy's arms.

He gripped her as they rocked back and forth.

"Welcome home, Punkin." His personal nickname for her stuck one Halloween when she insisted on carving what she called the punkin. "It's so good to have you back even if it's only for the weekend." His face dropped into a somber and dignified demeanor. "Are you doing okay with all that has happened? Your phone calls are always so brief. Why didn't you come talk with us? We might have been able to help."

Hope gazed into the intense, caramel eyes she inherited. "Daddy, I know you would have tried to protect me from the hurt. I had to do this alone. It wasn't your problem, and I didn't want to put you and Mom in an awkward position. It's already starting to mend somewhat."

"How can you say that? Your sister and your husband are still living together. It's sin, and they need to repent."

She reached up to cup his face into her palms. "Please trust me. I will take care of it. Josh, Susan, and I have made our peace and things are going forward. I will explain later." She hugged him again.

She looked back over her shoulder, touched by what she saw.

Mom's eyes glistened—hands clasped under her chin with the red and white checkered piece of cloth wrapped around one hand. A familiar pose Mom seemed to strike when she waited in anticipation of a hopeful outcome.

Hope pulled one arm from her father and grasped her mother's hand. "It feels good to be back visiting you. But this is going to be a happy time together. So, I will say this once, and it will be the end of it. We are not going to discuss what happened. Kenny and I are divorced due to his infidelity." She glanced into her mother's eyes. "Isn't that what the Bible says is the reason for divorce? He needed to fix it right away, but he didn't. End of discussion."

Her dad broke the physical connection and went down the steps to retrieve her bags.

"Mom, did you add some azaleas along the fence this year?" She gestured to the picket barrier that ran along the driveway. "They're beautiful. I love the way you've alternated the pink and red plants."

"Yes, I figured that color scheme would blend with the variegated roses that grow beside the front sidewalk."

"I believe that works." Hope pointed at the house and grinned as she poked fun at her dad. "Hey, Daddy, I love your new choice of colors for the house. What color is this? White?"

"Oh, my lord, that's outrageous." Mom's guffaw made them all laugh hard. Hope joined the laughter.

Suddenly, Hope broke for the door. "All this laughing is going to make me have an accident."

She heard both her parents' hysterics.

Friday night, the air wafted with Hope's favorite dishes of meat loaf, mashed potatoes with white gravy, green beans, and corn on the cob.

After dinner, Hope curled up on the overstuffed, micro-fiber loveseat and rested her head on Mom's soft shoulder. Why couldn't life always be this simple? She wrapped her arms around Mom's waist. She fought off a bout of melancholy when she realized this was the first time she had cuddled since the week before she found out about her husband two years prior.

Hope didn't want to fall deeper into the melancholic trap. Rather, she allowed childhood nostalgia to creep in. She could lie here like a kid and drop all her troubles at the end of the day just to be in Mom's arms. Her eyelids drooped.

Saturday morning, Hope rolled over and caught herself before she tumbled off the tiny divan. She shrugged off the light blanket and sat up, then rubbed her eyes. Where am I? The cool breeze blew into her face from an upright fan. As a slight, racing flutter slipped across her, realization dawned.

Sometime during the evening, Mom must have slipped out to go to bed.

Hope twisted her waist to get the kinks out from sleeping in such a small space, but she felt rested nonetheless. The rich coffee blends her parents preferred, which matched her usual flavor, wafted toward her.

She rose and shuffled to the kitchen where she found her daddy sitting at the dining room table rearranging the newspaper. The rustle of the pages sent another flood of memories and brought a chuckle from her.

His head lifted.

"You know you can get the news online nowadays."

"Naw, I love the feel and smell of the printed page." He flipped the sheet and folded it in half. "It separates me from the hustle and bustle of the outside world while allowing me to study it." He pointed at the top cabinet next to the sink to steer her to the coffee mugs. "Grab some brew. Sugar's on the counter—the fake sweetener in the cabinet—flavored creamer in the fridge."

"Wow, big changes in the Hart Bed and Breakfast. Flavored creamer in the refrigerator and sugar on the counter instead of hidden in the cabinet." She arched her brows.

"Smarty-pants. Pull up a chair and tell me what's going on at the company."

She poured her coffee, then dipped the spoon into the sweetener twice. After a moment of reconsideration, she scooped a third.

Her dad looked over the top of his paper. "Uhm. That's going to be your death."

"Okay, so I'm addicted to sweets. Sue me." Once her fix was in, she swung her leg over the back of the chair and sat.

"That's not very lady-like. You need to be more elegant like your mother." He grinned and extended his hand across the table to squeeze hers. "Or, you can be you."

Hope patted his hand. "You always know how to encourage my independence."

"Okay, little girl, what's been happening with Sparks System Logistics? What new gadgets have you installed since I was last allowed privileged information?"

She heard the scrape of slippers on the floor behind her and turned to see her mother shuffle through the door with a fist covered yawn and tousled hair.

Mom walked to the cabinet, retrieved her favorite cup, and emptied the carafe. "Continue. Did I miss anything, Charles?"

Her dad laid down the paper and slipped out of his chair. In two quick steps, he encircled his wife from behind and nuzzled her neck. "Good morning, my love."

Hope watched her mom lean back, tilt her head, and bring her fingers up to caress his cheek. She turned around in his arms and pressed her lips to his in a lingering kiss.

"Eww, old people kissing." Hope laughed. These two always showed such deep passion for each other. The devotion and intensity for one another had lasted for over forty years. It made her own marriage that much more of a farce.

They turned to her and grinned.

She jumped up and scooted over to engulf both in a tight hug.

When they all broke away, Hope and her dad returned to the table.

"Margie, our little girl was about to enrapture us with the adventures of Sparks Systems Logistics, Part Two. We won't discuss Part One. This is a new chapter, a new episode."

Hope reached across the table to grasp his hand. "Daddy, expansion might be in our future."

CHAPTER EIGHT

Mid-June, Springfield

"William, this coalition will make transferring parts easier." Hope showed him into the boardroom nearest her office.

"I agree, Hope. It will be more cost efficient for both companies since we buy and sell each other's components."

On William Scranton's return to Kansas City from a business trip, he swung by to see Hope at SSL in Springfield. This made it convenient for Hope as she wanted to present him with the new expanded prospectus. Hope had Susan look at all the legal ramifications of this proposal to unite the companies without either entity losing their autonomy. A sticky wicket, as the British called it.

Her nerve endings prickled when she considered her options of keeping him out of her business while benefiting from access to his. Despite those advantages, she kept a keen eye out for her own personal ethics. Corporate espionage was a real deal breaker. The meeting in two weeks with the lawyers would seal the contract.

Hope smiled at William and watched him scratch the side of his salt-and-peppered head as he settled back into reading.

When she reached for the doorknob to leave him to his reading, Scranton interrupted her exit.

"Hope, I forgot to tell you. Pastor Steve told me to tell you hello."

"Tell him I said thanks for thinking of me. Greet him for me as well." Hope's heart hammered. "I...I'll leave you to what you were doing.

If you have any questions, write them down and I'll try to answer them." She stepped out, closed the door, and sagged against the wall. Why did Pastor Steve affect her this way? He seemed to cause all kinds of impulsive sentimentality to well up. She closed her eyes and recalled similar anxiety that ran wild a few weeks ago while anticipating Josh and Susan's arrival as she sat in the corner booth of Al's Pancake Griddle.

Hope pushed herself away from the wall and back from her memories. She crossed the hall to Susan's office where her door stood ajar. Hope stepped through and closed the door.

Her throat tightened like it did when Susan was in her own realm. This looked like the old friend she loved and appreciated.

Susan's love and wisdom had been her center of gravity, and while separated, Hope drifted into the outer space of the toxic business world's void. Susan's intelligence had been the guiding star that moved Hope to excellence. Nothing but a toasty hug could describe her comfort level around this amazing woman. It surprised her that the girl chomped at the bit to start back to work so soon.

Josh had decided to gradually transition back, putting in a couple of hours per day to reacclimate to the job. He wanted to give his current employer, Carl, time to replace him. For the time being, overtime became the standard for their children's new nanny.

Hope stood spellbound seeing her friend's work ethic. She appeared as driven as Hope and nearly as focused. But Susan could drop everything and walk away if something else had priority. Right now, with her head down and her shoulder-length, wavy, red hair scrunched up into her left hand—elbows on the desk—number two pencil clenched between her teeth, she read some memorandum. An absorbed picture Hope had seen many times.

She reached up to wipe the moisture from her eyes. How could she have ever doubted Susan's devotion to her?

"Hey, Bozo. Want to take a break and walk with me into the plant? I have William reading that addendum to the contract in the boardroom and I don't want him to feel pressured."

Susan's head popped up and her eyes looked glazed. She shook her head with the appearance of shedding something from her thick red strands that Hope always called her clown hair. "Hey, Dopey." Susan's response referenced Hope's mind going into a deep place only the family knew about. She quickly glanced around the room. "Ugh, Ms. Sparks. Yes, I would like a break to escort you. Perhaps, I'll see my Mr. Hart-throb while out and about." Susan laughed at her own joke. "Maybe I'll talk him into a business lunch, if I'm not needed here.

"I'm going over the paperwork for the policy on interoffice relationships and I'm struggling with a couple of sentences that need to be reworded. With this new policy, it means my husband and I can't smooch even in the privacy of his or my office during work hours." Susan giggled. "How will we ever survive the day?"

"Get a room. Wait, let me rephrase that. Get a room off company property." Hope smiled as she shook her head. "Grab your pad, we have to look professional."

Susan snatched up a notebook and skipped over and gave Hope a hug—only the second between the two that morning. They interlocked their arms and headed to the door. As Susan reached the door, she released her arm, straightened her skirt, and pulled back her shoulders transforming into the dignified assistant her job required.

"I'm glad to have you back on my team. You are going to make it easier to deal with legal matters, especially when I decide to expand." Would the consolidation with Scranton, the challenges of expansion, and the problems here at the plant get complicated with the stress of reconciliation with Josh and Susan? And what about the added random thoughts about Pastor Steve?

A scotch sure would go down well right now. One couldn't hurt much. Could it?

CHAPTER NINE

Late June, Springfield

Hope's lips and nose were numb and her head foggy. She struggled to get her head off the tabletop. Someone's hand lightly patted her face.

"Come on Hope, wake up. We need to get you home."

She squinted to pull Tommy's face into the bull's-eye of sight recognition. The music sounded hip-hop and the lighting, bright and strobing. Which club was it again?

"I can't seem to focus on what you're saying." Her words slurred as her head dropped back onto the table.

Tommy's loud voice resonated above the din as he argued with some other man she didn't recognize, about something that didn't make sense.

Something sharp tugged on her shoulder. Without warning, she found herself standing against someone's side. She struggled to understand the conversation flying around her.

"I don't think she wants to go with you, buddy. I think she wants to stay here with me, so back off," the unrecognized male voice blustered.

"Listen to me really well, mister. This is my friend and she is drunk. If you don't want trouble, I suggest you let her go and allow me to escort her home before my friends get here." Tommy grabbed her hand. "Let's go, Hope."

Hope turned her head toward his voice. "Tommy, how are you? How is Annie?" Once again, she felt an arm tightening around her. She shifted her body to take in the face less than a foot away. "Do I know you? Who are you?" With as much strength as she could muster, she tried to push herself away from the stranger.

A gentle hand grasped her wrist and pulled her as she saw Tommy step back.

"Let her go!" Susan's harsh tone resounded. "She's in no condition to be around the likes of you."

"Where did you come from, Suz? My head feels like a bowl of cornmeal mush."

"Hey, lady. Hands off." The interloper clutched Hope to his side.

She waved her hand to clear the fog. Her eyes widened to bring in Tommy's face again.

The conversation made no sense. "What's going on? Stop playing tug-of-war with my body." She batted her eyes to clear the blur as she watched Susan hand the man a piece of paper.

"Sir, if you don't wish to find yourself in some legal hot water, then I suggest you listen to me carefully, as I am her lawyer." Susan's voice was stern. "This lady is beyond the legal limit and is unable to decide her own fate. Therefore, whatever you have in mind is without consent."

The man's loosened grip launched Hope to the end of the bench seat.

She grabbed the edge of the table. "Whoa. Stop the ride, I want to get off." Her stomach rolled as whatever was in it tried to come up. She fixated on the red-hair and blue dress before her to stop the oncoming vertigo. Without notice, the blue dress disappeared and was replaced by khakis and a yellow shirt with a logo on the pocket.

"I recognize that shirt. It's my shirt." She brought her hand up and traced the emblem with her finger. "S, S, L, Sparks System Logistics." She blinked and then scrunched her eyelids when a face popped up inches from hers. She smiled.

"Josh, what are you doing here? You don't even drink anymore." With another firm grip on her wrist, her arm appeared to fly up in the air and her body jettison into the atmosphere. Gravity adopted a whole new perspective. Her flying experience took a quick downward twist to pull her toward a yellow sea of cotton and polyester as she crashed over her brother's shoulder.

Clatter, clatter.

The sound grated Hope's sensitive ears as the wooden blinds opened to let the sunlight penetrate her pupils and puncture her brain. While she reached for the powder-blue pillow to hide from the glare, she scrunched her eyelids closed. She peeked around the edge of the cushion and watched Susan exit the room. Envy's sharpness crept in and stabbed her heart.

How could Susan keep up with her job all day, come home to the children, and still manage to maintain a spotless home? A mass of clutter filled Hope's own condo since her drinking had escalated. *Too bad I don't have someone to keep my place so clean.*

Though she pushed her tongue from the roof of her mouth past her lips, it seemed a chore. It had the texture of an entire package of cotton balls. She climbed out of the four-post bed in Josh and Susan's guest room and shoved her feet into the light-blue slippers. When she reached for the bathrobe on the back of the chair, she groaned. Everything was blue, just different shades.

"I guess I had better make my appearance. This isn't going to be fun." Maybe the children weren't up yet. Could she climb into her clothes and do her disappearing act? But as she scanned the room, Hope couldn't see her clothes anywhere. Maybe she wouldn't escape after all.

As she came down the hallway to the kitchen, she heard what sounded like utensils scraping across dishes and glasses clinking, along with muffled voices. She lingered outside to gather her courage while imaginary bees dive-bombed her insides. Before she pushed open the louvered doors, she overheard Josh's hushed voice.

"She needs a 'Come to Jesus' meeting, Babe. She's turning into an alcoholic. I'm sure you have noticed the well-stocked bar in her office."

"Yeah, I saw. But look what she has gone through in the last twenty-two months. If you remember before you became a Christian, you drank heavily. You remember the rough patch in our marriage. I would have been right there with you had I not been pregnant with Heather."

The slam of the dishwasher door created a momentary a lull in the conversation. "You know how she is. Unless she thinks it's important, you can't convince her of a problem. But, you're right. Hope either needs to go to rehab or start AA meetings. I love her, but I'm afraid that we are enabling her since our return to the company. This is the second time in a week we've had to go get her."

"Tommy told me this has been going on since the breakup." A chair scooted across the tiled floor. "She needs to fix this, or the company will suffer. This could affect us on a deep, personal level. At least with us being there now, we might be able to protect her and the people that work there, from her destructive path."

Does everyone know about my drinking? Could my mess ups be that catastrophic? The bigger question, can I get this under control?

But she couldn't just drop the business and go to rehab, especially not with the big meeting coming up. Reckless living looked like her current song and dance routine. She couldn't see herself doing the God thing. Somehow, she had to get her act together.

Hope shouldered the swinging double doors open. She pasted on a smile and entered the dining room.

Grated bay windows over the stainless-steel sink allowed natural light to bathe the ivory-colored ceramic tiles, which covered the kitchen floor. The sun's reflection illuminated her brother from his legs to his chest but kept Josh's face in the shadows. They weren't dark enough to hide his heart-piercing stare. She licked her dry lips and stepped farther into the kitchen area.

Susan turned toward her and leaned against the countertop with arms folded. A scowl etched her face.

"Last night was not a good one, guys." Hope stepped over to the coffeemaker and snatched a cup off the mug hooks. "Thanks again for bailing me out. I have no idea how you found me, but I'm glad you did." She glanced between the two and found only blank stares. "I've been thinking. I am going to find a good therapist and perhaps start going to AA meetings. I think I need some help with my problem." She smiled at Josh hoping to get encouragement.

Josh set his ceramic stein, which had turned from his beer container to his coffee mug, on the table, rose to his feet, sighed, and walked out the garage door.

This side of her brother stunned her, and she didn't like it. Before he became a Christian, he always had a snide remark. But Josh walking out hurt more than some smart aleck comment.

She grasped the sugar spoon and shoveled her usual three teaspoons into the steaming brew and allowed her sight to drift over to Susan. Her friend just turned back to the dishwasher and added soap to the dispenser.

Uh-oh. Not very happy. Surprised they didn't welcome her comments about getting help, it didn't look like they were going to coddle her like Mom often did. Maybe, they loved her enough to not put up with her bad behavior. Hope glanced back at her friend.

Susan gripped the edges of the sink with her head hung as her shoulders shook.

Hope pulled a chair away from the table and plopped down into it, disheartened. "I need to fix this. I think Monday morning I'll look up a therapist. Maybe restock my liquor cabinet at work with water and juice. Alcohol is not a good example for the workers. I'll do the same at home with waters and soda." She looked back at her best friend and watched her nod. But could Hope do it?

CHAPTER TEN

August, Kansas City

"Susan, it was paramount that you came to Kansas City with me. I needed you on this trip as legal counsel." The two women stood behind Baby in front of the hotel. She needed her best friend more now than ever before with Hope's struggle with the bottle.

"It wasn't necessary for me to be here. The contracts are pretty much cut and dry. His lawyers can't twist any wording around that might hurt your company." Susan looked down into the trunk. "Why did you bring so much stuff?" In order for her to grab her suitcase, she needed to move one of Hope's bags. She reached in, lifted, and grunted, then shoved the heavy case off her things and nabbed her own suitcase. "What's in that? Rocks?"

Hope grinned. "I brought the files to explain the direction we wanted to go with the merger."

Susan rolled her eyes. "What? You do know that you can download those onto an itty-bitty flash drive, right?" She held her finger and thumb an inch apart. "Or you could just look it up on your laptop?" She crossed her hazel eyes and slipped her tongue through perfect teeth. "Earth to Hope." Susan twirled her finger around her ear and twisted her lips to one side. It reminded Hope of the many times with a simple blank stare she could frustrate her friend and bring pink to her freckled cheeks.

Hope couldn't hold it any longer and exploded into laughter. "Susan, you should see your face. Of course, I didn't do that. I promised William that I would bring a couple of manuals for the robotic arm we were having troubles with. I know the tomes are extra thick and weigh a ton, but he thinks he might be able to make the connections more durable, so they won't short circuit as easily. If we go down, it could affect them." Hope smirked. "So, I brought what I thought he might need."

Susan put her bag down and glared at Hope. "I told you, I didn't need to be on this trip. You don't need my help." Susan gave Hope a blank stare. "I had plans for the whole weekend with Josh. Tori was going to keep the girls, but I guess this trip had precedence."

Hope's brows furrowed at this unexpected snit.

She reached in the trunk and grunted as she lifted the heavy case.

Later in the evening, Hope and Susan met William Scranton and his wife as planned. The quaint restaurant he suggested did not impress Hope. Sturdy pine tables with wooden benches for the booths and scattered sawdust shavings throughout the entire dining room set the cowboy climate. The servers wore western attire designed for a hoedown. Hope saw her fill of that around Springfield.

As Hope slid into the booth, the black-sequined, party dress snagged for a second. She glanced up at the open mouths of William and Gloria. She heard a snicker and turned to scowl at Susan.

Dressed in a pair of black slacks with a royal blue blouse, Susan slipped in beside her and bumped her hip into Hope's. "They said to dress casual."

The red head's snarky remark galled. Heat crept up Hope's cheeks.

Gloria recovered first. "It's fine. We should have explained better where we planned to have dinner."

Hope shrugged but glared at Susan. She wanted a drink to squelch the flame of her retort.

"They have quite an assortment of food here. Tonight, is on me." William smiled at Hope and turned to Susan. "Gloria, I would like to officially introduce Susan Hart, Hope's personal assistant, and, I might add, her legal advisor. She helped put together the new contracts, but we aren't going to talk about business tonight. We just want to get to know both of you."

Gloria reached her hand across the table to Susan. "I am so pleased to meet you. How long have you worked for Hope?"

Susan smiled. "Almost my whole life. I still haven't got it right." She elbowed Hope in the ribs. "We have been best friends since middle school and study buddies for life. Isn't that right?" She leaned her head over onto Hope's shoulder and batted her eyes at Hope. "But I really hang out with her for the fringe benefits. I get to be her sister-in-law, too. I'm married to Josh, the new CEO for the company."

"So, Hope, your company is a family business?"

"Yes. We are reestablishing management."

Gloria pointed over Susan's shoulder to the foyer. "William, look. Pastor Steve just walked in."

"Is he alone?" William curled his lip and squinted. "Doesn't look like he is with anyone."

At the mention of the pastor's name, Hope placed her hand over her fluttering stomach.

"Let's invite him over to dine with us." Gloria looked across the table at Hope and Susan. "Would you mind? He looks like he's alone."

"Not a problem for me," Susan said. "How about you, Hope?"

"No," she squeaked as she spun around to see the front door.

"William, go over and invite him. We have room and that way he won't have to wait for a single table to open."

Susan looked toward the lobby, and then back over at Hope—cocked her head—raised her brows and grinned.

Hope shifted back to face the table and stared down at the smooth surface of woodgrain. She worked on a nonchalant pose. Could she pull it off? Her breathing rhythm picked up. In her periphery, she watched

Susan turn on the bench. Hope would wait, not so patiently, to get another look at the gorgeous man in the entry.

"Very attractive. Good height and well-dressed." Hope's ginger-haired girlfriend rotated to face Gloria. "Is he single or married? Don't worry, I'm happily married, but she isn't." She pitched a thumb at Hope.

"He's single and a widower. Hope, haven't you two already met?"

Hope nodded as she took a deep breath to slow down her heart rate. "I didn't know about his deceased wife. We never discussed her."

Susan squeezed Hope's hand.

As the two men walked up to the booth, Gloria slipped out and embraced the reverend.

William sat down and shifted all the way over, then his wife moved in beside him.

William said, "Pastor Steve, I'm sure you remember Hope Sparks."

"Yes, I remember Ms. Sparks. We had lunch together just about three months ago if I recall." Steve smiled broad. "It's nice to see you again, Hope." He extended his hand to Hope. "And who, may I ask, is this beautiful, young lady?" He nodded toward Susan.

"I'm Mrs. Susan Hart. I'm Hope's sister-in-law."

"Pleased to meet you, Mrs. Hart." As he took her hand, he did an extravagant bow.

"Good looking and a gentleman," Susan said.

"Well, thank you." Steve turned his attention back to Hope. "Did you drive up in that magnificent automobile of yours?"

"We did. How is that beautiful pickup? Any new additions to it?" Grateful to speak on a safe subject her gaze traveled from his dark brown, casual shoes to his light brown hair. He looked even better in a suit. "How is Gus doing?" She squirmed on the lacquered bench in an effort to get comfortable. "Please sit and join us."

Steve eased down beside Gloria. "He's in the hospital. It doesn't look too good for him. His breathing seems sporadic. It's like he's slowly drowning."

Gloria brought her finger up to wipe her eye. "I'm glad he became a Christian and came to church while in his right mind. He will soon be with his Maker."

Hope saw a tear run down Susan's cheek.

"Sorry. I didn't mean to start the waterworks." Hope cringed and bit her lip.

Susan frowned. "You not being a Christian makes it hard for you to understand. He is family to us."

"Gus is dying from being infected with the HIV virus from a needle." With two fingers, William tapped his forearm at the veins. "He became a heroin addict, but he battled the addiction, then he found out he had the virus. It was the recognition of his use and the realization that he couldn't kick it by himself that he came to Christ. The Lord helped him fight until he was clean of the drugs."

Hope noted the quick glance from Susan. Would she say something about Hope's drinking? Susan nodded and raised her eyebrows again. Over the years, she said a great many things without opening her mouth. Hope dropped her gaze to her silverware.

The server brought over their drinks and set an amber liquid in front of Hope.

Hope looked up in time to see Steve glance at the glass.

An anguished internal cry screamed. *I know I have a problem.* "It's apple cider."

Steve smiled.

"Changing the subject." William gestured toward Susan. "Pastor, besides being Hope's sister-in-law, Susan is Hope's personal assistant and has her Master of Laws. She specializes in Corporate Law and helped write the new contract we will be going over tomorrow. She and Hope have been best friends since middle school. Both are pretty smart."

Susan's flushed complexion blended with her hair. "Thanks William, but I'm not as smart as Hope. You are looking at the Valedictorian of our high school and at university, Salutatorian." With her thumb, she gestured toward Hope. "She graduated with a four point two-five grade point average. And she has her doctorate in economics. The family is so proud of her. I know it hasn't been easy."

"Yes, she told me, and I'm impressed with both of your academic achievements." Steve's eyes sparkled as she glanced at Hope.

Hope's face warmed at the accolades. "I always strive to do my best." *Let's break out the champagne and celebrate my successes.*

"It was nice to see Pastor Steve. I didn't think I would ever see him again." Hope tossed her purse onto the hotel bed.

"You never told me you knew a well-groomed, good-looking man in this town." Susan smiled and bounced her eyebrows in a suggestive manner.

"He's not my type."

"You mean, because he's smart, handsome, and smells good?" Susan laughed while slipping off her shoes. "Lately, that seems to not be your type."

Hope sighed. "Okay, I get it, you're not happy with me." Hope rolled her eyes as far up as she could. Do I even understand what romantic love comprises?

She saw the profound bond that formed between her mother and father over the years. And when Josh and Susan are near each other, a special intense passion almost moves through the air. "Oh crud! That's why you're so surly. I stepped across the boundaries of your love life, and it's because I have no romance and no heart.

"You had a romantic weekend planned with Josh, and I pulled you away on business. No wonder you're not happy." Hope plopped down on the bed. "I know my choices in dates lately haven't been the best." She glanced up at Susan. Amends needed to be made. "Why don't we look at the schedules for you and Josh over the next few weeks. Maybe the two of you can take some time off." Her back and her resolve stiffened. "But regarding Pastor Steve, he's religious and I'm not." She glanced toward the bottom of the bathroom door and the same pain and emptiness of being alone night after night swept in like it always did which brought on the need to hide it under a bottle.

CHAPTER ELEVEN

Late September, near Conway, MO

Tap, Tap, Tap

A distant echo irritated Hope's semi-wakefulness. She rolled away and pulled her arm up over her head to cover her ear.

Tap, Tap, Tap

Once again, annoyance brought on an urge to scream. She shifted her body and mumbled, "Leave me alone. Can't you see I'm sleeping?" She pulled her jacket up to shield her eyes from the morning's brightness, then squirmed to readjust. "Why can't I move?"

Tap, Tap

"Ma'am. Are you okay? Hey, lady. Are you awake?" A man's muffled voice chafed.

"Go away." Hope shifted and bumped against the hard obstacle again with her knee.

"Honey, I believe she's waking up. Do you think she's hurt? Should we call for an ambulance or the police? Is she all right?" A lady's shrill questions reverberated in Hope's ears.

"Maybe she's sleeping off a night of partying, honey." The man rapped on the window again. "She's lucky she drifted off the road here in this open field."

Hope raised her head and craned her neck to look over her shoulder. She strained her eyes wide to draw them into focus. Once her eyes cleared, she glared out the glass at the couple and shifted to square herself in the car seat. She rubbed her knee and tried to arch her back.

The well-dressed man and woman stared through the driver's side window.

Hope's hand fumbled for the button to lower the barrier between her and these laborious people. Nothing. She grumbled her frustration. "Oh yeah, the key. Gotta turn the key on." The ignition key turned with a flick of her wrist, and she touched the switch again. Nothing. Following the previous steps, she tried again. Nothing. A dead battery? Her hand went to the door handle and fresh air rushed in as the door cracked open.

"Hi. How are you two doing this morning?" Hope presented a cheerful face even though her head thrummed like a bass drum. "I traveled a long way last night and got sleepy. I figured I had better stop and take a short nap before I continued. Apparently, I forgot to turn off my lights. I didn't want to endanger anyone." She pasted on a lying smile. "Thank you for stopping to check on me. I greatly appreciate it. It was very kind. Most people would just drive right by." *I wish they had.*

"Well, we were worried and thought you might be injured or something." The middle-aged woman dressed in pink and white gloves moved closer. "Is there anything we can do to help?" She leaned toward Hope, then made a sour face as she stepped back.

Hope took a quick inventory of herself. The ruffles down the front of her maroon blouse were plastered with vomit. The woman's reaction made sense.

She reached across the driver's seat and grabbed her purse, then searched for her phone. Once located, she retrieved it and checked to make sure she had some charge in her battery. Memories from her ordeal in Kansas City months ago and a fleabag hotel room drifted through her mind. If it hadn't been for Pastor Steve, she would not have found her car or help.

She turned back to the couple and raised her mobile phone. "At least my phone is charged. I'll call someone to come charge my battery." She smiled over at the man. "Thank you for stopping. I don't want to bother you folks anymore." She hesitated to ask the man if he had jumper cables. He wore a suit, and the woman appeared dressed for a fancy occasion. "Please don't let me hold you up from wherever you are going."

The man, who had graying at his temples, smiled at her and shrugged his shoulders. "I'm sorry about your battery. Do you have that insurance motor club thing that has the free towin' service? We can stay until someone comes."

"Yes, I do, and thank you for your offer to stay. Once I call them and give them my location it shouldn't be very long for them to get here." She looked around the surrounding area and did not recognize anything. She scrunched up her face and felt herself flush.

"Miss. Are you okay?" The lady in pink questioned.

"Yes, I am. I'm just a little disoriented right now from waking up. I'm not sure where I am. How far is it to the next town?"

The gentleman pointed down the road toward the morning sun. "Ten miles that way is Lebanon." He turned the opposite direction and gestured. "It's eight miles back this way to Conway and another twenty-one to Springfield."

"Thank you. I'll call my motor club and give them my location." She squinted her eyes to see the small numbers on the back of her insurance card and tapped them into her phone. Hope glanced between the man and woman. After a short conversation on the phone, Hope spoke again. "The tow service will be here in half an hour." She fidgeted with her phone. "Please, go ahead to wherever you're obviously dressed to go. Church maybe?"

"We don't want to abandon you," the man replied.

Hope wanted them to leave her alone but didn't want to offend.

"You have been most kind, and I appreciate it. Go on now, I don't want you to be late for," Hope waved her hand in the air, "whatever is on your agenda."

The couple walked back to their car parked alongside the highway, got in, and drove away.

"Wow, did I ever miss the mark." Hope rubbed her face. "How did I miss Springfield and end up twenty miles past my turnoff?"

She glanced down into the passenger side floorboard. Her mouth dropped open when she saw the empty pint of scotch on the carpet. "When did I buy that?" A faint memory caressed her thoughts of a conversation with a young lady on a bar stool in Mount Vernon. Hadn't the girl said something about a party she didn't have a ride to?

Hope looked out the side window and watched the passing cars. This wasn't good. No wonder they called it Blackout Drunk? She turned back, closed her eyes, and sighed. "Hope, you are a pathetic alcoholic. You need to fix this." When she opened them again, she stared out at the open field. *Josh said he had Jesus to help him. Gus did too.*

Hope climbed out of Baby and walked to the passenger side. After taking a deep cleansing breath, she popped open the door and leaned in. Another pungent blast of recycled alcohol smacked her in the face. She pictured the lady in pink's look of disgust and pulled back for fresh air.

Baby would need to be thoroughly detailed. Hope took another deep breath and this time held it long enough to grab the empty bottle from the floorboard. She popped open the trunk and tucked the pint into the corner. No way did she want to get caught with that up front and end up with a DUI on her driving record. Maybe she should start carrying mouth wash in her car. She could sure use some now.

Hope walked around to the driver's side and leaned against the fender. "This time it could have been tragic. I could have hit a tree and killed myself." She watched the cars fly by down the freeway. "Or worse, I could have killed someone else." Tears trickled down her cheeks. "I couldn't live with that. I have to fix my life."

CHAPTER TWELVE

October, Springfield

Hope laid out the orders she wanted Josh to take care of.

"Josh, we have those Barnes and Krieger contracts coming up. They could be vital to next quarter's profit margin. Could you look into those for me?" Butterflies fluttered. Maybe the old surge of adrenaline had returned with the chance of a new venture coming up. In the past, endorphins rushed through when her business radar tingled. Then again, she could simply need a drink. She licked her lips while Josh outlined the day's agenda for the plant supervisor Monday morning.

"Josh, while I'm thinking of it, I have Susan checking out the legal ramifications of purchasing Broderick in Farmington. Don't let this get out, yet. Expansion could be in our future." She paused long enough to draw what looked like a questioning look from him. "Can I depend on you to keep this quiet?"

"Absolutely. Sharing at this stage tells me that I am regaining your trust. That means the world. You can count on me."

"I plan to sit down with the leadership team within a few weeks to go over my plans and get feedback on whether it could happen." She stared him down hoping to show how serious she was despite the intense ripple in her stomach. "I want any outside negativity to be expressed openly. We can't afford the past lapse of having secrets within management." Would the not so subtle insinuation get the point across.

Her methods and business strategies had morphed a little in the two years of going it alone. Now, she had a group that she could bounce ideas off. Mixed feelings about sharing her thoughts made her jumpy. She watched Josh cringe.

"Yeah sure. Did you get that email I sent about the Davidson contract?" Josh tilted his head to the side.

"Yes, but I haven't had time to go over it. I'll look at it this afternoon. Thanks for getting right on it." She smiled. "Josh, since you have come back and taken over as CEO, things have picked up and are running smoother. You've eased some of the workload off my shoulders. I am free now to collect the data I need to go forward, and I can concentrate on some things I want to do with the company."

"I appreciate the encouragement. I'm going to do my best to help you move forward." He winked at her. "If I'm going to continue in that vein, I need to get back to my office."

As he exited, she leaned back in her chair.

Hope reached for her SSL mug and brought it to her lips. She scanned the office through the steam from the coffee and admired the freshly painted two-toned green and beige wall separated by the chair rail molding that she loved so much. She sputtered as the harsh dark coffee bit into her taste buds. Even sugar wasn't helping the aftertaste. Maybe just a touch of her special flavoring would help. Her eyes shot to her cabinet.

She pushed away the urge pulling her, but instead of the safety of clear thinking, it plunged her into the abyss of hopelessness. The vacuum of her private liquor cabinet sucked her in. She couldn't let it happen. Not now. Not here in the office. She had to fight it.

She grabbed her cell phone and tapped the phone directory app with urgency. "I need help." Finding the Springfield Alcoholic Anonymous locations, the panic ebbed. Browsing down the listings, she searched for a convenient and, as the group stated, an anonymous one.

She set her phone down in front of her and stared at the screen, then rubbed her temples. Her bullheaded determination shifted her resolve. "I can do this by myself. They don't have a monopoly on backbone. I'm strong enough." As the words spewed out of her mouth, the familiar taste crept in. She looked back to the phone app and cringed.

She fell back against her chair and sighed. Who was she fooling? She'd been drinking every single day and pretended it was to calm herself after a hard day at the office. Once the alcohol hit her system she couldn't stop. The last few times, she'd blacked out. Her finger scrolled down her mobile's page.

She set her phone aside, flipped open her laptop, and typed in Alcoholics Anonymous Twelve Steps. "I don't need a chaperon or meetings," she grumbled. Josh and Susan provided enough supervision. She hesitated. Had she been a responsible person?

Hope perused the Steps, but with the first line it hit her—she couldn't do it by herself. She read Step Number One, again. "We admitted we were powerless over alcohol—that our lives had become unmanageable."

The slap of reality jolted her. These people understood the truth of alcohol's pull. Hope scrolled down the list and noticed most steps referred to a higher being than the alcoholic herself.

At number four, she paused and contemplated its words. "Made a searching and fearless inventory of ourselves." Her chair leaned as she rocked backward. This needed to be thoroughly vetted. Had she really done a fearless inventory of her life? Could she honestly say she had?

Hope bounded out of her seat and marched to the entrance of her personal assistant's sanctum. She halted at the doorway and peeked in not wanting to create a disturbance, but her need overpowered her. She watched the ginger hair dip and bob behind a mountain of files and law books.

"Hi, are you real busy? I need some personal feedback on something

I believe is vitally important, but I don't want to interfere with what you have planned for the day. That's more important for the company. However, this is also significant and has possible consequences. It isn't pressing in an immediate way."

"I'm just finishing up a portion of the research on the local real estate laws for Farmington." Susan raised her nose and peered over the pile. "With the old zoning codes of the Lead Belt Region conflicting with the new environmental impact zoning codes, we will have to approach this in a very organized way when we go before the planning commissions in Farmington and the county of St. Francois." Susan shifted some documents to the other side of her desk. "Have you started any talks with Broderick Dynamics yet?"

"No. I wanted to hear from your report before I went forward. I didn't want to rush. Once we start, we need to have Josh and Tommy make a trip down to inspect the interior of the shops and the machinery to see what will work for us and what can be adapted to our needs." Hope leaned against the doorpost. "They may not even want to sell to me. Mr. Broderick didn't like me beating out her daughter, Carla, for Valedictorian.

Susan's lips pressed into a straight line, her eyes widened while her brows rose, then she tilted her head down to the side. She usually gave the same look when she had some tidbit of juicy gossip from their past. "Yeah, you messed up the grading curve big time skipping around and doing sixth, seven, and eighth grade all at the same time. Remember Carla wasn't the only one upset with that move. Janie was livid. Of course, Josh almost danced in the streets when you left our class."

Pressure like a large boulder crushed Hope's chest at the mention of Janie's personal attitude toward her accomplishments. Hope fiddled with her pen and tapped it on the doorframe. "Well, we can stay here all day and reminisce, or we can get some work done. I will let you get back to what you were doing. Will you be available by lunch to talk about the other thing? If so, maybe we can talk about your findings on the Broderick deal and make it into a work lunch for deduction purposes."

"I don't have anything pressing on the schedule," Susan said. "Let's make it happen. I will be ready, say eleven-thirty?"

"My plans are pretty flexible. I expected to take off early to pack for tomorrow afternoon's meeting with William Scranton."

Hope's stomach churned at the thought of having to go to AA meetings. Was it absolutely necessary? Maybe she could dry out on her own. But it hadn't worked in the past.

CHAPTER THIRTEEN

October, Springfield

Hope grimaced. From where she sat, Hope could almost taste the alcohol radiate off the bundled-up man with a dirty, knit skull cap as she watched him step inside the front door of the café.

Kathunk. A bottle slipped out of his fingers to the bottom of the trash container next to the entrance.

A cold fall draft blew over Hope as she and her best friend huddled in a far corner of the room away from the door. In Hope's mind, the lunch with Susan at the deli progressed on a positive path, and yet, witnessing the bottle fall sent a surge to indulge.

With a slow shake of her head at the sight, she remembered crashing the mission breakfast club in Kansas City a while back. Men and women struggling to survive everyday life. How they lasted the cold winter she couldn't fathom. She stifled a snicker as an image of a flock of homeless people flapping their arms flying south for the winter floated through her thoughts.

Hope tried to regain her composure. How could she be so shameful? She looked over at Susan and all the previous imagery drifted away like the breaking of a cloud as she watched. Her hand slapped her mouth as she snorted.

Susan's fingertip pushed the protruding bread back into her mouth as she mumbled her support of both the delicious turkey sandwich with cucumber and the idea that Hope needed something direct to reinforce the decision to curtail the excessive drinking. "What?" Some crumbs fell back to her plate.

Hope sputtered—coughed—pointed at Susan's plate, then waved away the thought.

With both of them tapping away, the Springfield AA meetings locales drifted across their phones. They each perused the schedules and looked for a time that would be conducive to Hope's schedule.

Hope lifted her coffee and swirled its contents. "Here's the deal, Susan." She gazed at a couple of ladies entering the café. "I never drink while at work anymore, and I usually do after a stressful day." Liquid splashed her wrist as it sloshed over. "Oh shoot." She grabbed a napkin and wiped the spill. Susan didn't have the market on sloppiness.

Susan scrunched up her face. "Stress is a daily occurrence, Hope. Tell me, when isn't there mental or emotional importance to your day?" She tossed over another napkin. "You may wait until you are home, but once you start?" She grimaced. "How you function the next day is beyond me."

Hope wondered that also. Some days she zombied through performing on rote in her efficient organized manner. On those days, she wouldn't allow herself to make major decisions for the company.

Hope stood and gathered the damp paper napkins. She tossed them into the nearest trashcan. Looking down at the garbage, she saw the empty bottle and all the self-control of her drinking flew out the window. She reeled from the smell that tried to tip her from sobriety to disaster. Reality hit her like a bottle in a brown paper sack to the forehead. She staggered away from the can. The intensity of the moment grew in her gut.

She returned to the table and stared down at Susan. "Girl, this pains me to have to admit, but when you're right, you're right." Hope curled her upper lip.

A large portion of white showed as Susan's eyes widened. Giggling, she whipped her phone up close to Hope's face. "Could you say that again? I didn't get that recorded. Your brother will be shocked at this confession. There will be top breaking news tonight."

They both busted up laughing as Hope plopped back into her seat.

After the outburst, the silence overwhelmed Hope as she pondered the monumental decision of which meeting place to attend. "Susan, I don't want to get mixed up with the dregs of humanity. I still need to feel good about myself."

Susan came up with a possible solution that would be close to the office on E. Kearney Street, but far enough away that her regular, consistent contacts wouldn't notice. "I'll go with you the first time you attend."

"If I'm going to conquer this, I need to do it alone. What happens when you're not there? I appreciate it, but you are busy with your family without having to run around as my chaperone. I don't see how you maintain your domestic responsibilities, along with the children."

"Yeah, it gets a little hectic sometimes," Susan said. "With Josh and me working I have had to extend Tori's hours with the baby. She has been such a Godsend." She leaned back into the soft, cushioned seat of the booth and toyed with her latté. "You know what Tori does sometimes? She does the dishes or vacuums while the girls are napping. She says she gets bored. She is a perfect picture of a virtuous woman that the Bible speaks of in Proverbs 31. She is worth more than you can imagine. Sometimes I buy her a special gift or slip a bonus into her pay."

"Aren't her children in school? What difference does it make? She has nothing better to do." Hope shrugged. "She could take some online college courses or something in her spare time to take out into the work force."

Susan grimaced. "Hope, sometimes you just don't get it!" She blew out a huff of air, shook her red mass of hair, then her voice softened.

"God gives everyone special talents according to their abilities. Yours is the capacity to present a great business model which in turn provides others with jobs, which they have the talent to do. Look at Josh and Tommy. Others have the proficiency to manage business law, like me." She drummed her finger on the edge of her cup. "Others, such as Tori, have the knack of expressing love and compassion through acts of kindness that the rest of us can't show as well."

"I understand all that." Hope stared out the window. Why would some people choose to settle for such a meager existence? She shook her head. "But she could do more for her family than what she's doing if she put her mind to it. If she is so good with children, why not become a preschool teacher?"

"If she did, then I wouldn't have a nanny for Heather and Ginny. She also picks up Ginny from preschool along with her own children while Josh and I are here helping you. So, you see, my friend, she is helping you and all you want to do is put her down."

The crushing blow of Susan's words added humiliation to Hope's fragile state of mind. "I guess I wasn't thinking about all the other things that she does, but rather why others aren't productive in my own little world." Maybe she did need some help figuring things out. Perhaps getting control of her life, and her drinking could provide some answers.

"So, Hope. What do you think of the meeting place on E. Kearney Street?" Susan continued the discussion.

"Is it down near the cola plant or closer to the big box store?"

"I think closer to the store near N. Glenstone Avenue."

"That might work. It's far enough from work to be discrete." Being extra careful not to slosh again, Hope swirled her coffee. "What have we found with workable meeting times?"

CHAPTER FOURTEEN

Mid-October, Kansas City

The gelid north wind blew autumn leaves across the highway. A beautiful collage of orange, yellow, and red adhered to the road's gray-black surface. The young trees shed their multicolored foliage in preparation of winter's onslaught of ice and snow.

Hope enjoyed this time of year the most, and this day she found pleasure in the scenery along Highway 13. With Bolivar in the rear-view mirror and Kansas City the next stop, she still had over an hour and a half of driving through the spectacular countryside before hitting the suburbs and metropolis. The partially lowered window sucked in the fragrance of the newly decaying variegated leaves.

She reached for her thermos of java and took a deep breath. The aromatic smell wafted below her nose. Not used to coffee without the Irish whiskey ingredients, she gasped at the scent. The change to this different brew wasn't easy. Staying sober became an unpleasant ordeal.

Her failures to remain alcohol-free lingered. Hope's desire to fall into the depths of a drunken stupor tarried until she coerced the thoughts back to her upcoming meeting.

Focus was the key, as well as having no distractions. Susan's presence would have helped. However, her own credibility needed to be established. Could she manage this alone?

A change of topic would prove helpful and wise.

In order to center her mind, she began the practice of talking to herself out loud.

"My goal is to hold my course and introduce my ideas to William by suggesting expansion while not revealing my plans to acquire Broderick's in Farmington. If things go well, we might be able to capture the business for a song."

Up ahead a large branch skittered across the road. Hope gulped and released a stuttered breath. "Good thing I'm not drunk now." She applied the brakes with time to spare. "That could have turned out much worse."

Hope cruised down the freeway without city congestion and entered the Power and Light District in downtown Kansas City. As she slowed down and passed the mission, she looked at the front door and saw the small cluster of unwashed homeless who huddled in the alcove.

Her shoulders sagged and her chest ached as her thoughts once again, traveled back to the morning she had crashed the homeless breakfast buffet after what she called her night of debauchery. Another thought followed of old Gus in his struggles with his addiction and his fall from success down to, from what William had shared, the man's recent demise. She wiped at her sudden runny nose.

"I guess my achievements could start to crumble if I let things get out of control. At least I haven't fallen prey to the clutches of biker-bars again."

But did she really have control of her life or was it an illusion? Could she drink socially while making a deal? Her back muscles tightened as a prickling sensation ran from her head to her tailbone. Could she let go of control in this area?

More memories flooded over her. Why did she have to marry a cheating husband? Would she drink this much if he hadn't cheated on her? She rubbed her hand over the steering wheel and stared at the brake lights on the car in front of her. "Why couldn't I have a relationship with someone with some class, like Pastor Steve?" The man probably treated his wife with respect. With the butt of her hand, she slapped the dashboard. "Stop feeling sorry for yourself and thinking these thoughts about someone who isn't at all interested in you."

Hope needed to get to her hotel room and read over the proposal for tomorrow without a drink. Maybe she should go to church with William and Gloria on Sunday. That should fill up her days. With a lighter hand, she tapped the steering wheel and nodded. This way, she could listen to see if Pastor Steve could really preach or if that day was a fluke. She'd even offer to take them out for lunch.

Bright and early Sunday morning, William and Gloria swung by the motel to pick up Hope for church. As they pulled near the front of the church, Gloria seemed ecstatic. "William, look at the new shrubs along the entrance of the parking lot."

Hope pointed to the message on the large marquee at the church entrance, which read, "When the world says, 'give up,' hope whispers try it one more time.'" Hope laughed. "That sounds personal. I didn't know they knew I was coming."

William chortled at her joke.

When Hope stepped into the foyer of the church, she half expected to burst into flames. It had been that long since she had set foot into the house of God.

She gawked at the size of the congregation, then leaned over to William. "The entire small church in Farmington where I grew up could fit in the nave of this one. How many come here?"

"The seating holds over six hundred people."

Once inside, they made their way to the right side, halfway down the aisle. The personal greetings between everyone continued for several moments. Hope met more people than she could possibly remember.

As they sat in their pew, Hope turned to Gloria. "My parents always had their special place they liked to sit. We took up a whole row with all of our friends. It was at church where Susan and I built our friendship that has lasted to this day."

After the singing and the offering, a lady sang a song which told of how Jesus Christ would carry you through the troubles of life.

The vibrations from the instruments rippled through the air and sent a tingle up Hope's spine. Not a demonstrative person prior to two years ago, she squashed down the ardent feelings.

The singer's melodious intonations flowed over Hope and the tension in her muscles slackened. With a calm, steady heartbeat, Hope closed her eyes and enjoyed the moment.

With no thoughts of the past and no worries about the future, she had no desire to be anywhere else. The message bore the weight of all her issues wrapped up into one neat package and allowed her to recognize God would carry her through the battles. If she would let Him.

Josh had spoken those same words the other day at work. Hope's mind drifted back to one of the worst meetings she and her staff had experienced.

Hope hadn't been able to get her sales staff to grasp the change of direction on the Gropperman shipment. Ready to fire the whole lot, her head had ached and her jaw throbbed from clenched teeth.

Josh surprised her when he stood up and requested the whole team go back to work while he and Susan processed with Hope.

Hope had shaken with anger and glared at her brother as the six sales personnel grabbed up their paperwork. As they walked out of the room several glanced back at her, their eyes wide while the others tucked their heads, stared at the floor, and made their escape.

Josh walked to her end of the conference table and sat, then motioned for Susan to come to join them

The scene continued in her thoughts as she recalled asking what he thought he was doing. She had been so enraged and wouldn't have been surprised if steam leaked out her ears as she set her jaw. The toxic words rang in her ears again. "You can't just dismiss my meeting! I'm the owner of this company. I'm the chairperson." The strain which had built in the muscles of her upper back and shoulders surprised her.

But Josh held up a finger which shocked her and caused her to pause. He turned to his wife, took her hands in his, bowed his head, and asked God to relieve the frustration. He'd even said she had a great plan of action. He'd gone on to confess that he couldn't comprehend what Hope wanted and asked God to help him understand, even to the point of admitting he needed help so he could relay the information to the rest of the sales staff.

Hope smiled at the memory. What a change had come over Josh after he prayed and both he and Susan came to understand her concept and idea.

Her thoughts returned to the present as the lady finished the song, Hope saw that Josh had asked a Higher Being to direct the explanation and understanding. He requested that God teach him the lesson that loomed too large to comprehend while releasing the pressure that she caused. Could God make that much of a difference? Could He carry her through the addiction? She whispered, "I sure could have used some help last night."

Pastor Steve's message had the same theme as the woman's song. He started reading about the paraplegic who was lowered into the house to be healed. It ended with Jesus Christ carrying His cross to be crucified so we wouldn't have to carry the burden of our sin. His final reading came from Isaiah 53:4-6, *Surely He has borne our griefs And carried our sorrows… And the LORD has laid on Him the iniquity of us all.*

After the services, Hope flowed with the exiting crowd.

As the individuals shook Pastor Steve's hand and made the seemingly obligatory remarks about his message, she watched and contemplated what she had heard.

Someone else carrying the weight of her actions, even if it was God, galled Hope. Why should she heap on someone else the issues of her own bad conduct? The right thing to do would be to take the full load of her own actions. Why would a righteous God, a supposed superior being, care to do that? She bore the responsibility for her own behavior, good or bad. She ran her own business without much help and held herself accountable for her own bad decisions.

Hope chuckled as a fireplug shaped woman hugged the preacher while her companion, a tall, Jack Sprat of a man looked on.

A vision of her arms wrapped around the handsome pastor popped into her mind. She glanced around and worried her neckline. Who turned up the heat in the church foyer? Did William or Gloria notice? But when she turned to find them, they were busy speaking to someone else. Hope inspected the tile flooring. Pastor Steve wouldn't be interested in a divorcee, anyway. He'd seen her after a low period and probably only thought about his deceased wife.

Hope trailed William and Gloria as they made their way toward Steve.

When Gloria stepped up to the minister, she gripped his hand with both of hers, smiled, and released one hand, then pointed back to Hope. "Great message, Pastor. You remember Hope? She and William are working out some issues between the companies and she decided to come with us to church. She has a question for you."

Pastor Steve turned to face Hope and his smile took over his face. "Thank you for coming, Ms. Sparks. What question do you have?" His crinkled grin weakened her knees.

She fought to gain back control as a dreamy haze floated over her. "Aah, yes," she stammered. "I'm taking William and Gloria out to lunch and would like to invite you to come. Unless you've made previous arrangements." She hoped not. Hope turned to Gloria. "Where are we going?" Why couldn't she remember the name of the restaurant? Her mind blanked because of the handsome man before her.

Gloria shared the restaurant's name, and thus saved Hope from embarrassment.

"Thank you for asking and I would be honored to go." Steve's smile curved his lips. He placed a hand on William's shoulder. "I have something to discuss with you and this would be a great opportunity. I planned on talking to you in a day or two anyway." He spun back to Hope. "Can I meet you there, say at two-fifteen? I need to take a couple of men down to the mission and depending on traffic, I could be back by then."

"Yes, that would be fine." The flutter in Hope's stomach intensified.

CHAPTER FIFTEEN

The upscale atmosphere of the restaurant leaned more to Hope's tastes than the previous eatery William and Gloria had chosen. She examined the large dining area with cylindrical lights of different lengths hanging from the ceiling. The carpet, a tightly woven pattern of different sized sunflowers stitched throughout, shrouded the floor. The chairs were covered with gray and white dots on a brown background. Booths along the walls of the restaurant surrounded the tables and chairs.

They followed the hostess to a square, ash table set for four.

William ushered Gloria to her chair and pulled it out. Before she sat, he kissed her on the lips.

Hope caught the mischievous twinkle that sprang from his wife's eyes. A warmth washed over Hope. True love and passion in other long-lasting marriages did exist, just like Mom and Daddy's. Was it possible that long-term, romantic marriages also existed outside that of her parents and fairytales?

While keeping her eyes on them, she fumbled for her chair. But as she reached for it, she jerked her head around in surprise. Pastor Steve had already pulled it out for her. She melted into his offering. The man had manners. Kenny did that for her while they dated and continued until six months into their marriage. She mouthed a thank you to her well doer.

He already showed her more respect than any of her dates in the last year. Would she ever find a loving, monogamous man who would put up with her strength, independence, abilities, and idiosyncrasies?

Would Pastor Steve show her much attention over this meal? It would seem so since they were both single.

However, he turned to Gloria. "I heard you are leading a women's retreat up at Saint Joseph." He sat down with his focus squarely on the older woman.

Gloria's attentive husband sat at the table beside her. Hope reached for a glass of water to put out the unbearable fire escalating in her stomach. Now this older woman had two men fawning over her. The water helped to quench Hope's disappointment. She stiffened her back. *Steve saw me at one of my worst times. He wouldn't be interested.*

Pastor Steve's eyes darted over to her as though he heard her thoughts. He smiled, then looked back at Gloria.

Her tension eased. Could the man be nice to a woman without an ulterior motive?

"Yes, I believe we'll have a lot of fun visiting the many sites there," Gloria said. "The church has a conference center and we're going to stay at the motel not far down the street." She turned to Hope with exuberant eyes. "Saint Joseph made the Wild West come alive. The Pony Express Museum at Saint Joseph shows the two-thousand-mile route traveled, which starts there and ends in Sacramento, California."

"So, besides the Bible Conference, you will be doing some sightseeing?" Pastor Steve asked.

"You bet. We're going to the Patee House, Jesse James Home Museum, Walter Cronkite Memorial, and the Wyeth-Tootle Mansion. Barbara Swanson went to a wedding there and said it is stunning." She gave Hope a sad smile. "Too bad you have such a hectic schedule. It would be nice to have you come along. I think you would enjoy the camaraderie of these women and you would be able to relax for a bit."

"Maybe sometime in the future." Glad for her busy life, Hope forced a smile. She reached for her water glass again and wished the water had some kick in it.

"So, Hope, how have you been?" Pastor Steve snapped open his napkin and laid it across his lap.

Hope glanced over to William. His head was hidden behind the menu. She brought her hand up to entwine her hair with her finger; her flirtatious gesture aimed at Pastor Steve. She regretted it immediately. The perspiration ran down her sides as she released the strand of entanglement.

"I've been fine. William and I have been going over some issues that have cropped up. I don't know if he told you about the problem we had in our shop with a robotic arm." She ran her finger over the smooth rim of her water glass to calm herself. "My brother came in and did some trouble shooting. Now Josh is back working for the company. I brought up the issue with William. He thought some connectors could be made that would stabilize the process and it looks like he managed it. It could have created disruptions in both companies."

Pastor Steve turned to Scranton. "William that's good news."

William glanced up from his menu. "Thank you, but no work-talk at this table. Hope and I get enough of it at the office." He looked over to Gloria.

Hope saw a slight grin cross Gloria's face.

William directed his comments back to the food choices. "This twelve-ounce Prime Rib looks delicious with the asparagus tips. Hope, if you prefer seafood, they have cold-water lobster tail and Alaskan King Crab Legs." He kissed his fingertips.

Pastor Steve laughed. "I guess someone got her message across loud and clear."

Gloria reached over to her husband and patted his hand in a manner that Hope took as a reward for a job well-done.

"I assume that it pertains to my job also." Pastor Steve grimaced. "I guess we will be discussing that other issue at another time."

"No, no, no," Gloria said. "You wanted to speak to my husband about a matter and you wanted his advice. He just needs some repose from the stress of his job. I always insist he take a full day each week with no discussion about work. The Lord took one day off to rest. We agreed that he is no better than the Lord, and therefore takes a full day off. Today is your workday, Pastor. What do you need?"

"Thank you, Gloria. I appreciate this. It is quite important and will affect the whole congregation. But I will hold off until after this delicious dinner that I understand Hope, our host, is providing. Thank you for this, Hope." He stood, removed his suit jacket and draped it on the back of his chair as the server walked up with her order pad in hand.

When he settled again, his pectoral muscles flexed and Hope gulped. She grabbed her menu as she tried to refocus her thoughts.

"Hope, this is quite a posh restaurant. The prices are a bit steep. Are you sure about this?" Pastor Steve wrinkled his nose.

"It will be fine. I can afford it. Order whatever you desire, my treat." She knew it would have been nicer if they could discuss business, so she could write it off. She shrugged. "I think I will go with the Alaskan King Crab Legs with a baked potato."

"And you ma'am?" The server asked Gloria.

"I'll have the same as Hope, but with a salad with Honey Mustard dressing," Gloria answered.

The young woman turned to William.

"I have to try the Prime Rib with asparagus tips and a baked potato."

"Okay Hope, if you're sure." Pastor Steve laid his napkin over his lap. "I believe I will have the cold-water lobster tail with a salad and Ranch dressing."

"Drinks?"

Gloria said, "Sweet tea."

"Sounds good. I'll have sweet tea as well." Hope licked her lips and reached for her almost empty water glass. Or a Tom Collins or a Lemon Drop.

CHAPTER SIXTEEN

After the meal at the restaurant, Hope and Steve ordered sugar with a touch of coffee. The server gave them a grimaced look as they both laughed. Apparently, he had a similar sweet tooth. William ordered a straight black coffee, Gloria, a lemonade. The afternoon crowd thinned and the atmosphere relaxed around the table.

The casual conversation mellowed Hope. Even the tension from sitting close to Pastor Steve eased. In hopes of catching a church conspiracy, a few apropos questions about his sermon were in order. "I wonder how you and the lady singer coordinated the song with your message?"

A perplexed look fixed on the minister's face.

"I don't understand. I haven't spoken to Charlotte in over two weeks. She's part of the worship team and I trust them with the worship time. I was out of town most of last week at a mission's conference down in your neck of the woods at First Baptist Church in downtown Springfield." He brought his coffee cup up and cocked one eyebrow. "I believe the Lord brought the two things together to get the precise message out to the right individual." He set his cup back on the saucer and wiped his mouth with a napkin. "What do you think, William?"

"I believe God sends a message for each individual with a particular personal need." William raised his cup to Hope.

"Are you saying that the sermon was for me, personally?" She glared at the pastor, then turned to look at William and Gloria. "I saw the marquee out front of the church. One of you told him I was coming, didn't you?" Anger rose and her throat tightened.

"No, they didn't." Steve reached his hand out and placed it near hers. "I did not speak with either of them all week until after the service and you were there. Don't forget there were over five hundred people in the audience who heard the same message. Why would I single you out?" He pulled his hand back to his side.

Hope's eyes pierced the preacher. She wanted to know the truth. Was she set up? "Yes, but all this seemed directed at me." She glanced to Gloria to see if the woman's face could be read and then she looked back to Steve.

Pastor Steve looked to the ceiling as though trying to read something off the light fixtures, then leveled his view at Hope. "It is like when Jesus Christ appeared to over five hundred after His resurrection. It is possible each person had a different perspective to what they saw and heard. They may have thought His message was directed at them in the same way you are doing now. The gospel is clear. He wants to carry your burden if you will let Him. You can carry it yourself, or you can turn it over to the Lord. The choice is all yours."

Hope eased back. Her eyes darted between the three.

Gloria's forehead creased and the corners of her mouth drooped. Her eyes glistened with moisture. Had Hope damaged any bridge of a relationship they had built?

Pastor Steve frowned.

Hope glanced to William.

William's lips pressed tight. His body crumpled into his chair making him appear a hunched old man. When their eyes met Hope knew she had hurt him.

"Hope, there are two things I want to say." William ran his fingers over the edge of his coffee cup. "First, you are a business associate of mine. To do something like that I would consider a breach of contract. To do anything behind one's back is deceitful and worthy of destroying our agreement which we are doing everything in our powers to strengthen. I would not do such a thing. Second, Hope, I consider you a friend, and a true and loyal friend couldn't do such a thing. I am dismayed you would think that of me, but I can understand why you would after what you shared with me about your past two years of dealing with betrayal. But I am still sorry you have thought this about me."

Hope's disquiet eased at William's words. "Then, why this message when I came today?"

"Perhaps God's Holy Spirit put the song and the sermon together for someone who is special to Him." Pastor Steve's eyes softened. "So, that individual might take it to heart and keep it as distinctive and exclusive for him or her." He picked up a packet of sugar and ripped it open. "Just think on that. We will change the subject as it has caused you distress. Anyway, I need to speak with William about my dilemma." As he poured the sugar into his coffee he turned to William.

"While in Springfield at the mission conference, I was approached with a proposal by the Senior Pastor at First Baptist Church. He offered me a position on staff as the Compassionate Ministries Director. I would be doing much of the hospital calls and helping with the homeless in the area. My other duties would include helping with the college age young men's ministry. Joe and Connie Barton are the leaders, but their helper finished with his doctorate and has accepted another position. He will be leaving at the end of the school year."

After hearing this new information, Hope threw off the thoughts of a conspiracy. Too many unsettling notions scampered across her mind and sent a tiny shiver through her. The stirring possibilities of having this man living nearby baffled her. "So, you'll be moving to Springfield at the end of the school year?" She took another sip of coffee as the battling emotions threatened to ambush her. Perhaps she might see him more often. Maybe, she'd attend church more.

"Hope, do you play racquetball, basketball, use a sauna, or lift weights? The church has all these to bring in the college and high school kids." He sipped his coffee again and turned his attention back to William. "Did you know there are ten colleges in Springfield with over thirty-five thousand college age students enrolled? This means I would have access to that many young people. Of course, there are more colleges in Kansas City, but accessibility to them is harder."

"So, the outreach would be less? What about the church here?" William scrunched up his forehead, one of the telling signs Hope noticed which seemed to help him tallying up all the options available.

"To be honest, as a widower and single, I feel uncomfortable when women come to me for counseling." He sighed. "I choose to leave the office door open with my secretary just outside for the women's and my comfort. It leaves the chance that our conversation will be overheard, which isn't good either." He glanced over to Hope. "I don't usually counsel women without Patricia, who is a certified counselor. She isn't always available since she's an advisor at the high school. I used to have Allison help the ladies."

"Well, Pastor, which way is the Lord moving you?" Gloria asked.

Come to Springfield! Come to Springfield!

"I feel pulled toward First Baptist, and it's not because of the bowling alley downstairs or the sauna." He glanced at Hope and smiled. Then his face took on a somber look. "William, Gloria, I don't feel I can do our assembly much good being without a wife right now. Sometimes, I am talking to a married woman who is godly and virtuous, and I think about Allie. Even though it has been two years, I want to run and hide from the memories. I think the Lord has opened this door to free me to serve Him in a new, different way." The last of his words seemed to catch in his throat and he wiped his nose with a napkin.

"Allison was such a wonderful young lady," Gloria reached over and squeezed his hand. "I'm sure the Lord will provide us with the right man and woman to replace you. What about the work you do at the mission downtown?"

"Bobby Connors and Chuck Hanford have been helping me and have actually put more time in down there. In fact, Bobby has made quite a connection and an impact there. He is well liked and has a heart for God."

"I believe the Lord has provided them to release me." He paused. "Thank you for discussing this. The questions you raised have helped me to see His path clearer."

Was God's path that clear? Did the right woman, like his wife, affect Steve in such a clear way? With Hope's independence, could she affect him or any man, for that matter?

CHAPTER SEVENTEEN

November, Springfield

Hope gazed at the huge, store-front windows which looked like billboards displaying a person's life to the entire world. She wanted this part of her life kept secret. But being near a busy shopping center on the main drag of E. Kearney Street exposed her addiction to the public. The meeting appeared to be in a storage facility's anterior office, and there, her humiliation would be unmasked.

A copse of northern red oak whose red autumn leaves intermingled with the orange and yellow foliage of the sugar maple and birch that would be denuded within weeks stood off to the side. Hope tended to relax this time of the year. She thought back to her hysterical laughter with Josh and Susan during their last golf outing with her then-husband, Kenny, right before her trip to the west coast. The fall always presented a challenge at the golf course. It didn't matter what color of ball you chose, it soon disappeared under the fallen leaves. It had been cold and after three holes they gave up and headed to the club house for a hot toddy of rum, honey, and a cinnamon stick. It had been the last get-together for the four of them before the tragedy of her failed marriage and the real start of her drinking.

Her hand gripped the door handle of Baby. With the thought of entering the AA meeting, a chill ran down her spine and it had nothing to do with the weather. After seeing the group congregated near the entrance, Hope worried she'd get cold feet and wouldn't be able to enter the building.

With a glance down at her dress slacks her gut tightened. Simple decisions almost crippled her today. Now, she wished she would have worn jeans instead.

Movement at the entrance caught her eye as two well-dressed women stepped out of the front door just as three other ladies approached from the parking lot.

"At least there are some women here." The pressure building in her stomach eased. She wouldn't consider going into the AA meeting if there weren't women.

"I'm not sure I have ever felt this naked in my life, even in a decent neighborhood like this. I'm glad I put your top on, Baby. I can at least lock you up." Hope smiled. At times like this, she could depend on Baby's discretion when she needed to carry on long, personal conversations with herself. And, this talk needed to be private. As she eyed the large parking lot next door, her heart beat faster, she wiped moisture from her upper lip, her eyes darted around. Would anyone she knew spot her?

After a quick glimpse at her Gucci bag, she shoved it under her seat. In this situation, perhaps it wiser not to advertise her assets. She climbed out of Baby, released a breath, and shoved her key deep into her pocket.

Hope marched forward and approached the entrance, then scanned the room as best she could from the outside. Once again, her heartbeat picked up its rhythm. Where were all of the exits? Would be better to know so she could bolt at the first sign of recognition.

Her eyes swept from one side to the other. Three rows of multicolored, metal folding chairs faced two white boards, at the front of the room. Built-in padded benches sat along the side walls. Other than those seats, the room presented a stark reminder of the hard life laid out to the dregs of society.

Murmured conversations around the room ran together.

Hope headed toward a planter with a fake fern that hid a bench in the corner and sat close to the exit. She slid onto the soft vinyl seat and slouched. But she looked down at her clothes and sat upright. Then reconsidered that when two men and a woman rotated around toward her and assumed the same pose.

Why were they mocking her? Did she make an unacceptable social faux pas? Were they letting her know they knew her secret and she couldn't hide?

Thoughts of escape screamed in her head. *Relax. They aren't out to get you. They don't know you. Breathe in, breathe out.* With as little movement as possible, Hope shook her arms and tried to slow her breathing.

Another group drifted in and milled about. Why had she decided to arrive so early? She ran her hands across the padded bench and gripped the edge. *Why did I have to be so punctual to absolutely everything?* She despised the arrogance of being fashionably late. Today, a case could be argued in its favor.

Hope watched a blonde walk in. Though a bit thin, the woman appeared well-kept. The black-and-white-checked gingham skirt she wore buttoned down the front with large, black buttons. Her blouse's pattern displayed small, close black dots with white background. Not a perfect balance, but the kind of contrast to pull your vision from the mismatched clothes to her bright and alert hazel eyes. Her eyelashes were long and thick. Real or fake? Hope couldn't tell. If not real, the work must have been done by a professional. Not a cheap fix. Her clothes didn't look discount either.

The slender, sandy blonde wandered over to the small group of women. She hugged two and patted the shoulder of another. The gracefulness of her interactions exuded a comforting charm. An air of sophistication surrounded the woman. It wouldn't be a surprise if she had a high level of education. Could she be the director here?

The lady scanned the room and her eyes landed on Hope, then

smiled and headed in her direction.

Not wanting to have any verbal exchanges on this first day, Hope shifted several times and looked up at the white boards across the room. Would the woman get the message? From the corner of her eye, Hope watched the female greeter seat herself about three feet away, and turn toward a young man wearing a baseball cap.

The lady sat with her legs crossed at calf-level, hands in her lap.

Hope smiled as she thought of how her mother had worked hard to ingrain that lady-like posture into her daughters. Janie could sit in that pose for hours and give off the appearance of grace and charm, then throw it off to flirt with a man like a common trollop. Hope, on the other hand, would cross her ankle over her knee like a man, and yet, almost run from the attentions of a guy.

Even after knowing Kenny for years, it had still taken months of pursuing her, before Hope even realized he wanted to date her.

With a glance at her cell phone, Hope raised her eyebrows. Wasn't it time for the meeting to begin?

And, the wait continued.

She looked around the room and wondered what these people's stories embodied.

A young man, maybe in his early twenties with sagging pants chatted with a middle-aged Latino guy wearing a straw cowboy hat. The older man had poorly crafted tattoos on his forearms.

An older woman sat off to the side by herself, her eyes appeared as slits and her head bobbed. Dozing? Looked that way.

A tall, skinny man stood, walked to the front, and shuffled some papers on the table. He whispered something to a dark-brown haired lady who sat opposite the table from him.

She nodded.

"Good afternoon. My name is George Cummings, and I'm an alcoholic."

The group responded with an unenthusiastic sounding, "Hello George."

"My sobriety—nine years and three days." He began the AA credo and the purpose of the gathering. He then read the *Twelve Steps*.

Hope looked back over to the drowsy lady, now slumped to her right side. Hope couldn't have agreed more.

George introduced Peggy, the brunette, who seemed listless and proceeded to drone out the *Twelve Traditions of AA* without much enthusiasm.

Hope caught a glimpse of the black and white decked out woman leaning over in her direction.

"Hun, I bet you're bored to tears." A slight Texas drawl rolled out but without the sleepy, southern comfort. "Why don't we slip out for a cup of coffee?" After she grabbed her purse, which wasn't Gucci but appeared upscale, and stood, she tossed her head in a come-with-me gesture.

Hope ran the purse through her memory banks. It wasn't cheap, but within reason, unless it was a knock-off. She could have gone that route, saved hundreds, and still had a nice bag. The woman had class and her style of dress was attractive, and yet, conservative. Hope rose and followed the lady out the door.

Half-way across the parking lot, Texas-lady stopped and turned to Hope. She extended her hand. "I'm Kelsey. Is that your Mercedes?"

"Yeah." Hope reached out to take Kelsey's hand.

"That's my older Lexus parked next to it." She smiled when she gestured.

They walked to their respective cars. The Lexus's interior looked spotless.

Kelsey opened her door and paused. "Are you pressed for time? Do you need to be somewhere right away?"

"No, I took the day off. I left the business in capable hands." She retrieved her keys from her pocket. "What do you have in mind?" Hope liked this girl, but still felt the need to be cautious.

"How about we go down to the coffee shop, and I'll buy you a cup? We can gab about these people." Kelsey pointed a sculptured fingernail back toward the meeting hall.

Hope unlocked Baby's door. Curiosity niggled in the back of her mind. Why would this woman want to invite a perfect stranger like Hope out for coffee? Puzzled, she threw caution to the wind. "Sure, why not? I didn't want to be in there anyway." *At least I tried. Sort of.*

CHAPTER EIGHTEEN

The coffee shop portrayed the upscale boutiques found in Chicago or New York City—minus the teeming, compressing masses—but more like someone would find in Dallas. It mixed the big city with the country. A hometown feeling that Springfield society could appreciate. The type of java retreat which would appeal to the opulent or society climbing, caffeine guzzlers.

Hope followed Kelsey through the heavy, hardwood door. The etched silk-screen across the window proclaimed the name of the establishment to the public, *When You Want to Brew.*

"The multiple meanings this coffee shop's name conjures is absolutely ingenious. Whoever thought of it was brilliant." Hope grinned as she stared at the beautiful glass panes.

"So, you got the meanings that were intended?" Kelsey held the door open and likewise gazed. A smile shone across her face.

"Yeah. Get the caffeinated fix you need while you mediate or work through your issues. I get it. I'll have to let the owner know that I approve of the message it sends. It guides the buyer to go beyond purchasing a beverage and return when life is tough or one needs peace and quiet."

Once inside, she glanced around to take in the ambience of the décor. Hope recognized prints of copies by modern impressionists which hung throughout the café.

Hope watched Kelsey waltz into the canteen in the same way she had at the AA meeting. The lady drew smiles from other customers as though she knew everyone she encountered. Kelsey had a way to tango with others even more than Susan. Still the sylph floated among the patrons.

Kelsey paused beside a young man who appeared college-aged and pointed to his laptop. "Are you getting good reception?"

"Yes, better than in the dorms."

She stepped toward a middle-aged lady and asked her a similar question about her tablet. The woman nodded and gave a thumbs up.

The lady had moxie. She came in and acted like she owned the place. Then it hit Hope. Kelsey did own the café. If she had it together as much as it appeared, why the AA meeting?

Kelsey came back to the table with two delicacy-filled plastic plates balanced in one hand and the coffees gripped by the other, the sign of a practiced server.

A red-haired barista yelled over to Kelsey, "Lauri called in. Said the baby has an ear infection, and she hasn't had any sleep. I called Sammy and he will take the shift if you don't mind. He says he could use the extra hours this week. Mid-terms aren't for another two weeks."

Kelsey nodded.

Hope she reached for the sugar before she took a sip of the rich blend, and leaned back in her chair to stare at her new acquaintance who eased into the seat across from her. "You run this place. No wonder you know everyone. Are you the owner or just the manager?"

"I'm an entrepreneur just like you, Ms. Hope Sparks of Sparks Systems Logistics."

"Wait!" Hope sputtered. She snatched up a napkin to wipe her lips. Stunned, a quick uneasiness passed over. "You know me? Did someone tell you I was going to that meeting?" She lowered her cup and glared into the blue-gray sea of twinkles in Kelsey's eyes.

The mysterious woman used a pliable knife to slice a piece of the pastry to include a portion of the raspberry fruit. "Don't freak out. I'm not a stalker." She stabbed the segment with a fork and with an elegant move stuffed the over-sized piece into her mouth. *"MMM. I love Danish."*

With gentle movement, she laid her utensil down on the plastic saucer and dabbed the edges of her lips. "Let me explain. I recognized you as I entered the meeting hall. I saw your picture in the business section of the *Springfield News-Leader* when you joined with Scranton Corp.

"Having been in the same uncomfortable situation a first-time person finds herself, I could tell if I didn't step in, you would probably not come back. That is unacceptable for what I assume are your needs. No matter how that may play out." With the corners of her mouth upturned, she raised her frothy Caffè Mocha near her lips. "The way I look at it, you went there for a reason, and it wasn't for the social graces of the participants. So, let's take an overall view of our current standing."

"Why would you care what I did?" Hope used her plastic fork to cut her dessert, but the prongs broke off. "Right there is an example of my life!" She stood up and walked over to the counter and retrieved another fork.

"Sit, Hope. You don't mind me calling you Hope, do you?"

"No." A little late to ask. Hope raised her right eyebrow.

"You were either there because you have an addiction problem and the courts made you go, or, you have decided you need some help. You made the choice to fix it yourself before you messed up the lives of everyone you know. As a business owner, alcohol could affect many people's lives." Kelsey raised her mug up in a toast. "Welcome to the club. I go because I'm an alcoholic and can't do it alone. I deal with it daily and have for six years. Because of my decision to deal with my problem, I have friends who love me and hopefully employees who can trust me."

"Do you have any family in the area?"

"No, Dad died when I was in high school from a heart attack. While I was away, right after graduation from college Mom died from cancer. I was too busy or too drunk to care until too late. No brothers or sisters."

"I'm sorry to hear that. That's sad. How do you deal with it? Without my family and my company, I would crumble." Hope cut into the Danish and munched it down in short order to evade more emotion than necessary.

"Thanks. It's a real grind some days." Kelsey cut into another piece of her pastry. "Now, let's talk about the riff-raff at the meeting." She waved the stabbed treat in the air. "You need to know what these drunks and druggies are all about before you start hanging out with them on a regular basis. But, if after I tell you about these characters, you decide not to return, you might want to go a different route called a Serenity Meeting. I personally go to both."

"Well, Kelsey, to tell you the truth, these meetings aren't necessary. Someone suggested it to me, not that I need them in order to stop drinking. When I drink, I continue until relaxed enough to fall asleep." Hope looked up at the prints on the wall to avoid the reaction she expected.

Kelsey raised her eyebrows again, then reached over, picked up both their empty plates, and took them to the trash can. When she came back, she stood by her chair and stared into her cup. "Mine's cold. Need yours refreshed?" Without waiting for a response, she grabbed Hope's cup and proceeded to the coffee maker. When she returned, she sighed and scooted the mug to Hope.

Hope sipped her coffee and waited. She watched Kelsey shift herself at an angle.

The lady's delicate hands wrapped around her cup. Kelsey lifted the drink to her lips and held the pose without so much as a taste. Her focus over the rim of her cup never left Hope's face.

Hope shifted in her seat, then shredded the napkin in her lap.

"I can relate to what you are saying. I said the same thing all the time." Kelsey lowered her cup and settled it on the tabletop. "The stress of work and all the garbage you must put up with weighs heavy on your mind. Everyone waiting for you to fail." Kelsey's eyes glanced to the steam rising from the mug and back up at Hope. "So, you come home to the lonely house to unwind. You have a drink or two, but when you wake up in the morning the bottle is empty, and you notice you didn't get undressed for bed. Yeah, I know the feeling." She lifted the cup and took a drink, but her gaze remained on Hope's face.

Hope looked down into her own drink. Who was she fooling?

"Let me tell you about a few individuals that were at the meeting." Kelsey lowered her Mocha onto a fresh napkin. "You saw the Ecuadorian gentleman with the straw hat? That's Carlos. Did you notice the prison tattoos on his forearms? Carlos spent six years incarcerated for vehicular manslaughter after he drove a truck into a crowd of pedestrians in a farmer's market. He was so intoxicated he didn't know he did it. The only thing that stopped him was a tent tangled up around his axle. Two people died and four others were hospitalized.

"You saw young Patrick. He also has the prison tats. He decided to party with some buddies the night his young wife went into labor. He rushed home and drove his wife toward the hospital to celebrate the birth of his first child. They never made it. Patrick ran off the side of a bridge. He swam to safety and walked away from the crash while his wife, who was pinned down by a double case of beer, drowned. He walked about a half mile, then laid down to sleep it off. He's been an emotional mess and can't hold down a job. He was released from prison six months ago."

"That's horrible. I wouldn't hire him."

"Let me tell you about another person." Kelsey pushed her drink away ever so slowly. "This lady finished at the top of her class in advertising and business administration. After graduating from Texas A

& M with a bachelor's degree, she landed a terrific job in New York City at a big advertising agency. As many new graduates do, she started at the bottom and worked her way up.

"She decided things weren't happening as quickly as she thought they should. So, she worked her way into a marriage with one of her supervisors who was a drinking buddy. Things still weren't going as fast as she desired, and she began playing footsie with one of the big honchos. He helped her out by making her his personal assistant. All the wining and dining took its toll on her marriage. She and her husband tried to work it out, but her drinking ended her dreams and her marriage. Her marriage and her career blew up in her face when she showed up at work drunk."

"Which lady was that? The one that kept falling asleep?"

Kelsey shook her head. "You're looking at her." She picked up her cup and gulped down another swallow. "I thought I had the drinking under control. I got to the point that I began to have blackouts. If I had stayed in New York, I would have continued to drink and probably ended up on the streets. Embarrassed by how my career fell apart, I decided not to go back to my hometown of Garland, Texas, and Dallas was too close to home, so I moved here. I needed to get my life back. The coffee shop is a nice distraction. Coffee is not my passion. My desire is to get back into the business world."

Hope stared down at the floor. "I never would have thought—I mean, you seem to have it together." Could falling asleep after a few drinks really be blackouts? What about waking up twenty miles past Springfield? And why did Kelsey even care?

CHAPTER NINETEEN

Throughout their shared lunch the next day, Hope told her best friend and confidant, Susan, everything the mysterious Kelsey had shared with her. After she wadded up trash and threw it away, she watched for a reaction.

"Hope, I'm uncomfortable with this whole scenario and want to speak further before we leave work for the evening. Plus, I want to pray about it." Susan munched down the remainder of her sub sandwich as they discussed Hope's first day at the AA meeting and her escape with Kelsey. "Let's talk after work. It'll give me some time to analyze it."

Thirty minutes before day ended, Hope headed to Susan's office as a plan took form. She paused in the archway of their connecting door. "Have you had a chance to think about what I told you earlier?"

Susan looked up from her pile of paperwork. "All I can say is, it didn't take Kelsey long to spot you and latch on."

"That's why I want you to meet her." Hope rested her cheek against the cool doorframe. "You know that I sometimes don't see things the way others do."

"By your description of her, she sounds like quite a smooth talker. Most con-artists usually are, and they spot where the money and vulnerabilities are." Susan shut down the lid of her laptop and carried her documents to her file cabinet. After she locked the drawers, she leaned against the repository. "You're right, I need to check her out. Right now, though, I'm running late, and Josh is waiting. We need to rescue Tori from the children." She chuckled. "Do you know what time

Kelsey goes to the coffee shop?"

"She says she gets there early to open up around six."

They walked down to the foyer where Josh sat.

Josh's teeth clenched—upper lip curled—a brow knit as he stared at his mobile phone.

"Whatcha watching?" Susan stepped over and placed a hand on her husband's shoulder.

"Some stupid video." He shook his head. "This guy's lucky he didn't get killed."

She turned back to Hope. "How about we have a planning meeting for nine at the coffee shop?"

"Are we moving our eight o'clock meeting? No one told me." Josh's scrunched up nose and curled lip had both ladies snickering.

"No, babe. This is after our staff meeting." Susan ruffled his hair. "Hope and I are going for coffee and rich, yummy pastries, and you can't go." She reached down and patted his stomach. "I'm going to meet her new friend."

Josh expelled a hefty breath. "What's his name and does he have a job?"

His remark stung, Hope set her jaw, "He is a she, and I met her at the AA meeting I went to. And for your information, she owns her own business called *When You Want to Brew*. It's a java retreat just off N. Glenstone." Hope looked at Susan to confirm. "Yes, nine will work for me."

"If Josh will watch the kids after dinner tonight, I can do a background search."

The next morning, Hope and Susan talked about Kelsey as they drove across town. What little Susan discovered with her research appeared to validate Kelsey's storyline. Despite the car's warm interior, a chill ran through Hope at the possibility Kelsey might scam her.

As they pulled into the parking lot, Susan rested a hand on Hope's forearm before they exited her Hyundai Elantra. "I want you to understand something. A good con-artist will set up a false personal history that can be checked out easily. I can dig in deeper with more time, so let's take this slow."

"Really, Susan? You've got to be kidding. I thought you were the one who didn't want to look at the negative side of anyone."

"I usually am. But things went too smoothly. It sounds to me like she opened herself up too quickly." Susan sighed. "I guess after the mess Josh and I made, and my decision for full disclosure to you, I've become a bit protective of my best friend." She touched her chest at heart level.

Hope stared at Susan's hand on her heart, then up to the soft pleading in her moist eyes which spoke volumes of her deep love to Hope.

Susan stepped out of the car and spun around to face Hope "Let's go meet this new friend of yours. She better not horn-in on our closeness. I'll fight her if I need to." She held up one clenched fist, and stretched out her other hand in a feline scratching pose.

Hope sputtered at the sight of her extremely feminine, and yet, protective friend. As they walked together toward the coffee shop, Hope grabbed Susan's hand to slow her. "I love you, girlfriend. You're so tough." She snickered. "Sometimes you treat me like a child or little sister, though we're only six-months apart," Hope laughed, "and though you think me naïve, I still appreciate your protectiveness." She winked.

Five minutes later, Hope eased onto a barstool and scooted up closer to the tall round table.

Susan stood gazing at the prints scattered along the walls.

Hope glanced around to check for Kelsey's whereabouts and waved when she spotted barista behind the counter.

The assistant manager tipped her head in acknowledgement while she steamed the frothy foam on a customer's mug. "Kelsey's in the back, signing for a drop-off. She should be finished in a few minutes. I'll let her know you're here."

"No hurry."

Susan wandered past each print and tilted her head from side to side. After making the rounds, she paused behind a stool across from Hope. Susan pursed her lips, her eyes darted and her brows furrowed.

Hope nodded her head as she scanned the portraits once more. "She has good taste in art, doesn't she?" From her position, Hope watched as Susan seemed to browse the entire café in a single eye sweep.

In a low voice, Susan said, "She's good, if she's a con. She's not dumb, that's for sure. I don't know why she would hang out at the AA meeting to shanghai anyone. Let's just be aware, okay?" She climbed onto her seat.

"There she is in the red blazer and beige leopard blouse." Hope leaned her head toward the coffee station, then watched Georgia whisper to Kelsey.

Kelsey glanced over her shoulder and smiled, then grabbed a couple of menus.

Hope watched Kelsey's panther-like grace as she moved in their direction. Black skinny-jeans and black pumps completed the woman's ensemble.

"Wow." Susan's reaction said it all.

"Good morning, Hope. How are you?" Kelsey set the glossy folders which displayed a variety of tasty desserts in front of both women. "What can I get you to drink?" She gazed at Susan as her lips turned up at the corners into a pleasant smile. "And you are?"

"You must be Kelsey. I'm Susan." She extended her hand.

Kelsey accepted Susan's offer and nodded.

"If you have a few minutes, and aren't too busy, I wanted Susan to meet you." Hope fingered the slick surface of the menu.

"I have about an hour before I have to go tally yesterday's booty and still have time to run the proceeds to the banking monopoly. My creditors don't seem to have a sense of humor when they don't get paid." She winked at Susan.

"I'm sure this place can get expensive with all the high-end coffees and rich pastries. I know this is personal and I shouldn't ask…and you don't have to answer if you don't want to, but do you have a big mortgage on this place?" Hope tilted her head.

Kelsey held up her manicured pointer finger to her lips. "Don't tell my slave labor that I don't have any debt as they may start a mutiny and demand a raise. I had enough in my coffers when I left New York to buy this outright. I learned how to handle finances while at my former place of employment and more so after I became a Christian. Our church is solvent with money in the bank to build a new sanctuary without going broke. The pastor says too many believers are depending on the Second Coming of Christ to absolve them from debt and liability." She smirked. "Some hold to the mantra, 'Leave it for the devil and his crowd!', but then they can't give from the heart since they are one step from debtor's prison. I refuse to be obligated to anyone. I am blessed."

Georgia carried over a tray with three drinks, a Caffè Mocha, a cappuccino, and a latte.

"Thanks, Georgia," Kelsey nodded to her employee.

"Now I feel guilty for thinking about borrowing for the possible deal I'm pondering." Hope reached for the latte knowing that Susan preferred cappuccino.

"Well Hope, if one borrows to improve themselves with collateral that will cover the loan in case of default, there's no issue. If you set it up to break even, and things go badly, it shouldn't be a problem because you can walk away not owing anyone. You can start fresh again on a level playing surface." Kelsey turned to Susan. "Does that answer your questions as to whether she should hang out with the likes of me, another alcoholic like her?"

Susan leaned back in her seat and stared. Maybe Kelsey wasn't the Black Beard con-artist after all.

Hope let her eyes flit between the two. Had Kelsey just issued a challenge? Kelsey didn't stand a chance against Susan. How long before Kelsey lowered the skull and crossbones and walked the plank? Hope smirked at her own wit.

"So, you own this lock, stock, and barrel?" Susan swept her hand to include the entire café.

"Yes, I spent some time investing while in the 'City'. Kelsey made air marks as she said the word. "I'm picky and quite conservative in my stock choices. I wished I had been more selective in my behavior before I ruined my career by showing up to work intoxicated."

"Hope told me that you were in advertising for a large firm." Susan made eye contact with Hope. "So, you lost your job because of drinking?"

"I was fired way back when alcohol became more important than my relationships, including my marriage. I even used the excuse that I was grieving my mother's death. I do have to admit it was a cancer that caused the destruction of my life. But not my mother's, rather the kind of disease you can buy in a bottle."

Kelsey toyed with her drink and looked straight at Hope. "Girl, every day you buy a drink, you poison your mind with the fallacy of 'I'm in control of my destiny'. There is only One who has mastered the future, and you need to look to Jesus, and Him alone. No man, no amount of money, no perfect job, not even your precious friend here can get you out of the mess that is your impending doom if you continue."

"And so, by telling me about all the stories of other people, you want me to realize I have a problem, and to stay the course with AA or the other place, the Serenity Meetings, at the mission. Is that how you think you can help me?" Between the hot coffee and the frustration, the burning acid reflux built in Hope's esophagus.

Hope peeked at Susan. Would she help to glean some wisdom? What she saw was a friend that looked in deep thought. Was Susan buying into the con act? *Hey Bozo, are you missing something? She mentions Jesus and you fall all over yourself?*

Kelsey's dialogue interrupted. "Hope, I told you those stories to let you know that they are no different than you, other than their financial standing." Kelsey touched the table near Hope's hand. "And, I'm too much like you. I see you as a possible friend I can relate to. I am highly motivated to succeed. I also see my failures. That's all. We all need direction, and it must be through Jesus Christ."

Susan nodded. "Sweetie, I made a bad mistake when I tried to protect you from the truth. It caused more heartache and separated you from Josh's and my love. The circumstances that caused it were horrible, but we should have been there to help guide you through the hurt, not hiding it from you." Tears trickled down her cheeks. "Our error threw you into despair and into the bottle. But, we're here now."

Hope took a sip of the latte as she stared at the silk-screen etching on the door. "Perhaps, I could use some direction. I'm not seeing this any clearer than I can see through that silk-screen window. If I don't fix this, I might mess up the new Broderick's venture. Kelsey, what night is that Serenity Meeting? It might be a better fit for me." But only time would prove whether it would.

CHAPTER TWENTY

December, Springfield

Hope laughed as she listened to the weather forecast. "Like they always say about the Missouri climate, 'If you don't like the weather, wait a few minutes it'll change.'"

She left home under frigid, cloudy skies. The overnight freezing rain left the roads slick with ice. Halfway to work, snowflakes drifted onto her windshield.

Throughout the day she watched the meteorological transformations out her office window. The sun broke out around noon. After work, the dreaded swarm of pounding rain drops returned. Hope grabbed her briefcase and headed out for the evening's Serenity Meeting a little earlier than usual. She cursed the cold sleet, it stung like a bee when it hit her exposed skin.

"Not good. Not good. Come on key get in there." Hope's teeth chattered as she shook from the ten-below-zero temperature. She cursed at her key fob which refused to work because of the cold, and she struggled to fit the key into the frozen car door lock. The freezing rain stuck to everything and ice wrapped around the door handle. Her hand fumbled in her purse searching for the small lighter. When at last she found it, she held it under the lock to melt the arctic crust, then warmed the key with the flame, and slipped the key into place. With the door welded shut by the crystals of frozen clear sealant, she tugged until at last it yielded.

"Okay, Baby, let's warm us up." The car's engine groaned and complained. She paused and tried again. This time Baby roared to life. "Thank you, honey." She patted the steering wheel with her fur-lined, leather gloves.

Hope leaned her head back against the headrest as the Mercedes heated. She had to analyze the latest disaster to befall the company. What a day! With the news of Loriann's accident the night before, everyone at the office scrambled to connect to their outside contacts. The pregnant Loriann had slipped on the frozen snow coming out of the grocery store and broke her ankle and wrist, but the doctor said the baby was fine. At least that was good news. What would she do without a receptionist since hers would be off work for a while?

Hope had to find a replacement temp. She hated temps. They could never keep up. Hot Irish coffee might take the edge off.

Necessity caused her to push aside the pressure to finish the Ashland order to allow for the weather to get to the Serenity Meeting on time. She'd been sober for three weeks and thought she had it down pat until this morning's fiasco over Loriann. The icy blur on her windshield mocked her. Could the defogger and heater keep the glass warm enough for the wipers to function, especially with the predicted snowfall later? She breathed out a huff of vapor.

She chuckled as she listened to the national weather forecasters on the radio speak of climate change.

Hope pulled out of the parking lot of SSL onto N. Kansas Expressway. Her tires slipped on the slick blacktop. In order to avoid the loss of control on the ice, she lifted her foot from the accelerator and eased toward W. Kearney Street on her way to pick up Kelsey at the coffee shop. Hope wanted to continue their discussion about the flow of the economy throughout the nation and how it affected small businesses like theirs.

With the frozen streets, rather than the usual fifteen minutes, it took her thirty-five minutes to go across town. She pulled into the parking lot and somehow managed to miss a young man shoveling the remnants of the snowpack from the lot's opening.

Hope grabbed her umbrella to ward off the freezing rain and quick-stepped over the clumps of snow while she avoided the slick ice. Glad for her boots, she stomped the clinging, white sludge from her shoes while she tried to juggle the parasol and briefcase. When inside, she moved to a corner table and set the case down. Once unencumbered, she went to make her selection.

The barista smiled when Hope approached the bar. "How can I help you?"

"An Expresso, please."

Georgia raised her head from behind the counter and grinned. "An Espresso? Rough day? Or do you have a long evening ahead?" She rose from her squat. "Cindy, this is Kelsey's friend, Hope Sparks from Sparks System Logistics across town. She usually takes a latte or an occasional cappuccino. I'll let Kelsey know you're here."

"Thank you, Georgia." She watched Cindy fumble a tall mug and managed to save it from sure breakage with her quick hands. "Careful. Nice save. Did you play softball?"

"Yeah, I played fast pitch. How did you know? Did you play?"

"No, but my older sister did. Pitcher and third base. She had a strong arm. I'm sure you made very few errors. Am I right?" Hope smiled. "I watched quite a bit. I was a nerd. Are you from Alabama or Mississippi?"

Cindy grinned. "'Bama. I'm going to Baptist Bible College over on E. Kearney Street."

"What's your major?"

"Elementary Education."

"Good luck."

"I believe it is right where God wants me, so I think there is no luck to it. I'll more than likely teach in a Christian school. Never know, I may meet Mr. Right and become a pastor's wife and teach."

"Don't jump into marriage too soon. Explore life for a while."

"I'm waiting for God to show me when. I'm in no hurry. It's all His timing."

Hope cocked her head. Interesting. That's what Kelsey said about life in general. Why was it always about His schedule? What about my timing?

Hope watched and listened to the young girl. She chatted about her plans and focused on the coffee at the same time. Not an easy job.

Hope knew a pastor she wouldn't mind getting to know better. She wondered if Pastor Steve had moved down to Springfield yet, or if he changed his mind? Maybe she'd ask William next time she talked with him.

"There ya go, Miss. Sparks, or is it Mrs.?"

"It was Mrs. But now it's Ms. Not a good marriage, so be careful with the hubby search."

Hope told Kelsey all about the day's happenings with Loriann over cups of brew.

"That's tough, Hope." Kelsey gripped her hot tea in both hands. "I agree with you about temp service. You seldom get someone that is compatible with your business. Can you grab someone from the lower ranks of your staff to replace Loriann while she's laid up?" They sat at a corner table waiting to leave for the Serenity meeting.

"I considered it, but all three girls are temps. They are business majors from Southwest Missouri State. I don't feel comfortable letting them into the inner sanctum of my company. They could work for a rival at some future date. They have specific jobs that don't overlap. I want to help with their education but not to that extent."

"Corporate espionage is an issue of small and large businesses. With the growth you are planning, it could occur." Kelsey leaned back, looked over at Georgia, then quieted as she sipped her drink.

Hope shuffled some of her papers back into her folder, then stuffed the file back into her briefcase. The time to leave for the meeting closed in. She liked the atmosphere of the Serenity Meeting more than the standard AA meetings. Though she had returned to a couple of those meetings when her addiction almost overtook her. She sensed an attitude at the mission that gave her a what? A peacefulness without the stress that brought on the drinking? Maybe so.

"You seem in deep thought, Kelsey. What's on your mind?" Hope lifted her cup to her lips. That the woman could compete on an intellectual level concerning business matters in general and their influence on the individual and corporate worlds impressed Hope.

Kelsey stood and collected their cups. "Let me think about your dilemma. How soon do you need someone, and how much in-depth in business knowledge does this person need to have?"

"Soon. I would prefer the person to have some working knowledge of how a business runs. Josh and Susan can help direct when I'm unavailable."

"Hope don't stress over it. It could send you over the ledge and restart trouble. You are already almost a month into your clean life. Go to God and pray to Him about it. We'll figure it out." Kelsey turned to set their cups on the counter.

Hope stood. "Let's go while it is snowing, so it covers the ice."

CHAPTER TWENTY-ONE

Early January 2012, Farmington

The top four managers of SSL followed Edward Broderick past the receptionist. Hope perused the portraits lined down the short, broad hallway of Broderick Dynamics. She recognized photos of Mrs. Broderick, Carla, and her brother during different stages of their lives and regarded the pictures of Carla's grandparents who had founded Broderick's some forty years prior.

A sale of the company looked destined to happen according to Hope and Susan's research. By Edward's accounting, the children weren't interested in the family business.

When Edward Broderick offered to set up a time for them to meet, Hope could not have been more surprised. And then he agreed with the inclusion of Josh, Susan, and Tommy to join in the meeting. A promising development for sure.

The beige hall opened into a small office with a medium sized computer desk. A tall brunette around forty-years-old stood guard by a solid white oak door with an antique brass thumb latch. Four windows, separated by beautiful white-oak mullion, stood behind the apparent personal assistant.

As Hope's group entered the space, Edward smiled at the tall woman still by the door. He reached for the latch and paused. "Carol, may I introduce, Hope Sparks, owner of Sparks Systems Logistics. This young lady is Susan Hart, Hope's assistant. These two men are Josh Hart,

C.E.O., and Tommy Jenkins, head of maintenance. Josh and Hope are brother and sister, and Susan is married to Josh."

Carol nodded at the visitors. "You seem to know them quite well, Mr. Broderick."

"They all went to school with Carla. I've known them most of their lives." He smiled and turned his attention to first Hope, then Susan, Josh, and Tommy, and he finally gestured toward his office manager. "Folks, this is Carol Baggerly, my assistant. She knows all the ins and outs of the business and keeps me on a short leash. She has been my trust-worthy right-hand for fifteen years. Carol, could you grab the file I prepared for Ms. Sparks and her assistant?" He ushered Hope's group into the room and pointed to the chairs. "Carol is currently taking a few courses in pre-law. She may have some beneficial insights or suggestions."

The five of them stepped into a larger office which appeared a cavernous space encased in walnut shiplap panels. The matching desk almost filled a quarter of the room. Hope stared in disbelief at its size.

Edward wasn't a large man and when he slid into his leather chair, it seemed to engulf him.

Manuals covered a shelf along one wall and a large collage of Edward's hunting expeditions hung on the far side. Hope choked and coughed, aghast at the avid hunter's display of dead animals. She glanced over at Susan and rolled her eyes.

Susan grinned.

"I see you are a hunter, Mr. Broderick." Susan gestured to the photographs. "Josh and Tommy like to kill the wild beasts, too. I am sure your wife appreciates that you keep them here and not at home."

"You will notice that several of the pictures are of my wife."

"See Susan, other women go hunting." Josh smirked.

"Maybe, but I prefer to track my game at high-end department stores. I have found some killer deals." Susan giggled.

"Mr. Broderick, I called Pete and he will be here shortly." Carol eased into the seat nearest Edward with a tablet in her hands.

"Thanks for remembering." In slow motion, he wobbled his head. "See, I told you she keeps me organized. Pete is head of maintenance. He will walk Josh and Tommy around the plant later. He's a good man, former Marine, and quite good at his job, but don't tell him I said that. His noggin is big enough." Edward chuckled.

Tap, tap.

A man poked his large head through the entrance. "Is it okay to come in, Mr. Broderick? Carol wasn't at her desk. Oh, there she is." He nodded at Carol, then stepped through the doorway with the grace of a swan but the body of a gorilla and stood by the collage with his legs splayed wide and his arms pulled behind him as if in a military stance.

Hope snickered, then leaned over to Susan and whispered, "He's huge. He could move a machine by himself with or without a forklift."

"Thanks for coming Pete. When we finish with our initial discussion, you can escort Josh and Tommy around the plant and answer any questions they have about the equipment."

After the primary meeting, Hope watched Pete, Josh, and Tommy exit. She shifted back in the chair across from Edward and glanced over to Susan, then to Carol. A quick adrenalin rush passed through her and her nervous energy spiked. Often, she would discuss business over drinks to help the opposing side relax their guard a bit. If she remembered right, Broderick was a teetotaler.

Carol stood and walked to a small portable file cabinet on casters, then maneuvered the repository beside her own chair. She slid open the top drawer, reached in, withdrew a thick file, and placed it on the desk to the left of Edward. The familiarity between the two—evident. Everything looked choreographed to precision which gave evidence of the length of time they had worked together in a close manner.

"This is the County of St. Francois' assessment of the property value." She pointed to the first document as she laid it to his right. She glanced up at Susan.

Hope bristled.

"As I am sure you have researched, there are no liens on the property and no current second mortgages. The first title is free and clear."

"I noticed that." Susan nodded.

Hope shifted in her chair and coughed.

Carol deposited another document to Edward's center. "Here are other offers we have received from different corporations. Some are very lucrative but required revamping the entire employee base. This restructuring is unacceptable. We have families from our area dependent on the jobs we offer. To bring in outsiders to fill these positions would be an insult. Mr. Broderick dismissed those propositions immediately." She gave a quick glance in Hope's direction but returned her stare to Susan. "What are your plans for the employees that live in this area? Are you going to toss them aside for your own profit?

"Mrs. Hart does not make those decisions. I do." Hope sat up more erect and bristled again. When had she lost control of the meeting?

As if reading Hope's mind, Carol re-directed her conversation. "Ms. Sparks, I do acknowledge you as the final say in this process." Carol let her eyes dart between Hope and Susan. "Mrs. Hart is a strong influence on you as your legal advice, and I assume you will not make a move without her counsel. Therefore, why beat around the bush? Why not be honest and straight forward?"

Carol suggested an interesting postulate, which Hope had not recognized, until now. Susan most definitely played a powerful role in the decision-making process.

Susan raised a brow and her eyes shifted to Hope. An upturned, crinkled smile materialized.

Edward laughed. "Hope, as you can see, we are nothing more than pawns in this game. Carol has expressed what my desire is for this company. This is a family-run business that has its roots planted firmly and deeply in this community." He shared with her his aspirations that the business would become solid enough to maintain full employment for his current employees and its connection to the community of Farmington.

Hope pulled out her tablet and made a couple of swipes with her finger. Her eyes scanned the screen to remind herself what goals she wanted to reveal and what details she needed to keep private. She winked at Susan as she realized how Carol had hit the nail on the head.

Carol, in turn, laid out more of the balance sheet to reveal the business ran in the black with cost analysis showing the steady dwindling of customers in a field that deteriorated with no real future.

"So, my projections are true that your electronics is no longer viable." Hope thought about all the research she had done on Broderick's products. Not being on her toes to new trends in SSL's specialty technologies could up-end her company like Broderick's.

Edward picked up the folders and handed them back to Carol. "Here's the deal, Hope. My son, Bobby, is involved in his career up north. Carla and her husband are wrapped up in teaching and with our grandchildren. They are not interested in this business which has no real future. My wife, Josie, and I are ready for retirement, but we feel somewhat responsible for these families and the community. I want Farmington to prosper. It's not easy out there." He gestured toward the large window to his side. Edward took a deep breath and stood. "It's getting close to lunch. Carol, tell Debra to take all calls."

Hope's father's own words rang in her ears. "To whom much is given, much is required." The mounting pressure of responsibility ascended. Her throat dried. A drink would help right about now. She shook her head. Maybe she needed the inner strength which Kelsey spoke of. Would God carry the burden which Pastor Steve preached about? Could she trust Him enough to ask?

CHAPTER TWENTY-TWO

Early January, Rolla

Hope's delight in how well the meeting with Edward Broderick went on Friday continued. Saturday morning started off at the elder Hart's breakfast table with a hearty breakfast. Annie helped Mom cook. Bacon, eggs, with biscuits and gravy crossed the table as SSL management team discussed the pros and cons of acquiring Broderick's business. Daddy sat off to the side and listened without offering any insights. Everything sounded promising.

Mom and Daddy seemed to have fun bunking with Heather and Ginny over the weekend at the Hart homestead in Farmington. Josh and Susan settled into Josh's old room and Hope stayed in hers. Tommy and Annie went to his parents' home across town.

"I miss all of my children being in one place." Mom wiped her eyes with her apron. Josh, Dad, and Hope each picked up their cups and walked into the living room without response.

Sunday afternoon right after church, Hope and the others climbed into Josh's eight passenger SUV and left with bunches of kisses from Grandma and Grandpa. The forecasters predicted possible inclement weather for later the same day, but the dark clouds cleared as they reached Rolla.

Everyone burst into tears of laughter when Tommy's stomach growled its empty discontent.

"Uncle Tommy's tummy is telling him, 'I'm hungry'," Ginny

squealed and pointed at his stomach.

Josh laughed. "Well, knowing Uncle Tommy like I do, we need a pretty big plate of meat and potatoes to fill it." He chose the next exit and pulled into Downtown Steak House and Grill which was in sight of the highway.

Hope exited the vehicle and stared at the front of the restaurant. Her sigh loud enough to grab Susan's attention. "If this place has sawdust on the floors like at the restaurant in Kansas City, I'm leaving."

"Hey Hope, you'll love the food here. Tommy and I used to come here occasionally while going to Missouri S and T." Josh rotated his daughter, Ginny, to his opposite hip and draped his free arm over Hope's shoulder.

"Yeah, when we could afford it." Tommy smiled down at the diminutive Annie.

"Ugh," escaped Hope's lips as they stepped through the door to the foyer.

"What?" Josh grinned.

"Really, dead animals and fish heads on the wall?" Hope snarled at her brother. "Didn't we just deal with this at Broderick's?"

Susan gripped Heather's car seat with both hands. "I find it charming. The only thing that could make it better would be Roadkill Salad." She batted her eyes at Josh. "Yum, yum. Hope, what did you expect from two hunters?"

"Maybe a little class without critters?" She watched the hostess walk toward them. "Susan…you, Kelsey, Annie, and I need to have a road trip for some fine dining and theater. Something upscale, where we can dress up."

"How many in your party?" the young lady asked.

Still smiling, Josh held up five fingers and then added, "A highchair and enough room for the baby's car seat." He shifted Ginny in his arms as Susan toted the sleeping Heather in her carrier.

"Follow me."

Tommy and Annie led the way with Hope trailing behind.

Susan stopped. "Why, look who we find lurking about in a country steak house. Hope, it's Pastor Steve."

Steve Burrow raised his head from the menu and gave a big smile. "Well, hello Mrs. Hart. How are you? Ms. Sparks? You're both looking well." He slid out of his seat and extended his hand toward Josh. "You must be Mr. Hart, Hope's brother. I see the family resemblance. I heard a little about you when I met your bride. We have a mutual friend— William Scranton."

Josh gripped Steve's hand. "Yes, I heard about you. You're William's pastor. Have you ordered yet?"

"No." Steve glanced at Ginny and then over to Heather in her infant seat. "Who are these two beautiful young ladies?"

"This is Ginny." Josh nuzzled her neck and she giggled. He then pointed to the sleeping little one. "This is Heather. Would you like to join us? I'm sure they can make room for one more. Unless you are meeting someone?"

"No, I'm here by myself. I'm coming back from a conference in St. Louis and headed home to Springfield." He turned and looked at Hope. "I would love the company."

Heat rushed to Hope's cheeks.

A waiter pushed two tables together to accommodate the expanded group.

Susan shoved Hope into the seat beside Steve.

She stared down at her plate while her heart pounded out the rhythm of a marching band as she remembered the gentle way this handsome man responded to each of her stressed out situations when they were together. Would her voice crack and betray her?

Hope listened to Susan do the introductions for the group.

From what Hope could see, she and Steve had little in common, so why did he affect her this way? The physical and emotional attraction almost bordered on unmanageable. While listening to the good looking, polite, and intelligent man speak, perspiration dripped down her sides only five minutes into the conversation. She reached for the glass of water and the cool liquid soothed her parched throat.

The conversation around the table turned a corner. All of them were Christians except her. Couldn't they talk about something other than religion? She brought her hands to her lap as her fingers clenched and unclenched. What did she bring to the discussion? What could she say if someone asked how they met? What if he offered that information?

Her stomach twirled like a ride at the town fair. How would she talk to him with everyone else here? She didn't speak the same language they did…at least, so it seemed. The slow draw of darkness pulled Hope to escape the confines of stress. Then Steve's calming tone reached in and eased her out of her anxiety and into the conversation.

"…settled in my new apartment. First Baptist has made me feel quite welcome," Pastor Steve continued. "Springfield is a new kind of city for me. Different from Kansas City in many ways. I've only been in town three weeks."

"I've heard some good stuff about First Baptist but there are some things I think must be rumors." Annie giggled and reached for her water glass.

"Like what?"

Hope's attention piqued.

"Well, I heard…and I'm sure this is total hearsay…that there is a bowling alley in the basement." Annie set her glass down and scrunched up her tiny nose. "That's crazy."

Hope saw her opening. "Isn't that what you told me, Pastor Steve?"

Steve's laugh boomed across the restaurant. "Annie, it's incredible but true. I have had the opportunity to participate at the lanes." He turned to Josh. "Do you play racquetball?"

"I've tried it once. Why?"

"We have a court downstairs and a weight room with sauna."

"I heard High Street Baptist has basketball courts and a weight room also." Tommy draped his arm over Annie's shoulder.

"We have basketball, too." Steve shifted.

His hip touched Hope's causing her to almost wilt.

Steve continued, "What church do you go to?"

"We're new Christians and are shopping for a church home. As of now, we are visiting Life Fellowship Church on S. Campbell," Susan said.

"I'm not sure where that is. I'm still learning the town. I've never been on S. Campbell as far as I know." He turned to acknowledge Hope. "Do you attend with them?"

Hope shook her head side to side.

"So, how is business?" Steve's question brought relief from the talk of church. "Have you seen William lately?"

"Yes, I have. We have some new directions we want to go, but right now we can't reveal any of the pertinent facts. That's part of why we are here." Good…business talk…she could do this. Show him her strengths. "We were in Farmington, our hometown, discussing strategies for the company."

"I was on N. Kansas Expressway the other day and drove past Sparks System Logistics. It appears to be in a good location." Steve grabbed his cloth napkin and laid it across his lap.

"Why didn't you drop in?"

"I didn't want to disturb you at work. Besides, I was running an errand for someone."

"Yes, we think the location meets our needs. It is close to the freeway and only eleven minutes from the airport." Hope shifted to see him better and immediately belly-flopped into the crystal-clear, blue pools of his eyes. Once again, her concentration strayed. She glanced across the table at Susan and Josh in desperation. Someone needed to rescue her from the topical stream that swept her away. She saw Susan fumbling through her purse and Josh arranging his napkin over his lap. Panic mounted. Her conversational footing couldn't get off the slippery, moss-covered rocks. Alarmed, her mind was forced under the rushing river of emotion as if she bounced off the submerged boulders battering her and her mouth flooded with saliva. She gulped.

"Pastor Steve, I hear you have a very nice pickup." Tommy's rescue couldn't have come at a better time.

"Yes, a 1970 Ford F150, long bed with a 302-small block."

Thank you, Tommy. "It's a beautiful Wild Cherry with baby-moons, four on the floor, and gray upholstery." Safe on firm footing, Would the perspiration show through her blouse? If she could steer clear of his almost sky-blue eyes, they wouldn't weigh her down and pull her into the deep end. His riptide-like draw kept her from escape. She grabbed a menu like a life-preserver and covered her face.

"Hope, didn't you say Steve did most of the work himself?" Susan jumped back into the conversation after wrestling her purse into submission.

This seemed to stir interest and the discourse moved to headers, cam shafts, and bore-to-stroke ratios. Hope understood and watched Susan and Annie's eyes glaze over. Being mechanics, Josh and Tommy handled most of their wives' car maintenance.

While listening to the men converse, Hope peeked at the list of entrees and engaged the ladies. "Susan, the other night when I had the meeting with Kelsey, she wore a square-necked dress with three-quarter sleeves, light gray from the neckline over her shoulders to just above her bustline, from there, charcoal gray with the last three inches brown. Her purse matched the brown." Hope smiled over at Tommy's wife. "You know Annie would look good in something like that."

"I don't know, Hope. Kelsey is taller and slim while Annie is tiny with curves."

"Who's Kelsey?" Annie asked.

"We go to Serenity Meetings together."

"Oh, is that at Springfield Victory Mission?" Pastor Steve's voice cut into the conversation. "I've been meaning to drop by there. Hope, it seems we once again have a common interest. It was at a Serenity Meeting when I gave my life to Jesus Christ."

Great Hope. Now you've done it.

The entire group grew very quiet.

Hope had feared this moment. This revelation of her alcoholism to the man who had become her dream-soulmate would dash all desire for even a hint of a relationship with him. Her body shivered as she looked around for an escape. The secret hiding place wasn't an option this time.

Where was the restroom? Should she bolt, or stay and face the cesspool of her life? Images swirled as she pictured her life flushed down the toilet in humiliation. She took a deep breath and raised her head ready to face the reality of her need for intercession. Wait a minute! The comprehension of what he had just admitted landed on her like a ton of bricks. He was where, when he became a Christian?

CHAPTER TWENTY-THREE

Bewildered, Hope's mouth went slack as she stared at Pastor Steve, his sultry eyes no longer overwhelming. The table grew eerily quiet as all eyes focused on the handsome pastor as he readjusted in his seat. Steve now faced all five without having to twist his body.

When Steve Burrow speaks, people listen. It seemed the whole table embodied a time-stopping moment. Then again, it could have been her. What he'd mentioned in a nonchalant response changed her anesthetized brain into an alert, curious mind, and now she hung on his every word.

"You see." Steve looked to each person at the table. "I was a party guy when I first went to college. I flunked out. Not because I couldn't do the work but because I was too drunk to go to class."

Hope gasped, then slid her hand over her mouth.

Steve picked up his napkin and wiped the corners of his mouth. "I got into some trouble and couldn't hold down a job. I was on my second Driving Under the Influence violation, and I physically assaulted a man in a bar. He was hospitalized. I didn't even know I did it until later. I became a blackout drunk."

"So, you went to jail?" Josh asked.

Hope recalled that Mom told her about Josh close to a similar situation a couple of years back. It happened right after the firings at S. S. L. and almost ruined his and Susan's marriage. Not long after, he became a Christian and his life turned around.

"No. I made the decision to join the Army." Steve shook his head and continued. "I had no real skills except from high school auto and metal shop. I became part of the government motor pool. Spent a year in Afghanistan and six months in Germany. While still overseas, I continued to drink but did my best to taper off. Finally, I got stationed at Fort Leonard Wood, Missouri." He looked at Hope. His eyes held such a sadness it almost crushed her. "That's where I met my wife, Allison." He scanned the group. "She lived in St. Robert. I went with a friend to church. Allie's friend drew my buddy's attention." Steve's voice seemed to catch.

"The pastor of the church encouraged the four of us to go down to the local mission and help out." Steve's smile tightened. "We went the night of what they called a Serenity Meeting. I didn't realize what it pertained to until we arrived.

"We listened to the testimonies of broken lives and devastation. I paid close attention when I noticed the most successful stories were the ones where Jesus Christ became the center of their focus and not themselves. They weren't selfish like me."

"I know the feeling." Josh's head dropped.

"Me, too." Tommy looked to his wife and wrapped his arm tighter around Annie.

Hope's own humiliation grew. Was she selfish as well?

"That night, I left and couldn't get their stories out of my mind." Steve took a sip of his water. "All the following week I wanted two things. One, I wanted to see Allie. And two, I wanted to go back to the meeting place and hear more. I did and the next week my life changed forever when I realized my need for the Savior. Allison and I were soon dating. We married right before I left the Army."

"Where did you go when you got out?" Josh leaned forward.

"I felt called to the ministry and applied at Southern Baptist Theological Seminary in Louisville, Kentucky. Once I graduated, I landed a position in Kansas City at Hope Harvest Community as an assistant to the senior pastor. The church grew in size and I grew spiritually from time spent in the Bible and alone with Jesus. I began to help out at the mission where *we* met." Steve gazed into Hope's eyes.

Hope gulped and ducked her head. Well, there it was, her open shame for all to see.

"After two years, the senior pastor fell ill and had to resign. I became the interim pastor and expected the board of deacons to get a more experienced man to take his place. They offered me the office. Then three years ago came the tragic news of Allie's cancer. It spread quick." Hope saw his forehead crinkle and watched him look down. When he looked up his eyes sparkled as his lips curled down. He sighed. "If it wasn't for my Heavenly Father and His Holy Spirit, I would probably have fallen into despondency over the loss and gone back to drinking. I still get the urges, but I know who I believe in and that He is able to pull me through."

Hope's fingers trembled as she reached for her napkin. Could it be that easy? Just believe?

Pastor Steve moved his hand over to cover Hope's.

Her head spun and her stomach flipped.

"Hope, I'm glad for Serenity Meetings. Regular AA meetings aren't enough. Christ must be the center of our lives."

Hope's voice came out a whisper. "It's not that simple. Is it?" A tornado of speculation overtook her mind.

Across Hope's thoughts drifted the memory of the morning she went to church with William and Gloria. Steve's sermon about how Christ would carry the burden for her replayed. She remembered the times she woke up without a clue as to her location or in a couple of instances, the identity of the man beside her. She considered her plans for expansion of the company and wondered if she could go forward while still a lush.

"Excuse me, I need to use the restroom." Hope forced herself not to run out of the restaurant but made her way to the lavatory on unsteady legs.

Her fingers gripped the edges of the sink as she lifted her sight to the wild-eyed image that stared back at her.

Was God the answer? In science classes they tried to explain everything apart from God, but there were so many questions that came up that haven't ever been answered. Her empty stomach twisted and she shivered. Both science and Christianity required a leap of faith. At least with God, the leap of faith was acknowledged. She looked down into the drain to ponder it more. Was Mom's and Daddy's religion right after all? Daddy said that it wasn't the religion but the relationship with God that changed a man's heart. With a shaky hand, she turned on the faucet and watched the flow. He also said it was the recognition of our sin in our association with a pure God that really transformed a person. Josh said the same thing a few weeks ago.

The bathroom door swung open and Susan stepped in. "Are you okay?"

"Yeah."

Susan stepped beside her. "Wow. That was quite a story." She stared into the mirror and their eyes locked.

Hope's line of vision dropped back to the basin. Her friend's piercing examination unnerved her. "I'll just step into the stall and be right out."

"Pastor Steve understands what you are going through. Kind of like what the Bible says that Jesus is like. The Lord understands what we need more than we do. I think Someone is talking to my best friend."

Alarms rang in her ears. "I have to…excuse me." Hope rushed to the stall and closed herself off from the rest of the world.

CHAPTER TWENTY-FOUR

Hope's illusions about her own ability to control the urges of alcohol turned upside down after Pastor Steve's revelation about his struggle with the bottle. Her mind screamed for her to run away and hide. Her answer—cower in the bathroom stall. Why did Susan have to interfere in the escape? Cornered like a trapped animal by her best friend, she listened to the water from the faucet on the other side of the stall door gurgle down the drain.

Urck, urck, urck.

"This soap dispenser isn't working very well. Hope, are you going to be okay?"

"Yeah, I'll be awhile. My stomach is giving me some trouble. You guys go ahead and order. I don't think I can eat right now." Hope's gut coiled like a snake ready to strike.

Steve seemed to already know her inside and out like Susan said. Almost like God gave him the answers to her life. How was that possible? She couldn't face the pastor right now. How could she get out of this?

"Are you sure?" The faucet shut off and the handle of the towel dispenser cranked. "Do you want to talk about it?"

"About using the restroom? Why would I want to do that?" Hope lashed out.

"No. About the other. You know you can talk to me about anything. Is it him or is it what he said?"

"Susan. I need some privacy."

"O-k-a-y."

The restroom door swished closed and the quiet grew spooky. Hope pulled toilet paper from the dispenser, then used it to wipe her eyes and nose. As a strong, independent woman, her business required many nights alone. Why did she feel empty and deserted now? The quiet stall intensified her loneliness.

Was she alone in this? Those she wanted to please the most couldn't help her. With a deep breath, she rose from the toilet seat and stared at the stall door. The man she wanted to impress was probably disgusted with her. She was pathetic and couldn't face him with the others around.

Hope forced her mind into business mode. She stepped out and glanced around the vacant lavatory. Carol Baggerly's efficiency and business knowledge was impressive. They could sure use her right now with Loriann out of commission. In an attempt to wipe away her urge to drink and thoughts of Steve's battle with it, she rubbed her temples.

Josh said Pete knew his job well and would be a great asset to the team, but Sally's analytical mind impressed him even more. Josh thought he could use her in other areas along with maintenance. Susan and Annie said there appeared to be more to Pete and Sally's closeness than the work.

Hope looked at herself in the mirror and frowned. Her confusion about her personal feelings regarding Steve frustrated her. Her hands wrapped over the edge of the sink. Could she face him after running out? Yet, she couldn't put it off any longer.

As she left the powder room, a lump rose to her throat. The restroom door bumped Hope's backside. Her heart raced. No, she couldn't do this. Though part of her knew the right thing would be to go back to the table with her friends, but her restless legs steered her out to the foyer.

Hope glanced over her shoulder to the group. Steve's head lifted and their eyes met. But she couldn't hold the gaze. She moved past the dining area and into the bar.

Hope stared into the dark liquid placed in front of her. How long had she contemplated the glass and its contents? It felt like hours but couldn't have been more than thirty minutes.

Several men approached to offer their company.

Her sharp candor sent them packing.

With a firm grip on the glass, she swished the drink and watched the ice cube circle inside, a habit she developed to help her mind wander when stressful circumstances rose. She could push the drink away or change its taste with the melting ice. Easy to do.

Her eyes drifted to the mirror behind the bartender who washed glasses for the next round of patrons, the reflection shouted at her, "You came in here looking to find solace in the bottle." Lined up in front of the reflective surface, several of her favorite bottled friends mocked her.

Movement behind her caught her attention but she ducked her head back to her drink to avoid eye-contact. Was it another man who thought she looked desperate? Did she send out an aura saying, "Buy me a drink I'm easy?"

Out the corner of her eye, she watched Steve slide onto the stool beside her.

Ashamed for her abrupt escape, she refused to acknowledge him.

The man behind the counter approached. "What can I get for you, buddy?"

"I'll have exactly what the lady is having. Exactly. And keep them coming. She needs it and so do I."

"You don't know what you're asking." The barkeep's comment brimmed with sarcasm. "It's strong. Do you think you can handle it?"

Hope stared at the counter and snickered. Did this man know what he is getting into with her? Would he be shocked when he took a drink only to realize it was cola without alcohol?

"They were worried, and Susan wanted to check on you." His comment surprised her. "I told her you weren't in the restroom, but I knew where you went and I would take care of you. I thought you could use some space, but I also believe you need someone who understands. We can talk or just sit awhile." He swiveled his stool toward her. "I'm here for you or you can tell me to leave. I don't want to abandon you."

Would throwing myself into his arms be an option?

"Hope, you're going to have to make a decision. Not for me, but for them. They're waiting. Would you like me to stay? Whatever you wish. If you want, I can send them home and take you to your place later."

"I think I would like that." Her voice whispered. "Do you want to be saddled with an alcoholic with a lot of personal issues?"

He reached for the glass in front of him and brought it to his lips.

"Do you really want to do that?" Hope watched him in the mirror knowing he took a chance of falling off the wagon. Her eyes widened as he paused and a smile crossed his lips. Her mouth dropped open as he downed about a third of the drink.

"Are you surprised with my choice of drink? The craving was strong. The temptation almost pulled me down." Hope frowned.

"I trusted you to do the right thing. If it had been a mixed drink, I believe you would have stopped me. Like me, you care about others and their welfare even if you are careless about yourself. I figured you wouldn't let the others…or me down."

He pulled out his phone and tapped it. "Josh, she's safe. I'm with her now. I'll take care of her and see her to her place. You can head home. It was nice to finally meet you. Maybe we can get together and discuss that work you suggested for the pickup." His voice paused. "No, she's going to be okay. As I'm sure you know, she's a strong individual. Have a safe drive home. She'll see you in the morning at the office." He laid his phone in front of him. "Your brother and I exchanged numbers."

"Thanks, Pastor." Hope placed her hand over his and gave it a quick squeeze before removing hers.

"Hope, I'm not here as Pastor Steve. I'm your friend."

His eyes along with his actions tonight—a panoply that draped her with something more than compassion. She warmed at the security and its possibilities. She stared once more into the dark fluid as her heart fluttered. Was friendship conceivable?

"Why don't we leave here and go back to the dining area? Let's find a table where we can talk."

Hope nodded as he extended his elbow to her.

As they exited the bar, her friends waited by the front door.

She looked at Susan. "I'll be okay. Drive safely. I love you guys."

Susan smiled and winked.

Josh stepped close. "Sissy, we love you, too. Call if you need anything." He hugged her.

Hope's head pressed into Josh's shoulder. She nodded, not trusting her emotions.

Within moments, Hope and Steve walked toward a table near the back of the restaurant.

"We'll have some coffee, please." Steve guided the chair under her. "Oh wait, Miss, I think we might order something. Hope, I know you haven't eaten yet, and I seem to have a hollow leg that still needs filling."

"Yes, I am a bit hungry."

After they ordered, they talked. Both loved nice cars and she found he had a taste for fine dining and appeared quite knowledgeable about some of the arts.

Hope shared with him about Kelsey and her café. Talk steered from artistic prints to sports and her feelings of inadequacy with things like bowling and racquetball, the activities available at the church. They agreed golf was fun with its combination of walking for exercise and relaxation but had its frustrations.

During dessert, their conversation grew quiet and the clanging of pots, cups, and silverware overshadowed their discourse.

"I guess it's time to head home. Some of us go to work tomorrow. The rest of us have the day off." The mischievous twinkle in Steve's eyes lit up the grin that spread across his face.

"Rub it in." Hope puckered her lips. She had begun to relax around him, but that twisted smile overpowered her. Her stomach churned and she worked to push down the tremors. How could he not feel the pull between them? Maybe there wasn't that draw for him. Perhaps he was being a friend like he said.

Steve rose and walked behind her to help her out of her seat.

They stepped through the restaurant door into the dark, brisk evening. The snow fell heavier, and the temperature had dropped. The drive home from Rolla to Springfield could be treacherous.

Pastor Steve and Hope bundled themselves in thick, down jackets and woolen mufflers around their necks. They laughed at how similar they were dressed, including the St. Louis Cardinal baseball caps, as they exited the steakhouse.

She quizzed and teased him about his plans for his day off.

As she stepped off the curb on the way to his pickup, she slipped on the snowpack that had turned to ice.

Steve caught her.

Under normal circumstances, she would assert her independence, but this time she allowed the man to continue to hold her elbow for support on the way to his truck. Her pulse throbbed in her neck and her mouth became as dry as the desert.

He opened the door for her.

She turned to say thank you. The words stuck in her throat when she glanced over his shoulder. Her mind froze as she watched a man hold open a woman's door, which would have been a wonderful gesture to witness under other circumstances.

Hope's entire body shook.

CHAPTER TWENTY-FIVE

Hope's vision blurred. She grappled to regain her composure as she stared through the blowing snow. A shiver started at her feet and ran up her spine. The chill seeped to her core. Her body trembled and enveloped her whole soul. She reached out to Steve with a silent, desperate cry for help.

Steve's brows furrowed. He looked her in the eye, moved beside her, and turned his head in the direction she nodded. He gasped.

"Oh, my goodness. She could almost be your sister." He chuckled and turned back to Hope. Over several seconds, the lines across his face deepened. "That's Janie isn't it?" He did a double take. "And that must be your ex-husband." He turned back to her and guided her onto the bench seat of the pickup. "What do you want to do?"

Hope craned her neck to see around Steve. Her body craved warmth. Despite her down jacket, the cold crept in. Desperate for heat, she wrapped her arms around herself. She watched Janie drape her arms over Kenny's neck while he pressed her against the car with a passionate kiss.

Hope could see it now. It must have always been about the romance and not just physical attraction.

She looked back at Steve. "I must have been a hiccup and distraction in their love." Hope stared into Steve's sky-blue eyes, then back at Janie and Kenny. In slow motion, she shook her head, twisted her body around, stepped up into the truck, and drew her feet up onto the floorboard. A numb emptiness enveloped her. "Please, take me home."

Steve closed the door and walked to his side.

Kenny and Janie walked toward the restaurant. They paused as Steve slowly pulled past them. Their eyes locked with Hope's as she glanced from one to the other.

Hope turned her head away when she saw their mouths drop open as recognition traversed across their faces.

The air thick with silence, choked her as Steve eased out of the parking lot. It portended a long drive back to Springfield.

After about ten minutes, she broke the hushed gridlock. Hope chuckled. "That went well." She turned to face Steve. "I've seen Kenny a couple of times since it happened but that was a first with Janie. From the expression on her face I think it came as a shock to her as well. I'm glad the others were gone before Kenny and Janie showed up. Thank you for being there, Steve. You calmed me and kept me from reacting. You complete me." She realized what she said and stammered out. "Ah, what I meant to say, you're good for me. Oh gosh, I mean—"

"Better stop while you're ahead." Steve's snorted laughter made her laugh so hard the tears came.

"You're right, I better shut up." She wiped her eyes.

"Do you want to talk about it? It took a long time to get over Allie's death, and I wanted to start drinking again. I know thoughts about my loss sometimes overcomes my better judgment and the bottle calls me again. I couldn't battle it without Jesus Christ in my life."

"Steve, thanks for the levity. I needed it." Hope took in a deep breath and blew it out. "I thought I could handle it. It's been over a year and a half since I saw Kenny last and almost two years since I've seen my sister. Seeing them tonight brought back the image of catching them together."

"I'm sorry. That can't be easy." He looked down the highway as they approached St. Robert. "I could use another coffee. Would you like something hot to drink?"

"Sure, how about some tea?" Hope giggled. "Most of the time, I would reach back and grab my thermos for some warm brandy or a hot toddy. My, how times have changed. It's been a whole month since I've had a drink. I came close earlier. You were a life saver tonight."

"Perhaps." Steve took the next exit and pulled into a mini-market. As he came to a stop, he looked at her. "Someone is taking care of you, and He sent me."

"You, my family, and friends have been my guardian angels this past month."

"Hope, I want to be there for you for as long as it takes." Steve paused for a moment, then snickered. "I just thought of something. Your ex saw you with another man outside the office for the first time since your breakup. I bet that might have been a bit of a shock to him, and her."

A guffaw exploded out of Hope. "That's rich! I wonder what is going on in their minds right now. I'd love to be able to eavesdrop during that conversation. You seem to sense what cheers me up. I imagine we messed up their romantic evening."

Kenny's and Janie's love interests gave her heartburn. The acidic taste in her mouth was bitter. The desire to spit venomous aspersions against them laid on the tip of her tongue. She glanced at the preacher and swallowed the vile words. "Let's drop this discussion about them. I don't think it's a good place for me." The tension tightened in her shoulders. "I don't want a disturbance like this to trigger any episodes like the one you witnessed the day we met, when my mind drifted into economic theory, and you thought I needed to be institutionalized."

"I didn't think that. I thought you were physically sick and couldn't think straight."

"If you say so. I must admit that when I went into the restroom earlier, I had to force myself out of that same state of mind again." Hope shifted to get comfortable. She needed to explain herself. "I allow my mind to drift as an escape from the pressures. It helps me cope. My family and Tommy and Annie know the pull stress has on me. If you want to be my friend, you will need to understand the draw it has and how it sometimes becomes a path to important insights for business. It's just a part of who I am and the intellect you have heard about."

"Hope, I want to be there for you, no matter how you are. I pray you get to know Jesus better. A relationship with Him could make all other encounters a bit richer. Think about it.

"To change the subject, I want you to tell me more about your friend, Kelsey. She seems a unique individual." He placed a hand on Hope's forearm. "I'll listen to any other issues you want to unburden yourself with. Not as a pastor but a friend. Sometimes it helps to confide in someone different."

Once back on the highway and her piping hot cup of tea grasped tight between her hands, Hope shared her knowledge of Kelsey. A stream of jealousy toward Kelsey's classy style seeped in, but Hope shoved a finger into its dike.

Steve continued the discussion. "Other than her love for the arts, Kelsey appears too upscale for me. I'm a down-in-the-dirt kind of guy like Josh and Tommy. I prefer working on my car and helping others that are struggling with addictions like we do. I hope you don't mind me talking about Allie sometimes. It's cathartic to speak of her but that kind of conversation is often uncomfortable with another man. But you are different from even other women. I feel I can speak openly with you about most anything." Steve raised his brows, then he gave a lopsided smile. "I hope you can do likewise."

Could she? Should she? And did she want to? She lifted her hand and wiped the corners of her mouth. Her eyelids drooped, and her mind drifted with desire and need. *Can you hold me when it gets unbearable?* She sighed. *I think not. Pastor, I don't want to compromise your position.*

CHAPTER TWENTY-SIX

Early January, Springfield

The to-do list on her desk stared back at Hope. The list of questions she prepared last Thursday to ask Edward before they ran off to Farmington over the weekend had most items checked off. The important components of her inquiries had been answered within her and Josh's queries. She still needed to transcribe her notes and jot down her opinions about what she learned at Broderick's. But she had reached a stalemate. A myriad of thoughts ran through her mind from business to Pastor Steve to her need for a drink.

Management's two o'clock meeting to discuss everyone's take on the deal that Edward Broderick presented would be full of pros and cons. As it stood, the positives outweighed the negatives. But last night's fiasco seemed to put a damper on the adrenalin rush that had been building in her over the previous weeks. The similar charge she experienced when she started SSL fizzled.

What to do about Loriann's fall became a priority. Hope had grabbed Bethany, the second-year student from Southwest Missouri State, to answer calls and act as receptionist until a decision could be made as to who would replace Loriann.

Bethany's pleasant telephone voice and alertness should cover any minor mishaps. Though it wouldn't work for her in this position long-term because of her other responsibilities, Hope considered a rotation of the other two college students. The idea dropped as fast as it had come since their jobs couldn't be disrupted either.

As Hope moved a document to another folder in her laptop, her mind drifted back to the chaotic day in Rolla. A simple lunch turned disastrous as her usual well-kept emotions created a haphazard mess and spawned disorder and confusion.

Her reaction fell into the typical response of past stressful encounters. She panicked and hid.

Around Steve, Hope floundered and behaved like a flustered teenager with her first boyfriend crush. Then the confession of his drinking. Her face flushed. Her thoughts conflicted. The remembrance of his expression of love for his deceased wife and his devotion to Jesus Christ caused a deep discomfort with Hope.

Now, even in the safety of her own office, the intense flutter in her heart grew. Hope rose from her chair and moved to the file cabinet. "Why does he stir these feelings in me?"

With her hand on top of the cabinet to steady herself, she recalled her vanishing act to the bar in desperation—her escape to the familiar.

Steve appeared to know where she would find solace and came in search of her. Why did he take such a great risk? Being an alcoholic like her, entering that bar could have caused others to question his judgement, or it might have destroyed him. Did he do it specifically for her, or was it something he would do for anyone?

Hope pulled the file she wanted, crossed back to her desk, and plopped down in her chair.

Ting…ting…ting.

She reached for the com button. "Yes, Bethany?"

"Ms. Sparks, a Ms. Kelsey Warren is here to see you. She doesn't have an appointment."

"It's okay. Send her in." Once again, Kelsey crowded into her thoughts about Steve.

The door opened, and Bethany escorted Kelsey in. As Bethany

moved to the exit, Hope saw the young lady's eyes widen as her gaze moved from Kelsey's face down to her feet and back again.

Kelsey dressed to impress in a charcoal-gray wool jacket with matching skirt. Underneath was a lime-green blouse. Black, leather pumps adorned her feet. Tucked neatly under her arm a thin, messenger-satchel. The woman and the outfit appeared to dazzle the young student.

Hope rose and came around the desk, then hugged her friend. Bethany lingered. Was it to watch their interaction?

"What brings you over to this part of the city?"

Kelsey turned to gaze at the receptionist.

Hope smiled at the crimson color that washed over Bethany's face and neck as she spun to leave.

"Oh, I decided to slum a little." Kelsey snickered. "Actually, I was wondering if you found anyone to replace Loriann?" She nodded toward the door. "Is this girl any good?"

"She's doing the job on a temporary basis. Her actual job is data research, and as a second-year student, she is progressing nicely. I prefer her back at her regular desk though."

"Good. I might have a temporary solution to your problem."

"Do tell." Hope pointed to one of the wingback chairs and moved back to her desk. "What is your remedy to my dilemma?"

"The answer is standing before you." Kelsey eased into the chair and placed her satchel at her feet.

"I'm not following. What about the coffee shop? Don't you need to keep an eye on things?"

"I trust Georgia to run things short term." Kelsey pulled out a folder from her bag and handed it to Hope.

"What's this?

"My résumé." Kelsey gave an award-winning smile. "We have talked about my past position while in New York, and how I sort of miss the everyday business hustle and bustle. The coffee shop has its benefits, but it is quite laid back. I designed it specifically for that. The problem is, I miss the ordinary push and drive required to close a deal."

"So, you thought SSL would give you the adrenaline rush you need." Hope raised her eyebrows.

Kelsey added, "When I'm here, your business would be my primary focus. And since this is a temporary position, I wanted to see if the old feelings I used to get from the business world would still stir or not." She pointed to her paper presentation in Hope's hand. "As you can see, I have the necessary qualifications to do the receptionist job and more, which will benefit your immediate needs. Regarding what takes place at the coffee shop, I will call there during my break time and stop off after work to check on things."

Through Hope's clear, acrylic work desk, she watched her friend cross her legs, place her hands on her knee, then lean forward—business ready. Did Kelsey ever relax her standards? Was she as aware of being on display as she seemed? Hope straightened her back and wriggled farther into her chair.

"What do we, at Sparks, get out of it? Why are you offering?"

"It's simple. First, you have an immediate dilemma that needs to be dealt with, which is stressful." Kelsey held up her hand and proceeded to count off on her fingertips. "Second, you are a friend in need, and I want to help. Third, part of running businesses like yours is risky. You are taking a chance that I will meet your requirements and you will profit from it. I am putting my business in a precarious position while earning some extra income to expand my own personal portfolio."

With Kelsey's business knowledge, could she be trusted around sensitive data? Had she been honest in previous conversations? Maybe it was time to find out. Hope took a deep breath. "Well, your interview for the position is complete. Now we'll discuss your pay and what I expect of you." Hope leaned forward and placed her forearms on the edge of the desk. "If the salary is agreeable, we can give it a try." How wise was this? Could she depend on her? She wanted to trust her. Would Kelsey meet Hope's goals? She smiled and moved the folder to the opposite side of the desk. What if Kelsey couldn't do the job? Could she fire her without destroying their friendship?

Kelsey accepted the wage negotiation and suggested she could begin the next day.

"Now that we have agreed to your hire, let's just relax for a bit." Hope rose from her desk and stepped to the matching wingback chair next to Kelsey.

"Don't you have pressing business to attend to?"

"That's what I like about you, my friend. You have a sense of what's important." With Kelsey's offer for the job and the acceptance of it, the anvil-like weight of filling Loriann's position fell by the wayside. "I can afford to ease up for a few minutes. While I'm thinking about it, I won't be able to make the Serenity Meeting this week. I have a meeting in Salt Lake City Tuesday evening and I will be in L.A. Wednesday. When I return Thursday morning, you are going to see the real me."

Hope raised her ankle toward her knee but stopped mid-rise. She lowered her foot down to allow one knee to fold atop her other.

"Sounds interesting." Kelsey looked down at Hope's adjustment and smiled.

"Business is business, but I'm not looking forward to Los Angeles." Hope curled her lip.

"What's up?" Kelsey's brows lifted.

"The L.A. client is an old drinking buddy." She flushed in remembrance, looked out the window, and sighed. "Not drinking will be a struggle around him. He will want to have the luncheon meeting at the hotel near LAX. I have been known to get comfortable while intoxicated." Hope shrugged. "Then, I fly out in the morning."

"I see." Kelsey scooted her chair closer to Hope. "Is your return flight out set for the next morning or is it changeable?" Her hand touched Hope's chair. "Perhaps a flight is available shortly after your meeting."

"I guess I could check."

"That could resolve both issues." Kelsey gave a slight tilt of her head to the side. "If you have a scheduled exit, you can avoid the drinking and, I assume, the undesired other aspect. It might cost a bit more to make the change but think of what it will cost you if you slip up and drink. And if you are able to return earlier, you'll also save on the hotel booking."

"Yeah, that could work. Thanks for the suggestion. Kelsey, you are good for me." Hope covered her mouth when she snorted, as the words she spoke to Steve the previous evening reverberated.

"What's so funny?"

"I said the same thing to Steve last night on our way back home from Rolla."

"Is this the same Pastor Steve you were telling me about?"

Hope grinned and squirmed to get more comfortable.

Kelsey leaned back and her brows lifted. "Well? I'm waiting."

Hope's excitement built like reaching the crest of a roller coaster.

CHAPTER TWENTY-SEVEN

Hope wriggled in her office chair as her heart drummed.

"I couldn't believe the management team stumbled across Steve in the restaurant. When Josh invited the pastor to join us for the meal, I almost panicked. Don't get me wrong, I was thrilled to see him and wanted to be near him." Hope grinned at Kelsey.

"Except?"

"I didn't want everyone knowing how we met. I haven't told anyone the whole story."

Kelsey smiled and nodded.

"Steve went into the army because he had a drinking problem." Hope whispered as she reached out to touch Kelsey's forearm as though she were leaking classified, national secrets about the man.

"Did you confess your drinking issues to him?"

Hope grit her teeth. "No. He pretty much let me know he knew without blatantly publishing it."

"Wow. What did you say?" Kelsey leaned forward as her eyes widened.

"Well." Hope scrunched her face. "I panicked and ran to the bathroom to hide. When I came out, I slinked off to the bar."

"Ahh, Hope. Tell me you didn't." Kelsey's southern drawl prevalent in her apparent disappointment.

"I didn't drink anything but a cola. Don't get me wrong. I was really tempted and confused." She spoke her words with emphasis as if they were sung. "Then, Steve came to my rescue. He offered me a ride home separate from the others and convinced me to go back into the restaurant with him."

"So, you went back to the dining area without drinking?"

Hope closed her eyes and let her mind drift back into her fantasy. "*Mmm.* Dinner was magnificent. Our conversation flowed easily. Then, as we exited the restaurant, I slipped on the ice." She quivered as she recalled the moment. "He caught me, and I thought for a second or two he would kiss me." After a brief chuckle, she opened her eyes and made a pouty face. "He didn't."

Kelsey's smile broadened.

"When we got to his pickup, the whole pleasant evening crashed in an instant." Hope locked her toes around the legs of the chair to keep her from bolting from it in her anger as the throbbing pulsed in her temples. "That's when I saw them."

"Who?"

"Janie and Kenny. My husband-stealing sister and my sister-stealing husband." A shiver down her spine produced a shudder throughout Hope. "It brought back home the devastation of their betrayal."

"That must have been tough."

Hope shared the conversation she had with Steve after they pulled out of the parking lot. She giggled.

"What's so funny?" Kelsey wrinkled her nose.

"I can't believe I said he completed me. He thought it was hilarious. I guess to him it would be."

Hope buried her face into her hands as the heat of embarrassment scalded her cheeks at her faux pas.

Ting…ting…ting

"Ms. Sparks, you have a phone call on line one. A Mr. Steve Burrow wishes to speak with you."

"Yes, could you tell him to hold for a minute? Thank you, Bethany."

As her heart rate jumped through the roof, she stared at Kelsey.

Hope held up a finger toward her friend. She wiped her lips with her tongue and swallowed down the dry wasteland in her throat. On unstable legs, she rose from her chair and reached for the phone, but plopped back down so she wouldn't fall. After a deep cleansing breath, she stood again and maneuvered around the desk, then glanced over at Kelsey who pointed to the door and shrugged. Hope shook her head and raised the phone to her ear.

"Good morning, Kind Sir. How is your day off? Did you sleep in?"

"Good morning, Hope. I was thinking of you and about last night. How are you doing?"

"I hope they were good thoughts."

"I became worried. I know that Sunday was a rough day for you."

"Well, Pastor Steve, you made it easier for me. Thanks for your care."

"Remember, I'm just your good friend, Steve. Of course, when you visit the church you can call me Pastor Steve. Is that okay, Doctor Sparks?" He laughed.

"Steve, thank you for what you did. Is that why you called or is there something I can help you with?" Hope's fingers twiddled with her hair as she stared down at the desktop. She sucked in her lower lip. Her eyes drifted over to Kelsey. Heat climbed up her neck like a three-toed sloth rushing for a new batch of leaves. Hope cleared her throat and slid her hand away from her hair. "How is your day going thus far?"

"I have already changed the oil in the truck, and I needed to get a few parts. I'm going to a store near you to pick them up. I was wondering if you're available for lunch or maybe an early dinner when you got off work? I understand if you are too busy. I just thought since I would be in your area, I would drop by to take you out." He paused and cleared his own throat. "I don't mean a date but something between friends. If not, maybe another day like Thursday or Friday night."

"I would like that. Today would be best for dinner as I need to leave town in the morning for business. Let me think for a second." She placed her hand over the mouthpiece as her jaw dropped. She looked over to Kelsey and whispered, "He's asking me to dinner."

Kelsey grinned. "Do it."

Hope rolled her shoulders and sat up straighter. "Steve, I have a pressing meeting with staff at two. How about you drop by the office a little before four for an early dinner so I will have time to finish packing for my trip afterwards, if it's convenient. I will take you on a brief tour of the plant."

"Hope, will Josh or Tommy be there at that time? I wanted to speak to them about the work on the pickup I talked to them about previously."

"I don't know what their schedules are at that time, but I will tell them you would like to talk with them if they're available."

"I don't want to hold you up any longer, I look forward to the personal tour."

"Don't get too excited. It isn't much to look at. I look forward to dinner. See you then, Steve." Hope laid the phone back in its cradle and released a deep sigh.

"Well?"

Jolted from her dreamlike state, heat flashed across her face. She moved back to the wingback chair and her friend.

As they discussed the call, the door between her and Susan's office swung open and Susan bounded in.

"You forgot to tell me you saw Janie last night." She stopped in front of Hope, then glanced at the other woman. "Oh, I thought you were by yourself. Hi Kelsey." Her head turned back to Hope and she raised her eyebrows.

"Susan, I fixed the Loriann problem. I hired Kelsey for the receptionist position. Now I can move Bethany back to her job." Hope smiled. Would Susan let the issue of Janie drop? "Kelsey will start tomorrow morning. I'll need you to help her fill out all the necessary paperwork and between you and Bethany line out some of her duties. I'll do the rest when I get back."

Susan turned her head, stared at Kelsey, and gave her red mop of hair a quick shake. "What?"

Kelsey looked up at Susan and smiled. "I'm just helping you guys out."

"Okay. Thanks?" Susan turned back to Hope. "We need to talk about this other matter. Your sister called, and she's upset."

Hope raised both palms up to shoulder level and shrugged. "It sounds like she has a personal problem and don't care at this time. We'll talk—"

The door between the receptionist and Hope's office banged open and Josh barged in. "Hope, we gotta talk! There appears to be a problem with Kenny." Halfway across the room, he came to a screeching halt. "Oh, I didn't realize you and Susan were in a meeting with someone. I'll come back later to discuss Kenny."

Hope frowned and shot a harsh look at Josh. Could this be a continuation of their betrayal of her and her company from before? Did she make the right decision to hire family again? Could having Josh and Susan back and trusting them prove to be her worst decision yet? Or were they trying to prove their openness? Determination set in her jaw. There would be no secrets behind her back this time. She would need to keep a close watch on them until she could know for sure.

CHAPTER TWENTY-EIGHT

The room rife with tension, Hope's eyes darted between her brother and Susan. Their anxiety level would be humorous under different circumstances. She took a quick glance at Kelsey who tucked her head down and seemed to stifle a grin.

Kelsey, I couldn't agree more.

Josh took a step back toward the door.

"Josh, I'd like to introduce Kelsey Warren. You heard me speak of her before." Hope gestured to Kelsey. "She is temporarily replacing Loriann as receptionist. Though she owns the coffee shop, her assistant manager will run things while she helps us."

"Ahh, it's nice to finally meet you, Kelsey. I've heard some good things about you and your establishment. I hope we won't tie you up for too long." He looked back at Hope, cocked his head, his eyebrows raised, and stared. "When can we discuss this other matter?"

"Remember we have a meeting at two o'clock concerning the Broderick deal." Hope allowed her head to slightly list toward Kelsey. Would he understand she didn't want to discuss this in front of her friend? "Oh, I almost forgot. Pastor Steve is coming by around four and wants to talk to you and Tommy about his pickup."

"Josh," Susan broke in. "could I see you outside for a moment?" She stepped toward her office door and reached out her hand. Her eyes shot several times toward the back of Kelsey's head.

Josh glanced to Susan, then back to Hope. "When can we talk?"

Frustrated, Hope grit her teeth and glared at Josh. "Later."

Susan escorted Josh out of the room and shut the door between the offices.

Kelsey stood, "I see you're busy. I'll be back tomorrow."

Hope nodded and walked her out.

The Broderick meeting went smoother than Hope expected. As people left the conference room, Hope heard footfalls from behind. She caught a glimpse of Josh as he sauntered to her end of the long table and plopped down in a chair next to her. He sighed with a deep, prolonged breath.

She ignored him as she shuffled papers into manila folders.

He sighed louder this time.

She reached for a pen and pulled out a notepad.

Josh folded his arms on the table and laid his head across his forearms, his face turned toward her with a sad-dog look. As a child, Josh used this annoying tactic to get someone's attention and, most often, it worked. At his present age, it looked pathetic.

Hope remembered she employed this same stratagem a couple of months back while mending fences with Susan. Hope coughed to avoid laughing.

Susan came in and sat on the opposite side of the table from Josh.

They were coming at her from opposing directions. What? Did they think they had to divide and conquer as the saying went?

Hope rose to her feet and ambled to the white board. With the eraser in hand, she wiped the surface clean. Could she wait them out? She couldn't let them gang up and manipulate her.

Hope didn't have long to wait before Josh blurted out, "Are we going to address the issue of Kenny and Janie?"

"It's not my problem anymore. If I wanted to deal with their issues, I would have called them." With a fast spin, she turned to confront them. "Why would I care what they want? Their choice. Now, they want to pull me back in after I went through that torment and anguish."

Her temper elevated. She squeezed the eraser tight. Though she really wanted to throw it across the room, she chose to spin back around to the board. After a deep breath of her own, she rested it into the tray and gripped the edges of the easel.

"I am doing my best to not get angry. I don't care if they are upset about seeing me last night. They didn't worry about my feelings when they destroyed my marriage and business."

"Sorry, Hope. We didn't mean to aggravate you," Susan said. "We weren't thinking again."

"It seems to me that their feelings are always considered above mine. I apparently have no heart." Hope turned to glare at Josh. "Isn't that the way you see it, Josh? Kenny's tender and fragile constitution needs to be pampered?" She slumped down defeated into the closest chair. She stared at the far wall. "If I wanted your input on this, I would have told you that I saw them pressed against their car making out."

"You're right, Hope." Josh leaned back and scrubbed his face. "We stuck our noses into something that was none of our business. Like Susan said, we weren't thinking. I thought it involved family issues. Some things aren't the whole family's business. It's just that we hope to get it resolved." He stood. "I was wrong. End of discussion. I should probably cut off any relationship with them to keep peace between us." He headed for the door.

"Stop, Josh!"

He paused with a hand on the knob without looking back.

"I don't want to come between you, Kenny, and Janie. Her and my issues shouldn't stop you from a relationship with her."

He nodded and walked out.

"I'm sorry. It was stupid. It's just, I worry about your mom and dad. The turmoil is hard on them." Susan walked to the chair nearest Hope, then sat and placed her hand on Hope's bicep.

"You don't think I worry about Mom and Daddy?" She glanced at Susan and watched the tears roll down her best friend's cheeks. "I do care. But do you think seeing Kenny and Janie last night was a picnic for me? In the state I was in already, I almost lost it. If Steve hadn't been there, the whole evening might have turned ugly. He is a God-send."

"So, how did your time with him go?" Susan scooted her chair closer to Hope.

Hope appreciated Susan's redirect of the conversation from her sister and her ex to something safer.

"We are going out for dinner after work this evening."

Susan grinned. "A date with an awesome man?"

"Not a date." She tucked her hair behind her ear. Goose bumps rose on her forearms. "We're just sitting down as a couple of friends. He's easy to talk to." But hard to be near.

"And easy on the eyes." Susan shot her a devilish grin. "What do you think are his plans?"

"We made it clear to each other. Friends." If Steve really knew all there was to her, would he even want to be friends? Hope lowered her head to the table. Why did every part of life become so complicated? Why couldn't people be rational and non-emotional? It would make life a whole lot easier.

CHAPTER TWENTY-NINE

At ten minutes to four, Hope jumped when Bethany chirped over the inter-com. "Ms. Sparks, Mr. Steve Burrow is here for his appointment."

"Please send him in." A rumba began in Hope's stomach. She scooped up her papers, slid them into a folder, and scampered to drop them into the file cabinet.

Bethany escorted Steve farther into the office than necessary. "Ms. Sparks, may I get you and Mr. Burrow a cup of coffee before I leave?" The young lady never took her eyes off Steve.

A dull ache coursed through Hope's jaw as she clenched her teeth. A flash of jealousy streaked through her as she watched the doe-eyed look of the receptionist. Reel it back in, girl.

"Bethany, this is Pastor Steve Burrow from First Baptist Church. Steve, this is my temporary receptionist. As she suggested, would you care for some coffee before we go?" her remark contained a tad more bite than necessary.

Steve extended his hand to the girl. "Nice to meet you, Bethany." He smiled at the almost drooling young damsel. "And, no thank you to the coffee."

"My pleasure, Pastor," Bethany squeaked and turned a light shade of pink.

"Bethany. I forgot to tell you something." Hope stepped back to her desk to close her laptop. "Tomorrow will be your last day at the front desk. You will go back to your regular job of data processing. While

Loriann is out, Kelsey Warren will be filling in. After she goes through some orientation in the morning with Susan, I will need you to help situate Ms. Warren for what she will need to start. If you are all caught up out front, you can leave for the day. Thank you for stepping in for a bit." She grabbed her purse. "Steve, are you ready to go? Josh will meet us at Tommy's shop."

With the tour of Hope's business completed, Steve told her he planned to swing by another auto-parts store after dinner. So, they drove their own vehicles to the small café

As Steve slid the chair out for Hope to be seated, he took her hand to help her sit down. He explained his preference for tables over booths.

"So, you are saying that in your opinion, booths are for business meetings or more intimate relationships, but tables are for friends, men or women. Please clue me in." She snickered while doing her best not to burst out laughing at the silliness of his explanation.

Steve grinned a cute dimpled grin.

"Okay, hear me out, let's try a metaphor." He grabbed a saltshaker and the pepper dispenser along with a sugar packet. He placed them on the table between them.

Hope spoke before he could speak. "Who's the salt and who's the pepper? Why are there three? It's only you and me."

"The sugar is the table, whether booth or not. What do you want to be, the salt or the pepper?" Steve chuckled.

"I better be the pepper. It's more my personality." She laughed.

"First, let's look at the booth. For a business meeting, things can be laid out on the table to shuffle around in order to explain things."

Hope nodded. "I can see that."

"Secondly, in the booth, an intimate dinner begins when the man and woman sit on the same side and can whisper to one another." He moved the salt to the same side as the pepper.

"So, I assume there will be no whispering going on tonight? I won't be hearing any juicy gossip about your parishioners?" She gave a forced snicker as disappointment played in her mind.

Steve shook his head with a slight smirk.

"What about the table with chairs? What's your take on that?"

"Well, tables with chairs are for friends and the possibility of future friendships or the progression toward a conceivably more intimate relationship."

Hope's heart skipped a beat with visions of his kisses and cuddles in one of the booths.

"You see, this" he waved his hand between them "is not a business meeting with papers and memorandums nor is it a couple of lovebirds. Distance is paramount while not standoffish."

"So, that is what this is?" She motioned between them.

"I want to get to know who Hope Sparks really is. If something were to develop further in any relationship whether friends or romance, I want it to be what we have in common more than a physical attraction."

The waitress wandered over. "Are you ready to order?" She looked at Hope.

"I'll have the country-fried steak, mashed potatoes, and whole kernel corn and a cola."

"That sounds good. I'll have the same, but with lemonade."

"Can't handle the strong stuff, Steve?" Hope tittered as she remembered the trusted moments of the previous evening in Rolla.

"No, but the caffeine keeps me awake." He smiled at the young server.

As the girl walked away, Hope decided to pursue the conversation. "What I am hearing, is that you want to expand our friendship."

"Not in a romantic sphere. As of yet, I don't know enough about you and you don't know enough about me."

Hope took a chance and reached across the table to touch his hand like Susan had.

He smiled and eased his hand back a bit.

"Oh." She slowly pulled her hand back. What an idiot I am.

"Hope." His hand shot out to snatch hers before she could hide it under the table. "That was stupid of me. I shouldn't have pulled my hand back like that. It was pure instinct. I am used to keeping my hands away from women for discretionary purposes. It was an impulse. I am always aware of the position of a pastor and so I guard myself from any impropriety. I am sorry you misinterpreted my actions and maybe misread my intentions toward you."

"Maybe I should go." She grabbed her glass and chugged some water down to squelch the acid reflux. So much for being together as friends.

"No, please don't go. At least let me clarify myself." He extended his other hand and wiggled his fingers. "Hope, too many times, we imperfect humans screw things up by not being clear in what we mean. I don't ever want that to be a problem between us. We have already had some misunderstandings and we don't need anymore."

She nodded as her stomach knotted.

"What little I know of you is that you are a very smart and complicated woman. You, like myself, have struggled to keep your feet under you. We have, through some of our discussions, found we have quite a bit in common. However, we need to delve into each other's lives a bit more before things could even begin to move forward." He tipped his head forward and stared at her. "Don't you agree?"

The words wouldn't come. She gave a quick nod.

"Let me ask you this. You told me that you knew Kenny most of your life since he was Josh's close friend. You said that he and Janie dated in high school. Did you really know your sister and ex-husband back then, or were you so focused on school and the future that you were unaware of how they interacted with each other?"

"I guess I didn't. And yes, I was focused on school."

"You also talked about growing up in church and being baptized, but you never said anything about a personal relationship with Jesus Christ."

"Yeah, I think that is private between the individual and God. I don't think that a god powerful enough to create the universe is that interested in Hope Sparks. What does this have to do with a relationship two people might share?"

Steve exhaled. "Since I am a committed Christian and I try to follow the Bible as best as I can, I can't go into a full-blown relationship with someone no matter how I feel about our compatibility in everything else, if we don't share our beliefs and faith in God. The Bible says to not be unequally yoked together with unbelievers. That is why I want to get to know you better. I haven't been this comfortable with someone in a long time but I'm also uncomfortable."

"So, what are you saying, Steve?" Though she didn't want to, she withdrew her hands from his, then wiped them against her leg. "You don't want to see me again if I don't see eye to eye with you regarding God?"

"No, no, no. That's not what I'm saying." He pulled his hands back and slid them under the table. "I wanted to come out tonight to get to know you better and understand where you are in relationship with Jesus Christ."

The server brought their food and placed it in front of them.

Hope's eyes focused on the tabletop. What she learned in school and about God scrambled her feelings. Why couldn't relationships be like simple equations? Add A to B divide by C, problem solved. But right now, she wanted to run away screaming.

As the server walked away, Steve cleared his throat.

"Why don't we eat, then maybe we can discuss this further?" The smile from his eyes looked full of expectation. "Do you mind if I ask a blessing on the food and our evening?"

Hope's numbness blurred her vision. She bowed her head in response.

"Lord, bless this food to the nourishment of our bodies, and I beg you to help me explain what I mean to Hope before there is any misunderstanding…"

Hope raised her head and looked across the table to watch Steve as he spoke to God. His face seemed content and relaxed while talking to this supposed super being. She liked what she saw.

What should she do about this? Should she confess God, for the sake of a relationship with Steve? Did she need to pretend to be religious in order to get along with him, like she did with her parents? Did she want a relationship founded on lies? Wasn't her marriage based on lies? Would that make her any better than Kenny?

Steve was smart and very observant. He would figure out her deceit in no time and walk away from any type of relationship.

When his prayer finished, Hope picked up her fork to start but paused. "I will be honest with you as to why I am not a Christian. Two loving parents raised me in a Christian home. My mom and Daddy tried to nurture us in a religious bubble in contrast to what the rest of the world did. I witnessed what some of my friends' parents in the church engaged in behind closed doors. Their behaviors were similar to the world. What my parents taught appeared contrary to what everyone else thought and did. Even though I love her, I saw my mother as a devout fanatic. I rejected her belief."

"Hope, keep in mind, not all people in church are Christians. I haven't met your parents. I don't know them, so I won't discuss their motives. However, I have met Josh, Susan, Tommy, and Annie, and though new in the faith, they seem to be headed in the right direction."

"Yeah, since Josh became a Christian, he has changed. I struggle to understand him and Susan. She and I can exchange ideas without her going off the religious deep end." Hope sucked her bottom lip in. She didn't like talking about this. Her gut turned. Why should she have to restructure her life just to date him? She would keep doing her own thing and forget about him.

The remainder of the evening, Hope deflected any return to the subject of Christ as her imagination ran wild. Any hope of a romantic relationship between them crashed and burned with no survivors.

As he walked Hope to her car, he asked to see her again for dinner or lunch the following week.

Hope shrugged. A deafening silence hung between them, but in her heart, screamed the insult that she wasn't good enough for this man. So be it!

About four blocks from her condo, she pulled into the Fast-N-Friendly convenience store parking lot. She didn't need him. She didn't need anyone. She only needed one thing. Quick steps took her inside the store where she would find another companion for the night.

CHAPTER THIRTY

Early January, Springfield

Buzz—buzz—buzz

Hope swatted at the offensive little box that had the audacity to annoy her enough to pry open welded-shut eyelids. The bedroom remained fuzzy as she scrunched her eyelids and reopened them only to bat them to clear the blur.

Her broken sobriety scoffed at her.

Hope wanted to forget the previous evening with the preacher. And, she needed to get ready to leave for her flight to Utah.

"I will bury myself back into business like before. Why do I seem to attract betrayal?" She grumbled as she flipped off the comforter and slid her feet into her slippers. "Why did Steve need to express his interest and then dash any hope of a future because of our religious differences?"

She shivered. Why did the bedroom feel so cold?

She looked down. Though she had managed to remove her blouse, her slacks now bunched at her knees. She failed to take off her pants to put on pajamas when falling into bed.

Though a struggle, she managed to stand, then shuffled to the bathroom. As she stepped into the cold room, the image in the mirror caught her attention. Mascara streaked her upper cheeks. While crying had never been a necessity for her, this time the bottle didn't bring enough of an emotional respite for the mood rolling over her after a night of rejection. She swiped at the black streaks on her face. The grief of a relationship at this time was something she did not need. The bitterness in her heart tasted like rum.

Hope slid open the shower stall and turned on the water. Once again, the taste of alcohol drifted up from her stomach, and she forced it back down. As she stepped into the water-spray, she glanced at the wall clock to see she still had three hours until her flight's departure.

After she cleared airport security, Hope perused her client's file. Steve's special ringtone gave her pause.

"Good morning." His voice sounded timid.

"Good morning. How can I help you? I'm pretty busy preparing for my meeting before my flight." Hope glanced around the gate area at the other passengers who also waited to board. With any luck, she could get through this call without drawing attention to herself.

"Hope, we need to talk about what happened at dinner."

"Not really, you made yourself perfectly clear. We're just friends and will continue as such. I get it. I have other Christian friends and I am sure you have non-Christian friends, such as me. I don't need to talk about it."

"Maybe not, but I do."

"Please Pastor Steve, I am trying to get ready to deal with a customer and I need to focus on those details right now." A tremor in her hand tried to dislodge the phone from her fingers.

"I thought we agreed for you to call me Steve, as a friend."

"Yeah sure, I need to go back to my paperwork. The flight leaves in half an hour, so I really need to go. We'll talk when I get back, Pastor Burrow."

Only dead air answered her.

"First call for Flight 2046 to Salt Lake City, boarding at Gate Four."

Hope disconnected, stuffed her cell phone back into her suit jacket, and collected her papers.

She settled into her first-class seat. She reached into her pocket and retrieved her phone to put on airplane mode. Before she could do so, the cell vibrated with a text.

Susan. "Have you boarded yet?"

She texted back. "Yes. You caught me right before I shut down my phone. What's up?"

"Just wondering how things went at dinner with Steve."

"We'll talk later about Pastor Burrow."

"Pastor Burrow? What happened?"

"Not now, please. I'll call between my meetings with Collins and Dinkins. Talk then. Got to go." But after she and Susan talked, Hope planned to have another meeting with Johnny Walker or Jose Cuervo.

"Ms. Sparks, didn't you say you were coming in this morning?"

The question seemed odd seeing it was only Wednesday morning. Was it Wednesday? Wait. Didn't she meet with Robert Dinkins on Wednesday? Hope planned to return home Wednesday night after her meeting. She rolled over, pulled the sheet over her head, and released the phone next to the pillow.

"Hope? Are you okay?" Kelsey's voice crashed into Hope's ravaged brain. "I thought you were coming in today. Weren't you meeting with Josh and Susan this afternoon?"

Hope dragged the phone back near her head. "Today's Thursday isn't it?" She flopped to her back and stared at the ceiling. "Kelsey, did I have any scheduled appointments? I can't remember."

"No, you wanted to make sure you were well rested before speaking to any clients. You wanted to organize any notes about Collins and Dinkins who you just met with." A long pause added to Hope's misery. "Are you feeling well? Are you coming down with a virus? If not, I can come to your place and we can work from your condo."

"Kelsey, I'm still in Los Angeles. I didn't make my flight." She sniffed the air. Cigars. Robert Dinkins smoked cigars. With a slow scan of the room, she spotted her briefcase and purse sitting on the lone chair across the room. She rolled onto her side, glanced into the trash can at the spilled cup, and groaned. What a mess. "I have to call the airline and get a flight. I'll try to get back as soon as possible."

"Hope, why don't you get ready and I'll call for you. I'll try to find one for about four or five hours from now, so you will have time to get there. How far are you from the terminal?"

"About a half mile. If you can book it within two hours, I can get cleaned up, pick up my luggage at the luggage storage where I left it during the meeting with Robert, and get to the terminal. My briefcase and purse are with me. Hopefully, I will have time to grab a bite before the flight."

"When you get back, if you want, we can talk about the trip." After another long pause which echoed across the distance, Kelsey added, "And anything else you want to discuss. Also, Pastor Steve has called twice already today. He seemed very concerned about something."

"I'll talk to him later." Hope's glazed eyes drifted over to the side-table and the half-filled bottle. "I'll call after my shower to get the flight information." Her hand trembled as she extended her arm to grasp the neck of the bottle.

She worked her way on wobbly legs to the bathroom sink and tilted the golden-brown contents into the drain. "Let's start this again with day one of sobriety. This time without my head in the clouds." Her thoughts drifted to the minister and his convictions. Could she *just* be his friend? And what about Jesus Christ? She needed some help. Maybe she did need to talk with him as a friend first and stop trying to manipulate the results. The bottle slithered through her fingers and hit dead center at the bottom of the trash receptacle. Bullseye. A first step.

CHAPTER THIRTY-ONE

A little girl's squeal jerked Hope's attention to the baggage carousel.

"Amber! Get over here. You're going to make me drop your brother."

A woman struggled to pull a stroller off the conveyor as she clutched an infant in one arm and tried to control a toddler with her knees.

No one seemed to care.

Hope ran up and grabbed the stroller. "Let me get that for you." She raised the stroller over the toddler's head while she also used her knees to help keep the child under control. "Which is your suitcase?"

The woman pointed.

Hope pulled the large suitcase off the belt. "It looked like you were herding sheep and couldn't corral them." Hope smiled down at the toddler.

"Sometimes that's what it feels like. Their daddy is running late from work."

What would it be like to have a family? A career, a working husband, and little ones. Did she want children? That was a definite, yes… with the right man.

Hope looked up at the woman and, over the mom's shoulder, spotted Kelsey coming into the terminal. Kelsey strode across the terminal's floor with her usual grace and a look of determination.

"Do you think you have it under control?" Hope spoke to the busy mom.

"Yes, thank you very much."

Kelsey already seemed more like an assistant than a receptionist. She wasn't a newbie. After all, she had been a personal assistant while working in New York City for the advertising agency and admitted she wanted to get back into the business flow. But how deep did she want to jump back in? Hope did not know. Why Kelsey wanted to do this, despite owning the coffee shop, boggled Hope's mind.

With Kelsey's efficient scramble to get Hope an earlier flight out of Los Angeles, they would miss Springfield's rush hour traffic. She had a way of making Hope feel important despite what Hope currently felt about herself.

Kelsey stepped to Hope's side and pulled out a tablet.

"Ms. Sparks, Mrs. Hart sent me to pick you up and called Bethany to cover at the reception desk." Her use of Hope and Susan's surnames in a public arena portrayed professionalism. Kelsey smiled at Hope. "How was your flight?"

"Very good, thank you." Hope glanced around the area and noticed several people watching their interaction.

"Ms. Sparks, you have a four o'clock meeting with Mr. and Mrs. Hart. Pastor Burrows would like you to call when you are available." Kelsey raised her brows.

Hope scrunched her face.

"Are we going to your condo first, or straight to the office?"

Hope pointed at the baggage carousel.

Kelsey reached out to grab Hope's valise and garment bag as they came by.

"To the office." Hope took the handle of the suitcase from her and rolled it toward the exit.

As they made their way to the parking area, an idea took shape.

The injured Loriann expressed a desire to remain as the receptionist since she didn't want to travel once the baby arrived. An assistant traveled from time to time.

But Susan's time ran thin and she also struggled with leaving the babies while traveling as Hope's assistant along with her duties as a legal advisor. Hope remembered their last discussions about the future. Susan expressed a longing to start her own law firm and take on several clients for legal business advice after the children were in school.

Hope didn't want to make a decision yet, but she contemplated whether Kelsey could be the fit as an assistant. She appeared to be an experienced personal assistant and because she was single, her schedule seemed to have more flexibility.

Hope glanced at Kelsey, tablet in hand with the daily schedule at the ready. She already knew Hope's drinking weakness, including this weekend, and as far as Hope trusted, Kelsey hadn't blabbed it to everyone. She had her own life and no family.

Hope's smile grew, then it faded fast. What if Kelsey had ulterior motives and wanted to harm the company? Hope would watch her closely. Her charm could be subterfuge. *Mental note to self, talk to Susan after I see if Kelsey continues to support my agendas for the company.*

The two women walked to where Kelsey had parked. Hope closed the door to the car once they were both inside. "I've fallen off the wagon for three days. I need to get my head back in the game. I'm almost positive nothing else happened." Did she do more than drink? That was the proverbial question. Would Robert Dinkins be honest?

As they walked through Hope's office door, Kelsey handed Hope her garment bag. "Ms. Sparks, when you are ready to head home, let me know and I'll drive you."

"I can call a cab. I don't know what time I'll be leaving."

"What you need is some rest."

"I'm not sure I can trust myself to be alone right now."

Kelsey stepped to the door between Hope's office and the reception area and closed it. "Hope, remember, that at the end of my workday, I am no longer your employee but your friend, and in some ways your sponsor regarding the bottle. I want to help you succeed in life. Your mastery over drink benefits you and me, as it helps with my own continued recovery. If, after you leave here, you want to talk, I'm available as a friend."

With her private life exposed and unprotected from Kelsey's prying eyes, Hope pulled out her cell phone to cover her discomfort. "I need to make a call. Thank you for the offer." Could she find some answers about the previous evening from Robert Dinkins? She hoped so.

Kelsey turned, opened the door, and left.

Hope checked the time and mentally adjusted for the time difference. "It's three-thirty here and one-thirty there. Maybe Robert is in the office." Hope punched in the number as her stomach clenched.

"Hello Hope. How are you feeling today?" Robert didn't sound too great.

"Maybe I should be asking you the same." Though she wanted to sound uplifting, her worry and fear wouldn't allow it.

"Well, I still feel hungover. We really went overboard. I haven't done that in forever." He chuckled. "It took a bit to get you onto the bed."

"Robert, I don't remember checking in to my room, or much else after going dancing."

"That's probably because I rented you a room."

"Oh, I see." She waved her hand in front of her face, stood, and walked over to turn down the heat in the room. "You weren't there when I woke up. How did my briefcase and purse get to the room? Didn't I leave my briefcase with the hotel concierge before we went to the lounge?"

"When we left, we grabbed it before we went upstairs. Listen Hope, you weren't in an emotionally good place. Your crying was desolate. You lamented about lost love all evening. Are you still dealing with your ex? It sounded like someone else. You appeared devastated at the loss."

Hope sighed. "So…we didn't…?"

"Hope, I would never take advantage of you or any woman under those circumstances. You passed out in the elevator. I could barely function myself." He snickered. "I called a friend after I put you on the bed. She came, put you into bed, then took me home."

"That explains why I was fully dressed when I woke up. Robert, thank you for being a gentleman. I appreciate it."

"Whoever he is must be special." He paused. "But he must have hurt you. By the way, I've been seeing *a friend* that I'm interested in."

"I hope it works out for you. Thanks for the information. I hope you get to feeling better." She sagged back into her chair. How she wanted to believe he told the truth. Outside her window, the blustery sky morphed across tinges of gray. Despite the clouds, it had just become a brighter day due to Robert's good report.

Ting…ting…ting.

"Ms. Sparks, Pastor Steve Burrow is on line one. He requests a few minutes of your time."

"Yes, I'll speak to him. But before I do, Kelsey, I'll take you up on the offer of a ride. I should be finished with the meeting with Josh and Susan around five."

"Sounds good."

"Thanks. Go ahead and patch the pastor's call through." Hope reached over and picked up a pen. When she heard Steve's voice, she doodled on a notepad. Her stomach clenched.

"Hello, Hope."

"Hello Pastor Steve. How are you today?"

"I'm fine. And you?"

"A tad under the weather but not too shabby. What can I do for you?"

"First, can you call me Steve, Dr. Sparks?" A brief suppressed laugh escaped his lips.

"Okay, I give up, Steve. I guess we can be friends. So, how can I help you on this cold day?"

"How about we go out to eat and then go bowling at First Baptist Church? I know someone who has an in and can reserve the lanes. But it must be a Monday, Tuesday, or Thursday evening. We could go in the afternoon, but you work."

"I don't have bowling shoes or a ball."

"Do you have some shoes with a soft sole? Not tennis shoes. If not, stocking feet works. As for bowling balls, we have a large assortment to choose from."

"I'll check my schedule with Kelsey and get back with you on which day would be best."

"Hope." An audible sigh followed a long pause. "I feel bad about how things were left in the air the other night. Do you think we can use our bowling evening to fix things between us?"

"We'll talk. We need to know where we're coming from or stop the charade. I'll call when I get home to let you know. Bye, Steve." Hope hit the END button and stared at the phone. If she let him get to her again, could she survive the hurt? Bowling might not be such a good idea. She glanced to the heavens. *What do you think?*

CHAPTER THIRTY-TWO

Hope set the phone down, rose from behind her desk, and walked over to the office window. She gazed out at the traffic cruising by. People headed to their respective lives. Some traveled south toward downtown Springfield. Red, blue, and silver sedans and coupes moved in a methodical pattern to or from a destination. Maybe students rushed home from classes. Semi-trucks, cars, and pickups journeyed north in the direction of Bolivar, Independence, Kansas City, and the far northern states or to destinations beyond.

A man maneuvered over the ice and snow drifts at its entrance. A minivan fishtailed out of the parking lot across the way. Hope's life swayed all over the place in similar fashion. She needed to get back control.

The news from Robert Dinkins in L.A. had been encouraging. Yet, depression wrapped around her like a rain-soaked blanket as she viewed the gray skies over the shops and restaurants. "Such a gloomy day, and to think earlier I could have basked in the warm weather on L.A. beaches. What a contrast my life has become."

Hope's stomach grumbled. She doubted she should ingest anything other than saltine crackers or her stomach might start a rebellion. Even with brushing her teeth three times, and using mouthwash, the taste of alcohol and its acidic essence drifted upward from the pit of her stomach.

The aftertaste, the upset stomach, and her bad behavior should be enough to keep her from coming within ten feet of alcohol for the remainder of her life. So, what drew her back to it again and again?

She watched the north bound transit and wished she could run off and avoid some of the issues in her life. But she needed to face it and recapture what she'd lost.

Hope clutched the window ledge and stared out at the company parking lot. Was it her own life anymore? What about family? Mom and Daddy, Josh and Susan depended on her to keep a clear head. And what about the company? Tommy and Annie, and forty other employees banked on her for their livelihood. She tried to set aside her personal feelings and look at it from a business standpoint. If not successful, the company would fold, and they would all be out of a job. The thought made her cringe.

Hope cast a look over her shoulder at her desk and the efficient cavern called her office. Tuesday, management had a meeting regarding the acquisition of Broderick's. There would be more lives to consider. Was she capable of holding the lives of a hundred people in her hands if she couldn't even hold her own life together?

Hope stepped back to her desk and considered the winds of turmoil she brought on her parents. Sadness blew through her. Academics seemed like a no brainer since she always landed at the top of her class. A child with her aptitude couldn't have been easy to deal with for her parents.

She stared across the room at the outer door to Kelsy's area. What about her willingness to step into a submissive position even though she owns her own business? She said her life would be in the gutters if she had not joined with Jesus, and yet, she never pressured Hope.

Would she ever get so desperate that she would need Jesus, too?

"And what do I do about Steve Burrow?" Her words bounced around the substantial office. How could she carry out a friendship with him when she wanted more? Could she have his Christ centered life and stay friends when Steve consumed her?

She picked up the com-line. "Kelsey, could you bring in my schedule for next week?"

As the two o'clock meeting about the acquisition of Broderick's finally approached, the tension mounted.

Hope's breath caught as her pulse pounded in her chest. She touched the window with her fingertips as she watched her staff's preparation through the glass door of the conference room. "The Hunt" is what she lived for. She scanned her employees.

At first glance, what played out before her looked to be discord and unrest as the members of the team shuffled papers. Small squabbles cropped up.

Her neck's veins throbbed while she observed the individuals scramble with last minute details.

Susan shuffled through title documents and memorandums.

Josh stuffed customer order forms into a folder.

Tommy stapled his requisition forms for potential maintenance, repairs, and refitting of equipment at Broderick's.

Bethany and the other two young interns ran in and out as requested for each department head. Hope's buy out of Broderick's became these young people's first opportunity to witness firsthand a major transaction in the making.

Hope cracked open the door to listen.

From the other door, Kelsey plowed into the room backward with a pile of papers in her arms. A vibrant look pasted on her face. A moth drawn to the light of the business world. She handed Susan a document.

"Thanks, I wondered where it disappeared to." Susan smiled.

Kelsey stepped over to Josh and handed him what looked to be order forms from clients. She received another smile.

"Thanks, Kelsey."

She stepped left and laid a yellow note pad and a couple of pens in front of Tommy. "You may need these today. Better get your writing boots on." She patted Tommy's shoulder.

Kelsey strode to the head of the table and put files, presumably for the Broderick deal, at Hope's place. She walked out and a minute later returned with her tablet and sat in the open chair beside Hope's chair ready with a sparkle in her eyes—nose flaring—flushed face.

She's loving this. Hope grinned as she analyzed the woman's degree of efficiency. The look on Kelsey's face told Hope her veins pumped business blood the same way Hope's did, which made everyone's job easier. More of a facilitator it appeared, she loved being part of the game without the added stress of being in charge. Could Kelsey be protecting herself against her own drinking problem?

Hope shivered and stepped into the adrenaline pumped room. "Okay, Sparks System Logistics's Expansion to acquire Broderick Dynamics is open for discussion." *Here we go!* "Josh, could you bring us up to speed with your interaction with Edward Broderick?"

"It seems Edward is interested in selling the plant to us. We are the front-runners to buyout Broderick's. When going over the transition between their capabilities and our needs, we found it to be quite favorable and cost effective." Josh tapped his pen on his file folder. "Susan and Tommy have more details. After reviewing employee records, we found a few we might not be able to grandfather into a viable position for our needs. While you were on your trip to the West Coast, the department heads looked through the files to see where these people can be trained."

"Susan, your findings?"

"All the title documents are cleared of any liens as Carol Baggerly stated. Taxes are up to date. I checked on all the employees' regarding legal documentation into the country. One is still pending. There are no easement issues since the property is open to all streets from the property itself. And there are no encroachment problems. Everything looks clear. Carol is one to definitely keep with this acquisition."

"Tommy?"

"There are a couple of small equipment problems. I spoke with Pete and Sally and they think it will be minor. I have contacted some parts manufacturers and we can have the components within a couple of weeks of ordering except a few belts and bearings which are backordered."

Several other topics, such as, why Broderick's products became outdated, were covered. They discussed how long it would take for Broderick's to complete previous contracts and commitments. Soon, the meeting tapered off.

"Good work, everyone. Josh. In your opinion, is it a go?"

"Yes."

"Susan. Is it a go?"

"Yes."

"Tommy?"

"Yes."

"Thank you all for the effort and hard work. Other than Josh, Susan, and Tommy, you can all return to work. We'll let you know when everything is complete."

Hope watched the others file out, then turned to the remaining three. The next step needed to be handled with special care. Hope prayed it would be a good fit and Tommy would accept. Otherwise, she'd need to go with someone else and wasn't sure Broderick's plant manager was up for the task.

"Now, let's discuss a few paramount issues with this procurement. Tommy, I want you to talk with Annie and see if she is willing to move to Farmington or Rolla."

"Why would she move there?" Tommy scrunched up his face.

Hope chuckled. "Well, Josh, Susan, and I believe that is where the plant manager of Sparks System II should be living. I am sure Annie would like to live there with him."

"Huh?"

Josh laughed. "Give him a few seconds, it'll sink in."

Tommy's eyes darted to every face at the table. His eyebrows shot up and his eyelids lifted.

"Hope, do you mean you are offering me the position of plant manager of the new operation?"

"You deserve it. Your hard work and loyalty are beyond dispute. Go home and discuss it with Annie. In fact, if you need some time off to go over it with her, do it. Give me an answer by Friday." Hope stood. "Tomorrow morning, we have a conference call with Broderick to present our offer. Josh and Susan, please be in my office at eight o'clock for any final adjustments."

Hope turned back to the table. "Tommy, if you don't take off and are available tomorrow and not too busy with maintenance issues, you are welcome to stand in. You have been a part of this since the beginning, a faithful and valuable resource to this company." Hopefully, this decision would prove one of her best…especially since other decisions of late had not.

CHAPTER THIRTY-THREE

Mid-January, Springfield

Hope blinked several times and stared into the dressing table's mirror. Would it give the approval she needed? The scheduled bowling night had arrived, and a kaleidoscope of butterflies put her on edge.

She glanced at her outfit laid out across the bed, then looked at her eyeshadow. "Oh great! The wrong shade." With a wet-wipe, she scrubbed off the dark tint. After dabbing her lids dry, she held up the lighter hue and compared it to her blouse. Her shoulders relaxed. This could work.

She hoped her blue, Jazlyn lace up soft-sole, Hushpuppies would work for bowling shoes. Years had passed since she last bowled. Could she keep the ball out of the gutters? It should be fun. But her competitive spirit needed to stay under control.

Her quick check on the time revealed twenty-five minutes until Steve's scheduled arrival. A tremor rolled down her shoulders and down to her freshly painted fingernails. She gripped the edge of her dressing table. "I've got to get control, or I'll never finish putting on my mascara. Why am I this jittery for a date? No, remember, this isn't a romantic date. It's simply time out with a friend. I love being around him." Hope looked at herself in the mirror and cocked her head. "Then why does he keep me so off balance?"

With only two minutes left, she slipped on her boots and touched the soft soles of her shoes.

Ding…Dong

Startled by the doorbell, Hope launched off the side of the bed like a runner after the starter's pistol for the hundred-meter dash. She stopped at the full-length mirror by the front door to inspect her casual attire. "We are just friends. No need for seduction." As she reached for the doorknob, her eyes drifted up. "What do I do if Steve brings you up, Jesus?" Out blasted a breath through pursed lips. "Oh great! Now, *I'm* talking to You, what next?"

Hope swung open the door. "Good evening, P…Steve."

"Wow. You clean up nice." Steve's perusal obvious as his eye brows raised and his eyes drifted from her head down to her boots.

Warmth rose to Hope's face. "I'm concerned about my shoes. Will these suffice?" With shaky hands she raised her Jazlyns to expose the underside.

"Those should work great." He offered his elbow. "Shall we go? We'll grab some burgers and shakes first, to take with us. There will be other people on the campus, but we have full access to the lanes. There are several lanes. It isn't as noisy as a public bowling alley. I expect the racquetball courts, weight room, basketball courts, and the teens' arcade room will be in use. It's a busy place."

"So, we won't be alone to talk about the things we need to talk about?" She slid her hand through his proffered elbow. Was that a shiver when she touched him? Her eyes darted up to his intense sky-blues. Did their touch affect him as much as her?

"Oh, there are places to have a quiet conversation. Hope, above all. I want to get to know who you are, and I want you to understand where I'm coming from. But, let's not get into that right now because I'm going to kick your tail bowling." He grinned. "I hope. Unless you have hidden the fact that you are really a pro bowler."

She smirked.

❧ ～ ❧

When they arrived at the church, Steve walked around and opened his pickup's door for her.

Hope slid out and gawked at the First Baptist Church campus. He wasn't lying. It looked like a college or high school campus and covered an entire city block with its parking lot included. A three-story facility dwarfed the large church Pastor Steve had ministered at in Kansas City. She let her vision scoot from one end of the building to the other. "It's huge. There must be quite a few people here to run this operation. I see offices and classrooms but where is the sports arena?"

"Oh, it's in the basement an underground lower level."

"You mean there are four stories? This is outrageous for a church."

"It is an outreach for the community. Christianity isn't just church. It is a lifestyle. Here, we can touch the lives of hundreds of youth and young people every week. It keeps them off the streets at night. And it engages families."

They strolled toward one of the side doors.

"Magnificent. I noticed the four columns at the front. The portico is stupendous."

Once the bowling began, the laughter and banter overshadowed the inevitable conversation that Hope dreaded.

Two young couples bowled in the next lane which helped relax Hope.

She teased him about his release posture.

He laughed hysterically when she rolled the ball down the alley from between her feet.

"Are you thirsty, Hope?"

"Yeah. I could use a drink."

Their eyes met. A deep understanding passed between them.

"Why don't you rest for a few minutes, and I'll grab us a couple of soft drinks."

Hope smiled. "How about water?" A flashback crossed her mind of the steakhouse and the bar where Steve took the chance on drinking the cola.

Steve walked away, and Hope's desires followed him around the corner.

"Oh man, you both got it bad." A girl's voice caught her off guard.

"Excuse me?" Hope spun to face the young lady.

"It's not just Pastor Steve, either." A young man added "Are you his girlfriend?"

Hope's face filled with heat. "Ah, we're just friends. We met when I attended a meeting in Kansas City." She scrambled for the right answer without giving away where she met him.

The girl extended her hand. "I'm Theresa. You can call me, Terry. Pastor Steve helps in the College and Careers Class." She grinned. "He needs someone to look out for him. Often, he seems to hold back his feelings but overall, he's a great guy. But around you, he seems relaxed. Don't tell him we said it, but we saw him checking you out."

Hot blood rushed to the surface. *Where's a fan when I need one?*

"That's true." The other couple nodded in agreement.

"I think he's lonely." Terry added.

"Yeah, his wife passed away a couple of years ago." Regret sunk in like quicksand as Hope's words escaped. Why couldn't she keep her mouth shut? It was none of their business nor was it hers.

"Did you know her?"

"No. Mutual friends told me she was an awesome woman. It isn't for me to talk about, so I will shut up." She drew a line across her lips for emphasis. "I don't think he is interested in me in that respect. You see, I'm not a Christian."

Terry laughed. "Oh, he's interested. I guarantee that. I saw it in his eyes."

Hope glanced at the banners on the far wall. Faith. Hope. Joy. Peace.

Her mind yammered at her with a thousand unanswered questions. She gazed to the ceiling. *If only, Jesus.*

"Hey, what did I miss?" Steve juggled two bottles of H_2O and two bags of chips as he skirted the corner.

"I met Terry. Though I didn't meet her friends." She reached for one of the containers and turned back to the girl. "By the way, Terry, I'm Hope."

The second girl's date grinned as he looked up at Steve. "I bet you are."

"I don't get it." Steve crinkled up one side of his nose. He, then, introduced the college kids. "Clay and Terry are dating." He gestured to the young man sitting beside her. "Reese and Sarah are not but from the looks of it, they are hoping." His laugh drew out the red in Reese's cheeks. Sarah's head dropped to her chest.

"You got that right." Clay's full-throated chortle chimed in.

Hope smiled at the ease with which Steve interacted with the young people.

"Guys, there's more to this lady than a mediocre bowler." Steve laid a hand on Hope's shoulder. "Have any of you heard of Sparks Systems Logistics?"

"Isn't it up on N. Kansas Expressway?" Reese sat up straighter. "Do you work there?"

"Meet Doctor Hope Sparks, founder and owner," Steve spoke with pride.

"Wow, you're a doctor?" Clay stood up and stepped closer to Hope. "I have a rotator cuff problem from baseball. Could you check it out?" He rubbed his shoulder and rolled it forward.

Laughter rolled from each of the younger people.

"Doctor Sparks, do you have any words of advice for us?" Terry shifted forward in her seat.

Hope drew her brows together and placed a hand on Clay's shoulder. "Stay in school, be diligent in your studies, and especially, you, Clay, don't go into standup comedy."

Reese rolled over onto the small bench-seat in belly-grabbing laughter.

"Hope, I'm about tapped out on bowling." Steve pointed toward the racquetball court. "Would you like a tour?"

"Sure, I guess it's your turn." She rotated away from him to the group behind her. "It was nice meeting all of you." Hope brought her finger to her lips.

Steve extended his hand to her. "Shall we?"

Hope clasped his hand and fell into step. "So, this is when we get serious?"

CHAPTER THIRTY-FOUR

So far, the evening had been a blast. Fun like this had eluded Hope for years. The teasing banter while she and Steve tried to keep the ball out of the gutters escalated. Now finished with bowling, she wondered what the remainder of the night held.

Hope focused on viewing the lower recesses of First Baptist. With her eyes dashing from one side to the other, her inquisitive mind raced forward. As usual, her business inclination ran rampant.

"Steve, Annie will be so jealous. I can't wait to give her the details that support the rumors about this place. This gives me an idea for the company. I might add a gym membership or company picnics for bonuses, like the big IT corporations do—something to bring unity and motivation between the two plants."

She marveled at the liveliness that surrounded the activity center with college and high school-aged kids running around. Laughter rang down the halls. The good-natured ribbing at the struggles of athletic endeavors astounded her. No one used vile profanity like most did at public venues.

"I miss the joy of good clean fun. I guess the church is the last bastion of virtue left in our society."

Steve's smile spread as he nodded.

Wistful longing drifted into her thoughts. Hope wanted this back in her life. Had she been tainted by betrayal and through extension, her own bad behavior? Could she get back what she'd lost? If so, how?

The betrayal and her bad behavior could be remedied by a good man like Steve in her life. Did he even realize that he still held her hand? Could he perhaps be rethinking his view about her? Maybe a romantic evening loomed ahead after all.

It took great determination not to look down to their hands. Instead, she drew pleasure from the skin to skin contact. The contrast of her soft palm to the odd combination of his smooth palms and calluses on his fingertips intrigued her.

Hope forced her eyes straight ahead toward the wall. A poster of a cross with a thorny crown caught her attention. **What does Jesus want from you?** in dark red, bold font, topped the hanging and below, in another sentence with a lighter, and more flowing print read: Nothing but a relationship full of love, forgiveness, and friendship.

With a loud crash, bowling pins slammed into the back of the pinsetter and broke the moment.

At that instant, Steve released his hand from hers in a slow movement.

Hope's eyes slid down to the space that grew between them like an untethered astronaut. A cold void almost like the vacuum of the cosmos replaced the warmth. Panicked, she envisioned herself at the end of the unfettered cord floating away from the docking port of a relationship.

Once again, with his words Steve drew her back from the ethereal emptiness. "Hope, I did you a great disservice the other night at the restaurant. I used Kenny and Janie's high school relationship to move our conversation toward Jesus. I should have been upfront with you about my intentions at that time." He slowed his pace. "I let my own personal fondness for you intermix with my pastoral duties." He blew out a heavy breath. "I must be honest with you. I have been interested in you since we first met. However, I deeply wanted to speak with you about your spiritual condition." They paused by the heavy plexiglass window of the racquetball court and he looked at the players. "As you can see, this is the racquetball, handball court."

The players swatted at the ricocheting little ball with tiny tennis-racquets.

A man skidded to his knees, scooped up the blue sphere, and launched it into the corner of the wall.

The other man dove to the floor on his stomach only to miss the ball.

"Just like this game, our emotions and actions seem to bounce off the box we call life." He rested his fingers along the windowsill. "We never know exactly which way things will go. Sometimes, I get mixed up and let my feelings dictate my actions."

"How long did it take for you to come up with that analogy?" She tried to chuckle but it fell flat. Dissatisfaction grew and hollowness joined it. Hope reached to the ledge near his hand and watched as the two players, sweating profusely, high-fived each other.

"It would be an even greater injustice to our relationship to be dishonest about how we feel."

She braced herself for the disappointment coming. She scrunched her eyes shut instead as everything around her sucked into the black hole of her life's secret hiding place. Her stomach twisted. Her heart pounded as strength dropped out of her arms. Was this what an anxiety attack felt like?

The tightness of his grip on her bicep and the fear transmitted through his voice shocked her back to reality.

"Hope, are you okay? Let's step over here to these chairs." He took her elbow and guided her to a padded folding chair near the weight room. "Do you need a drink of water?"

Hope shook her head and stared down at the floor. She struggled to pull herself together. Was he thinking that he just dodged a bullet from the crazy woman? She needed to grow up and face reality. The gray shade that always covered her mind when emotions and stress fought lifted.

Could God be so cruel as to put Steve this close and then jerk him away from her? What about that relationship full of love and friendship the poster said? Did she need it with God in order to get him?

He knelt in front of her and waited.

She blinked and refocused on his penetrating eyes. They seemed to burrow into the depths of her emotions to draw her mind gently back.

His patience—similar to Susan's, her best friend mastered the lesson through years of trial and error. And yet, he appeared a natural.

"I'm okay, Steve. I'm just fearful of the future. I have this new acquisition going on and the stress has built to an enormous level."

"Maybe, we should hold off our discussion until after the urgency of your business deal has lifted. What do you think?"

Overwhelmed with her shame, Hope glanced down at his shirt unable to face him. She'd never recover if she allowed her business life to bleed over into her private life. "No. I think it would be just like a pressure-cooker ready to explode rather than releasing the building steam."

Steve pulled another chair around to face Hope. "Do you need a few moments to compose yourself?" He leaned over to rest his elbows onto his knees. "Would you care to use the facilities or get another drink?"

"I'm fine," The lie floated off Hope's lips far too easy.

CHAPTER THIRTY-FIVE

The night of bowling had turned upside down. Hope swallowed the rising bile that choked her. She glanced across the hall at the plexiglass window of the racquetball courts and wet her lips.

Steve's soothing voice pulled her gaze back to his face. "Hope, I care about you. More than I have a right to. Please let me know if anything I say makes you uncomfortable. Okay?"

She nodded. Moisture blurred her vision and she feared broken-hearted crying might be on the agenda.

"I have dated a couple of single Christian ladies. Things never clicked. Though they were wonderful young women, we knew it wasn't God's will for us to be together. So, each relationship ended. This is just coincidence and perhaps a play on words, but a spark didn't ignite." Steve laughed at his own joke.

Hope couldn't help but smile. Her stomach fluttered around emptiness. How could this night possibly end with a positive outcome?

"I never felt relaxed around them, and our interests didn't gel." He pulled at his shirt's neckline as though it might strangle him despite his loose collar. "One woman sensed I would never love her and give my heart to her completely because she thought I was still clinging to Allie." He sighed. "She was probably right, at least in regard to her. Allison was my first love and may be my only love. But," Steve took in a deep, slow breath, "I don't think the Lord wants that for me. I believe He has something planned that opens my heart to love again."

"Do you think love is in the cards for either of us, Steve?"

"Of course, I do. That is why I want to be open and honest with you." He reached toward her with his hand open.

Hope watched him check himself and withdraw his hand.

"Unlike these other ladies, I feel comfortable, and yet, uncomfortable when I'm around you." Steve shifted in his chair. "I enjoy your company and we have so many things in common. You know some of my history, and I know a bit of yours."

"Yeah, not too flattering is it?"

"No, not for either of us." Steve's head dropped. He didn't move for several moments.

What did he find so interesting in her shoes or the floor that would take so long? "So, what now? Where do we go from here?" The ends of the wide hallway sucked in around her. Claustrophobia could soon force her to run. She took a deep breath, then exhaled to ward off hyperventilation and to keep the pressing walls pushed back. "Do we call off the friendship?" With a shift in her seat, she continued, "I am not sure that I can handle some of this."

"What part?"

"I would miss the fun of being around you and the occasional jest of a shoulder bump." She grinned, but a tremor ran down her arms at the thought of losing contact with this man. "To be truthful, I wonder about being around you without the closeness. What if you do find love and it's not with me? Could I stay friends and watch? Would it send me back to the bottle?"

"You bring up a good point." He glanced at the ceiling." I know I have no right to put you into this situation." He looked back at her. "All relationships are fragile even with Jesus."

"I thought you were in solid with Him. I was under the impression that once you were in a relationship with Him everything was good."

"To be honest, the problem isn't with Jesus, it's with us. We sometimes break our bond with Him." Steve rubbed his neck. After several silent moments, he released it. "I know this is none of our business, but let's look at a relationship we both know, you more than me."

"Okay."

"Look at Josh and Susan. You are in an intimate relationship with the two. He is your brother and, she, your best friend. Is there ever a conflict between them over you?"

"Yes. But it usually is brought on by my issues."

"So, one chooses you and the other doesn't. Correct?"

"Yes, sometimes, and sometimes neither sides with me."

"What about within their marriage? Is it always smooth sailing?"

"No."

"Has the marriage suffered because of it? I have to assume it does to a point. But in most cases, one is at fault and to fix it the offended party forgives with or without an apology to restore the bond of matrimony." Steve reached out and took both her hands into his. The smile on his face sent comfort deep within.

"Hope, the connection between the believer and Jesus is similar to Josh and Susan's. It is a marriage contract dealing with daily life…not just on Sunday at church. It is a bond between two people that is even closer than a marriage contract. The problem is that men and women are imperfect beings in a relationship with a perfect God. So, all fault is with us. We betray the marriage vow and break the link necessary for interaction with the Savior. We sever communication due to our sinful nature. We then must rebuild the connection, which only happens when we agree with Him about our sin. Once the agreement takes place, we are as close to Him again as we were when we first met Jesus and became one in marriage. That is what the Lord wants for believers and for the rest of the world which includes you. He is my family and I want you to be close to my family. Any believer would desire the same thing for the person they may spend a lot of time with and possibly their entire life."

"Is that what you want with me, Steve? Are you saying you want to spend your entire life with me?"

"I want that for any Christian woman I choose for my life partner."

"So, someone who is a Christian. Someone other than me." Her chest tightened.

He shook his head. "I want my soulmate to be my entire soulmate which includes my whole family. I want to share the depths of my love for Jesus with the woman I become involved with. It won't work any other way."

"I need to take a walk and think about what you said." She watched him lean back, he massaged the muscles in his neck again, and close his eyes. "I promise I won't run away like I so often do."

His eyes opened and he nodded.

Hope stood up. "It takes me a bit to digest the data. I may not even come up with a solution tonight. But I will not flee the premises, nor will I fall back into the bottle…at least not from this."

"Take your time. I'll hang out here."

Hope turned and headed back toward the bowling lanes. Could she stay friends with him without being more? Why did she have to meet him? Was it a mistake? Wouldn't it end in disaster?

Before she entered the bowling area, she glanced up and spotted the poster again. **What does Jesus want from you?** The response caused her pause when she put Jesus as Steve's family. "Nothing but a relationship full of love, forgiveness, and friendship." Hope read the words from the bottom of the poster.

"A relationship full of love, forgiveness, and friendship is what I crave with Steve," she whispered. "And Jesus is a main part of his life. Can I be part of that family? Most of my own family are. Can I give my life up for Steve?" She turned the corner and entered the arcade area. After two laps around the teen center, she headed back still without an answer.

She looked again at the poster, and she remembered her daddy's words. "What would Jesus do?" The question stressed her and a familiar taste flooded her mouth. "What would Jesus want with me, an alcoholic? I don't know, but I want a drink in a bad way." She shook her head. "No, I can't go there any longer." She gazed down the hall in Steve's direction.

His body knelt over his chair in prayer.

Was he praying for her? What would it be like to have a man pray for her every day?

CHAPTER THIRTY-SIX

Late January, Springfield

Perched on top of the world with her scepter in hand, that is, the pen she used to sign for the purchase of Broderick's, Hope smiled at William Scranton.

"Congratulations on the buyout of Broderick Dynamics." A broad smile passed over his face.

Hope straightened herself and gave a quick glance around her throne room, that is, her office. "Thank you, William. I believe this expansion will benefit Scranton as well as SSL. If everything goes as planned, we might be able to produce some of the more difficult items your company and ours have trouble accessing. My question is, do we adapt the current products to avoid the ongoing copyrights fees, or avoid the design costs and keep paying the fees."

After the official paperwork had been filed and the title of Broderick's switched to Sparks System Logistics II, invincibility had crowned her majesty.

"Yeah, that's where it gets complicated. It would be nice to pick up the rights but it could be expensive. All I can say is, this is a bold move and I wish you success. I will advise you though, go slowly and don't allow your emotions to outrun your resources and capabilities. Stay organized and efficient."

"Thank you, my friend." Some of her dream projects were coming to fruition. Pride filled her. "I considered every aspect I could think of to foresee any flaws in the buyout. As you know, I put together a good base of talented people. My management team dug into the pros and cons. Now I feel we are on solid ground."

"What about Dynamics' employees? How many are there?"

"There are thirty-five plant workers and three office personnel. We're going to retrain them in our system. Their way of thinking needs modification and modernization." Hope picked up a folder and laid it to her right. "From what we are looking at, the base group is solid in their work ethic. There seems to be some good people."

The office door swung open and Kelsey came into the room carrying a tray with two steaming cups, packets of creamer, and a bowl of sugar.

"Here you go, Mister Scranton." Kelsey balanced the platter on the front edge of Hope's desk with grace and poise.

"Thank you, young lady. I appreciate this. I didn't grab my usual morning cup before I left the motel." He reached for the heavy-duty mug Hope kept for him.

"According to Ms. Sparks, you drink coffee straight black." Kelsey glanced at Hope and grinned.

"I understand you are helping out Hope while Loriann is out of commission. She told me you have your own coffee shop?"

"Yes, I am glad to help out. My assistant manager is quite capable of running my business while I'm here." Kelsey reached across Hope's desk to set Hope's favorite SSL mug in front of her, then placed the sugar bowl with spoon beside it. "Ms. Sparks, is there anything else you need? If not, I need to sort through your notes and organize your schedule for tomorrow."

"There's nothing else for now. Thank you for the coffee."

"Mister Scranton, it is an honor to finally meet you." Kelsey turned to exit the room.

"It was nice meeting you too, Kelsey."

They watched as Kelsey closed the door.

"Wow! That girl amazes me every day." Hope dipped the spoon into the sugar. "William, you need to drop by her shop to really appreciate her business sense and style. But, here's the thing, the coffee shop doesn't seem to be her goal. It is nothing more than a means to an end. She says she has a passion to get back into the business hunt."

"Didn't you say she worked for an advertising firm in New York?"

"Yes, but circumstances changed that." She glanced at the doorway. Kelsey had a flaming desire for business, but she did the mundane and grunt work, which set up the drive to succeed. To Hope, that separated failure from mastery. So far, the background check hadn't found anything different from Kelsey's story to suggest a sinister agenda against the company. The news thrilled Hope.

William departed to head back to Kansas City. Kelsey laid a small pile of customer files on Hope's desk and left her alone.

Hope flexed her fingers in preparation of a hard day's work. With the O'Brian file in hand, she gazed at the paperwork and caught sight of O'Brian's first name—Steven. A sharp flash to her temple caught her off guard, followed by a dull ache at the back of her eye.

Her hand swept to her mouth to cover a gasp, when last week's bowling excursion tumbled back into her memory. Their evening ended with Hope still unsure how to respond to Steve's presentation about Jesus and relationships. Her stomach churned each time she recalled their conversation regarding her feelings about their discussion. It relieved her to learn he had to make a four day trip out of town; he would return this evening, but she still wasn't ready to talk.

Hope hid O'Brian's first name with another piece of paper. Even the pastor's written name invaded her space. Her head ached as she pulled the sheets of paper from the folder.

Would having Steve around be a loss or a gain for the company? Could a profit be made? Her eyes blurred, and she squeezed her eyelids shut tight. "I'm getting confused. Who am I dealing with? Which Steve?"

Hope wiped the moisture from her upper lip. She couldn't even concentrate on the simple task of organizing her customer notes. She shoved the pages back into the folder. Hope grabbed her keys. "A clear head is what I need and time alone with Baby will accomplish it.

The old familiar tang invaded and overpowered her taste buds.

Hope licked her lips and whispered, "Yeah, that's what I need. A drink." Her chair seemed to catapult her from behind the desk toward the office door.

Somehow, the knob turned, and Kelsey's desk came into view.

As she pushed through the door, Hope forced her sight to the distant exit. "I needth a vreak. I'n going for a drive to clear my head." Her feet propelled her forward.

Kelsey jumped from her seat and swung around to face her with arms extended. "I don't think you want to do that."

The side door to Susan's office opened, and Hope glanced that way.

Her friend entered with a huge smile. From the file in her hand, she looked up. "Hope, I got great news regarding the information Carol sent." Susan stopped dead in her tracks and her jaw dropped.

Josh and Tommy's laughter brought Hope's attention to the outer entranceway.

"Hey Kelsey, is Hope in her office? We have good news about—"

Tommy almost ran into Josh at his abrupt stop. Tommy's smile fell.

Hope tried to focus on the pair as Josh's face seemed to enlarge, then shrink far away.

Hope looked back to Kelsey. "Whas wiff the fathe?" She staggered sideways half-a-step to step past her.

Kelsey's movement blocked her.

The panic went straight to Hope's throat and closed it tight—her breath came in gulps—the room spun and extended arms rushed toward her as the blackness descended.

CHAPTER THIRTY-SEVEN

Early February, Springfield

Beep-beep…beep-beep…beep-beep.

What's that infernal noise?

Beep-beep…beep-beep.

Hope buried her head back into the soft pillow. She wanted to return to the pleasant dream of Steve but somehow couldn't. Her desire to feel his tender kisses and the way she imagined his soft touch on her cheek sent a shiver throughout her body. His fingers brushing through her silky hair brought a delightful tingle to the left side of her scalp. The desire to snuggle against his muscular chest grew. The scent of his cologne wafted to her nose mixed with another smell she couldn't quite figure out. Could that be cleanser? Maybe Steve's hand cleaner in his truck?

Beep-beep…beep-beep.

Was that the alarm? Could she be running late for work? She needed to get up and get ready.

Most mornings, she could spring up out of bed. Why not now? Perhaps one of those paralyzing types of dreams held her captive?

Hope struggled to free herself but couldn't. Mixed feelings played through her—she needed to leave the wonderful dream, but more so, she wanted it to continue. Why would anyone want to leave that kind of pleasure?

A moist splotch dripped on her forearm. Water? Where is water coming from? Another drip. She tried to move her arm to dodge the drops but couldn't.

No sound came from her mouth as she tried to call out for help. She needed to calm down and evaluate her situation. Was she still asleep? If so, how could she climb out of the dream that seemed to be hurtling toward a nightmare.

Her one option: use her intellect and heightened senses.

Question one. What do I feel? Wetness on my arm. She concentrated on her fingers. Wiggle those on my right hand. They are sluggish. Go to the left fingers. Nothing? Numb? Asleep? Until those wake up, my hand will be useless.

"Heavenly Father, I beg You." Steve's soft voice pushed into her dream and increased in volume. "Please Lord. I need my friend. I'm desperate. I can't lose her. I can't let her go without You. I love her though I know it is nothing compared to Your love for her.

"You showed Your love to us while we were nothing. When we were full of sin, You died for us. Let Hope live until she knows the truth about Your love and receives You as her Savior. Please Jesus. I will do anything that she might have eternal life with You."

His words were so personal and touching.

Beep-beep…beep-beep.

Confounded alarm. She fought to concentrate on the words he spoke.

"Jesus, she has become so much to me."

Why do my eyes seem to be superglued shut? Steve, I'm right here! She grabbed at the empty blackness.

His imploring voice drew her back.

"…troubled mind rest in You. If Hope were Your child, I could let her go. Let Your Holy Spirit bring her to where You want her…" His voice quavered.

Hope zeroed in on his words.

What was that sensation on her left forearm? Did someone touch her? She wasn't sure, but she wanted to ignore it so she could focus. What did Steve say?

"I will give her up if it means saving her from the stress. I would rather go off into the sunset than allow her health to suffer. I can't go through that again."

Alarmed, she tried to thrash about. Her breathing became rapid. Claustrophobia clawed at her. Why couldn't she wake up from this nightmare?

Beep, beep, beep.

"What's happening?" Steve's tone became sharp and intense as it moved away from her. "Nurse? Nurse? Something's happening. We need some help here."

Fast footsteps rushed toward Hope. "I'm here." The steps came close. "What happened?" An unfamiliar female voice moved to her side. "Her pulse is up."

"I don't know, one second she was breathing normal and the next it became labored, like she was trying to catch her breath."

"Were you speaking to her?

"I was praying."

"Did you say anything that could cause her stress?"

Why are they ignoring me? They needed to listen to her. Her mind screamed, but no words came from her mouth.

"I don't think I said anything that would upset her. Is she going to be all right?"

"Her blood pressure has elevated, also."

Why won't anyone listen? Just help me wake up.

"She seems agitated." Steve sounded concerned. "Look at her eyes. They're moving under the lids."

"Yeah, that's the most movement we've seen for several days. I'll give her something to calm her and help her rest. The more she sleeps the better chances for recovery."

But she didn't want to sleep.

Their conversation faded.

Did you hear what he said? an unfamiliar velvety voice asked from deep within her new dream, as if from inside her, yet not. *He must care a great deal for you. He is willing to give himself up for your eternal soul, but he's incapable because of his own sin. Hope, would someone be able to sacrifice himself for another's eternal life? Perhaps, that's an important question for you to ask. Is it possible for someone to love you enough to give themselves for your eternal soul?*

Troubled by this Dream Stranger's questions, Hope said, "As a child, my parents told me that Jesus did that. So, I guess according to that, Someone did."

Then, why haven't you let Me be that sacrifice for you? The soft words enveloped her in accusation.

The light stung her eyes as she did her best to force them open. Squinting to avoid the brightness, she scanned her surroundings. Then the unfamiliar quickly registered—a hospital room. As her vision cleared, she saw Steve sprawled out in the chair. He looked so uncomfortable with his head cocked to the side and his arms limp over the armrests.

Hope scrunched her eyes shut, then willed them back open. She tried to speak, but a plastic mask covered her mouth and nose. With her right hand, she swiped at it enough to dislodge it. Her throat scratched with rawness as she screeched out a small squawk.

"Hope? Are you awake?" Steve scrambled to his feet and rushed to her side.

The strain to talk exhausted her and her eyelids drifted shut again.

"Are you in there? Hope, please speak to me."

"I...luff...ooo, Stheve." Her fingers yielded no strength as she did her best to squeeze his hand.

"Nurse! Susan. Mr. and Mrs. Hart. I think she's trying to wake."

The sound of scurrying feet caused Hope's breathing to increase.

"Steve, are you sure?" Susan's inquiry sounded shaky.

"I can't be sure, but she tried to speak, and her eyes opened for a few seconds."

Hope listened and felt the tremor in his fingertips that clutched her palm.

His hand slid away.

A great emptiness settled over Hope as though love drifted like a small boat drawn away with the tide. She tried desperately to run after it and pull it to safety. Finally, she gave up.

"Honey, are you awake? Daddy and I are here."

The sound of more feet rushed toward her.

"Excuse me. I need to get to her." Once more, the unfamiliar female broke in.

The recurring gray fog of sleep took over.

Come to me and I will give you rest and peace. Once again, the Dream Stranger's soft whisper comforted.

Such love. "If I go with you, do I lose him?"

Hope, you can seek the kingdom of God, and his righteousness, and all these things will be added to you. Or, you can choose your own kingdom and forfeit it all.

CHAPTER THIRTY-EIGHT

Hope tried to open her eyes. Nothing.

"…never seen anything like it." A man's voice came crashing in through the haze. "He only leaves to go to the bathroom or to get some water. He hasn't eaten in almost six days."

In the background, the irritating beep-beep called out.

Hope struggled to clear her mind. Now, she recognized Josh's strained voice.

"We need her back. Susan, I can't lose Sissy. Can you believe Janie and Kenny have been downstairs all this time?"

"I'm worried about Janie. She doesn't look good." Susan's words sounded exhausted. "She hasn't stopped crying since she first heard about Hope."

Someone hadn't eaten? Kenny? Steve? Janie was crying? What were they saying about her? Hope fought to retain her drifting focus.

Josh's next words cleared some confuse for her. "Steve's fasting shows his love and dependence on God."

Fingers lightly brushed her hair. A breeze passed over Hope's arms, then the warmth of cloth covered her.

"I have never seen such trust in God as he has displayed. Steve loves her. I can tell." Josh's comment appeared to catch in his throat. "I saw him talking to Kenny in the waiting room. I thought Kenny would crumble when Steve approached him. I even asked Steve what they talked about, but he told me they spoke in confidence."

Why couldn't she open her eyes? Hope attempted to thrash about—

her limbs stayed welded to her sides. Frustration built as the darkness tried to envelop her again—her breathing accelerated.

"He must have spoken to Kenny as a pastor." Susan sniffled. "Josh, I'm afraid. Hope's the driving force that moves our family. We would all just drift through life without her.

With a familiar gentle touch, fingers wrapped around Hope's hand and light strokes grazed her upper arm. Her hand rose and a tender kiss touched her palm.

"Please, sweetie, come back to us. We need you."

Hope tried to call out to them. But again—nothing but silence.

"Josh, anything?" Mom's desperate and weakened timbre begged.

"Nothing, Mom." Josh's tone remained flat.

The fatigue took over and a deep darkness overshadowed Hope.

But right away, an intense brightness forced Hope's eyes to spring open. It illuminated all corners of an indistinct hazy room. She squinted at the brilliance.

You're getting some much-needed downtime. Once again, the Dream Stranger's voice sounded cheerful and trustworthy. *However, everything else you want is in Me.*

Her body tensed. Her eyes darted about seeking the speaker.

Your struggle should be to open your eyes to your spiritual condition. You have complicated any real search by filling it with bitterness and strong drink. Your selfishness keeps you from what you need.

"Who are you? What do you want from me?"

I only want your love. I know you are not ready yet, but we'll get there.

"Get where?"

Are you ready to move on with your life? You have obstacles to overcome. Forgive so you can find peace that will fill your soul before resentment and hatred fully contaminate it.

Her eyelids drew heavy as sleep, like a wave, washed over her.

Hope's eyes eased open. She took in the soft florescent lights overhead and the white tiled ceiling.

"Please, Lord, I can't go through this again," Steve's whispered tone pleaded.

The muffled words drew her gaze down to the light-brown hair pressed to the bedsheet.

She swallowed and grimaced. Small tubes attached to her nose pumped oxygen into her nostrils and caused rawness to her throat. "Hey." A raspy sound seeped out. "Can you keep ith down? I'm trying to take a naf." Her hand eased over to stroke his messy hair.

His head jerked up with widened, red eyes. "Hope? You're awake!" He extended a shaking hand to her shoulder. "Let me get a nurse. I'll call your family." He stood and turned to leave.

"Pleasth wait," Hope whispered.

He turned back, "We were so worried."

She watched the tears streak his cheeks.

"I take ith, I'm in the hosfital?" Hope sunk back into the pillow to gather her thoughts. "Wha happen? Did I trif and fall? Do I haff a concuthun or something? My head hurts."

"We'll talk in a bit. Let me grab a nurse to let them know you're awake." He stepped to the curtain, pulled his phone from his pocket, and hit a button. "She just woke up and she's cracking jokes."

Hope watched Steve disappear behind the hospital door.

A weighty speculation crept in as Hope did a quick inventory of her body. Sluggish movements weren't quite right. A heaviness in the left arm and the prickly itch on the left cheek troubled her. *Why did my speech slur when I talked to Steve?*

She twisted glanced at the heart monitor. Unable to keep it in sight long enough to decipher its reading, she sank back into the pillow. The tape holding the intravenous tube that piped liquids into her veins itched and irritated her right forearm. She wanted to scratch, but her left arm wouldn't move. If she could only wipe off her clammy hands.

A picture of herself strapped to a bed permanently popped into her mind. Her heartbeat pounded in her ears as panic closed her throat. She struggled not to scream. Perhaps closing her eyes while she waited would help her figure it out. Her eyes drifted shut. *What kind of major catastrophe have I gotten myself in to?*

The scraping sound of the curtain jerked Hope's eyes open.

A middle-aged, brunette nurse scooted past her and checked the bag hanging above Hope's head. "Fluid levels look good." She released the tube and turned her attention to Hope. "Hey, young lady, I see you have finally decided to join the rest of the world." Her eyes darted back and forth between heart monitor and Hope. "How are you feeling? Are you in any pain?"

The blood pressure cuff inflated around Hope's bicep. "No pain. Jus tafe itching." She looked down at the IV needle. "Wha haffened to me. Did I fall an haff a concuthun?"

The nurse carefully pulled the tacky strip holding Hope's IV.

"Ahh." Hope grunted from the sting.

With the tube in place, the smiling nurse pressed on a fresh piece of tape. "No, Ms. Sparks. The doctor isn't sure what took place, yet. We called him to let him know you're awake." The nurse pulled the blankets to cover Hope's chest while leaving her arms out and brought the call button cord down for her to reach it. "The doctor is on the way. He'll explain it. Push this button to call us." She turned to leave and called over her shoulder. "I'll be back in a couple of minutes."

Hope's face tingled. She glanced down. Her fingers on her left hand were curled under. *Is my hand attached to a lead weight? I can't seem to lift it.*

After several moments of struggling, she raised her right hand with slow movement. With her fingertips, she probed her cheek. Nothing. No feeling at all. Why did her lip sag? The skin on the left side seemed droopy. This isn't good.

CHAPTER THIRTY-NINE

Hope drew back when the hospital room's curtain rustled. Mom and Dad flew in the room with Susan and Josh on their heels. Their rapid movement and tense faces sent a shock wave through Hope.

"Oh, sweetheart, we were so worried." Mom practically threw herself across the bed to encompass her.

Through the loose strands of Mom's graying, strawberry-blond hair, Hope glanced to her daddy and watched tears cascade down as he scooped up her limp hand. He pulled her fingers up to his lips and choked out, "Punkin."

"Glad you're back, Sissy." Josh rocked from side to side with nervous energy, his eyes wet and red-rimmed.

A whimper drew Hope's attention from Josh. Pulled back in a scrunchie, Susan's Raggedy Ann-hair looked disheveled. Her usual pale complexion appeared pasty white, and her lower lip quivered as her fingers white-knuckled the railing at the foot of the bed.

Hope tried to smile, though her mouth didn't want to cooperate. Still foggy, her eyes swept the room searching for their target—craning her neck toward the doorway and back to Susan. Consternation rolled over her. "Where—?"

"Steve's telling the others. He'll be back." Susan moved to the IV stand side of the bed and gripped Hope's hand. "He hasn't left your side the entire time."

"How lawn," Hope gasped, "haff I veen here?" The oxygen tube in her nose chaffed.

Susan patted her shoulder. "Six days. And he has only left to go to the bathroom or get water."

"I think the man is in love with you." Mom's soft fingertips caressed Hope's hair. "He has fasted and prayed the entire time."

"Janie?" A deep-seated need to see Janie washed over Hope after overhearing her sister's name mentioned earlier while semi-conscious.

"I think she snuck in here at least once a day and stood outside your door for hours." Daddy's gentle squeeze locked in childhood memories. "Since she came days ago, she hasn't left except to eat and clean up. I don't think she's stopped crying either. She sent Kenny home. There's been tension between them for more than a week from what I could gather."

Hope's brow twitched. Steve might be the key to all of the questions plodding through her.

The nurse reappeared, followed by a short, thin, dark-skinned man sporting a white medical coat. "The doctor needs you all to leave for a while. He wants to examine her."

A white gleaming smile spread across the doctor's face and the skin around his eyes crinkled as he fiddled with his stethoscope. "Young lady, you had quite a few people worried, including me."

Hearing his cheerful East Indian accent and seeing his bedside manner calmed Hope's racing heart.

"We need to do a few more tests to figure out what caused this episode and find a solution." He turned to Hope's parents. "Give us an hour and a half and you can come back for a short time. Please don't overtax her."

"Doctor, what happened to her?" Mom wrung her hands. The only thing missing was Mom's dishtowel.

His soft eyes seemed filled with understanding as he looked down at Hope. "Do I have your permission to discuss this in front of these people?"

Hope nodded.

"Yes, I'll be happy to inform you then. We aren't yet sure if it is something gone haywire with your metabolism or Transient Ischemic Attack, or TIA? Our preliminary tests are still inconclusive. After we dealt with the immediate threat, we allowed your body to do its own repairs. TIA is like a mini-stroke that is most often temporary. It was probably brought on by stress from work." He shifted closer to Hope's side. "You're a little young for that. Your brother said that you were under a lot of mental and emotional strain. The problem is that this is affecting your arm and part of your face. Things are starting to look up now that you're awake. I will wait for the final diagnosis until after the tests." He turned back to her parents. "We are taking her down for another MRI. So far, so good. After that, I will talk to my patient here and let her decide if I share more information with you all."

Though the results were still out, Hope liked the guy.

"Hope, try to get some rest." Josh came forward, leaned over the rail, and kissed her forehead. The stress had fallen off his face, and yet, the moisture still remained in his red, road-mapped eyes.

Susan bent down and cheek hugged Hope. "Dopey, don't you dare scare me like that ever again."

"Doctor, can I haff Suthzun sthay here wiff me? She's my lawyer."

The doctor smiled and nodded.

Good-ole Daddy herded the other two out leaving Hope and Susan alone with the nurse and doctor.

"Okay. Doctor—" Susan leaned forward and squinted at his name tag. "—Singh, what are you not telling us?"

Hope rested for a while after the examination. Mom helped into pajamas before the rest of the family returned.

Then, Mom and Daddy inched closer on either side of Hope. Their tender touch euphoric.

"Mum and Daddy, I know you thought I mighth die, but you staring at me maketh me uncufutable. I neethud someone to vee here to helf with the doctor and nurse. I wantud Suthzun since she is my lawyer. I hope you diddent mine? Ith was easier." She glanced at Mom, shrugged, and crinkled the right side of her nose.

"Honey, I don't work and can stay here so Susan can go back to work." Mom squeezed tighter.

"Mom, what I think she needs is some legal advice to read all the hospital paperwork." Susan grinned big. "I can tell you are struggling to understand Hope. She knows I understand her slurred speech. Many times, I've been around her when she was drun—" Her face scrunched up. She fiddled with her necklace and turned away.

A typical Susan move, blurt it out to family. When Susan glanced back at Hope, Hope stuck her tongue out.

"Hope, we understand Susan being the one you need." Daddy chuckled. "After all, I don't think anyone knows you like she does." The lines in his face softened. "I'm surprised she doesn't read your mind and speak for you like a ventriloquist." He winked. "You were joined at the hip growing up. You're closer than many twins."

Susan snorted, then cleared her throat with a cough. "The doctor explained her problem." Susan looked over to Josh who sat near the door. "Hope let me know there are some things I can tell you but other items she wants to keep private." She shot Hope a look.

Hope's feeble squeeze of her parents' hands didn't ease the tightness in her chest. Still, she nodded for Susan to continue.

"Well, here we go." Susan went on to remind everyone of hers and Hope's special facial and eye communication along with certain hand and finger signals that developed over the years.

"I always knew you girls had something going on." Mom's titter sent everyone in the room into laughter. "I thought I had it figured out and then things would change. You were both too smart for me."

"Yeah, like twins and their special language." Josh repositioned his legs and chortled. "I would listen and watch them in class. The teachers were clueless. And speaking of clues, what did the doctor say?"

"You remember he said they believe it was a mini-stroke, not a full stroke. He believes the chances of a full recovery are good since we caught it just as it began. Still, she has another problem that, when mixed with the stroke, caused the coma. The coma was her body shutting down to start the repair."

Hope's stomach churned at Susan's words and the shocking possibility of no recovery.

"What's the other problem?" Daddy's furrowed brow glanced to Hope. "If you want to tell us."

Hope's quick nod to Susan continued the explanation.

"Substances that are normally found in the human anatomy can accumulate to toxic levels if the system fails to dispose of them correctly. Some examples are ammonia due to liver disease, carbon dioxide from severe asthma attack, or urea from kidney failure. Drugs and alcohol in large quantities can also disrupt neuron functioning in the brain." Susan sighed and looked to Hope.

Hope gave a prompt tilt of her head knowing her privacy was about to crash and burn.

Susan expelled a large breath through pursed lips. "Mom, Dad. Hope has a drinking problem and has been in the process of fixing it for a while. The toxin levels caught up with her body and it shut down temporarily. This process triggered the stroke. We are hoping her left side will recover completely. She will need physical therapy." Susan fiddled with the sheet. "Kelsey and I will work here while she's still in the hospital. Loriann has recovered from her injuries enough to return to take over at the receptionist desk. Once Hope is released, we'll work at my house. Josh will handle the running of both plants."

"I'm gething tired." Hope looked up at her mom.

"We understand, honey. Get some rest. We are staying at Josh and Susan's until we hear of some improvement. So, we'll be close for a while. We love you." Mom leaned to kiss her forehead.

"Love you, Punkin." Dad grasped her hand and brought it to his lips.

"Call me when you can, babe" Josh kissed Susan and lightly swatted her backside. "Talk later, Sissy. Rest."

After everyone left, Hope looked at Susan. "Ith Janie still here?"

"I believe so. Why?"

"I want to see her. Ith Stheve here?"

"No, but he told me he was running out to grab a shower and something to eat. He said that he would be back soon. Do you want me to call him?"

Hope smiled. "Go sthell Janie not to leave. When Stheve comes vack. Vring them voth."

"You want to see Janie?" Susan's eyes widened.

Hope pointed to her wrist—two fingers—head tilted to the side with closed eyes—held up one finger and made a circular motion.

"Yes, you want to rest one hour, then I'll bring Steve and Janie." Susan turned to leave. "This ought to be interesting."

What would she say to her sister? All the drama needed to end. The hurt had to go away. The Dream Stranger was correct in that. Despite the cold winter outside, the cozy room and bed warmed her. She shifted her feet under the blankets. Kenny and Janie were in love. Would it matter how angry she continued to be? Hope settled back into bed and the pillow seduced her into slumber.

CHAPTER FORTY

Hope flinched at the soft pressure on her forearm and her eyelids fought to open.

"Hope, it's been an hour. Do you need more rest?" Susan seemed to step through a cloud of blurred sleep.

Disoriented, Hope batted her eyes to bring the room into focus. As her mind cleared, her stomach turned rock hard as the realization of her location scared and depressed her. She rolled her head away from her friend as she hoped to hide from the reality.

She stared at the tubes and wished she could wipe her wet cheeks.

Beep-beep…beep-beep.

"Hope, are you okay?"

"No, not really," she whispered so softly it barely registered even to her. "I know my fathe is drawn down. I can feel it. I muth look horrible."

Susan touched Hope's shoulder. "I trust you will recover.

Hope cleared her throat. "Gif me a few seconds."

"Steve and Janie are both outside. How do you want to do this?"

But she didn't want to do it. Hope pictured a moss-covered rock with a hole under it and wished she could crawl into it. She licked her lips. What did the Dream Stranger say? Her selfishness kept her from what she needed and had created obstacles she would need to overcome. Hope's anger at Janie had built up a barrier she had to get over. But how? Once again, the Dream Stranger's response, *Forgive.*

Hope turned back to Susan. The potential of a visit with Janie created terror like a bubbling cauldron. Not trusting herself to speak she pointed to two chairs and directed Susan to place them side by side.

"What next?"

"Stheve, firsth." Hope's finger pointed at the chair to the left closest to her. "You there." She gestured to the right.

"Here?" Susan sat down. "You want Steve first, then Janie?"

Hope nodded.

Susan raised her brows. "Do you need anything from the nurses first?"

A headshake gave her response. She scrunched her eyes shut to stop the vertigo.

"Are you okay? Let me pour you some water." Susan stood and reached for the pitcher.

Hope gave a thumb up and squinted one eye to slow down the room's tilt

"Are you sure you're ready for Steve?" Susan played with her necklace again and tilted her head.

Hope opened both eyes, blew out her breath, and smiled. She watched Susan exit.

Time seemed to stand still. One minute, two minutes, a long third minute and she heard the door open.

Hope's heart skipped a beat when he came around the curtain.

With a quick and direct pace, he approached. A wide grin plastered to his face. The stressful look that covered him when she first woke up from the coma had sloughed off. His beautiful white-toothed smile replaced it. The twinkle in his eyes stirred the boiling pot in her stomach.

Susan trailed right behind.

With no hesitation, he leaned over the bed-rail and kissed her sagging, numb cheek.

Beep, beep, beep.

Hope and Susan's gaze connected and Susan grinned.

Hope's fingers brushed the spot of the kiss still feeling the sensation from his lips. She didn't want their first kiss on the side of her face, but there it was, a friendship's kiss.

If what she heard while coming out of the coma was true, why this type of kiss?

Earlier, Hope had shared with Susan what she overheard from Steve when she fought to wake up.

Susan raised her palms up and shrugged.

She continued to caress her cheek. *Maybe he thinks I'm hideous with my face all drawn down like a melted wax figure. Maybe he thinks he can hide his feelings and back out gracefully if this is permanent.*

Beep, beep, beep.

Anxiety built—her breathing labored—eyes darted. Try as she might, the numbers and equations didn't come. Where did the secret place disappear to when she needed it?

"Shhh. Take a slow breath. Don't fight it. We're here now." Steve's tender touch stroked her sweaty hair. "It's going to be okay. Do we need to call a nurse?"

With great concentration, Hope shook her head.

His fingers slid down to her cheek and pulled her hand away with slow, gentle pressure. "It's okay. I know you're scared. I know you fear it will always be like this. I believe my Heavenly Father will completely heal you, but if not, you are still beautiful to me." His sky-blue eyes sparkled out a smile.

Hope's heart flooded with love. The heart machine went back to its normal tempo.

"Thankou. I neethud that." Hope glanced to Susan and watched the tears streaking her face. Susan knew her private pain and Hope loved her for that. "Suthzun, can I gith your heff?"

Susan scooted closer. "Pastor Steve…"

"Please call me Steve. I'm only a pastor while at work."

"Okay. Steve, over the years Hope and I have developed a special way to communicate without many words. There isn't much going on in her life that I am not aware of. I am here to help her talk to you."

"I understand." His eyes never left Hope's face. "As independent as she is, she needs some help right now." He glanced at Susan for a second, but then shifted his gaze back to Hope. "She may buck, but I insist she let us help her in any way possible. At least until everything is stabilized."

"Thankou for sthayin with me. You are a good friend. I luff you for ith." The wetness rolled off her chin.

He reached to wipe the tears. "I'm ready when you are." He eased back in the chair.

Hope held up a pausing finger, looked to Susan, then pointed to the door where her sister sat outside.

"Yes, Janie promised to wait until you're ready for her."

"Are you sure you don't want to talk with her first? She is your family." Steve's forehead creased.

Hope shook her head and gestured to him with the number one.

"Hope wants you and I to be here when she sees Janie since you have spoken to her. She wants your take on it before that.

"I'm sure you do. However, I spoke to her and Kenny as a pastor, not as a friend. There are certain discretionary confidences that I cannot share. I promised. If she wants you to know, she will tell you." Steve's lips tightened into a straight line. "Hope, I would do the same for you or anyone."

Her shoulders sagged. She knew of pastor confidentiality.

"I'm glad you understand."

"Steve, Hope has some personal things she wants to speak with you about." Susan's chair sat close enough for her to reach out and touch Steve's arm.

"Some personal things?" Steve took Hope's curled left hand in both of his. "Are you sure you want to involve another person? I have nothing to hide and have no problem with Susan in this, but some things should be kept private. Don't you think?"

Hope shrugged.

Steve stood up and walked to the window. He pulled back the curtain and looked out.

Hope could see light snow drifting past the glass.

He turned. "Let's do this."

Her tension floated away like those snowflakes.

Once he settled back into his seat, he leaned forward to brush a loose strand of hair from her face. "Your caramel eyes are so full of promise and hope for the future. Full of life. No matter how this health issue plays out. You will figure it out and overcome it."

Awash with love by his words, Hope prickled with warmth. "Thankou."

"Hope, shall I start with what you heard?" Susan's brow lifted.

A nod. Hope's right hand squeezed his.

"What did you hear? Some rumor?"

She shook her head.

"Steve, we all thought she was completely unconscious and couldn't hear. But apparently, she was in and out of consciousness. She picked up bits and pieces of conversations and wants some of it clarified. She heard some of your prayers."

Hope tried to force her right-side lips to curl to what she hoped was a smile. Ahh, Pastor Steve blushes.

Hope held up her hand to stop Susan from continuing. "Things persthonal beetheen him an me, later." She replaced her hand on his and nodded for Susan to continue.

"Okay, we won't go there. I think she wants to talk to you about how she should approach the Janie and Kenny issue."

Hope shook her head. "Not, Kenny. Only Janie."

"What? You have to deal with the main issue." Susan's mouth

dropped open.

"I think I understand." Steve's face turned serious. "Kenny is secondary, but Janie's family. I get it. Since I have spoken to them already and softened things, you want me to broker a deal. Maybe an armistice between warring factions or perhaps a possible peace treaty?"

Hope shrugged.

Maybe some negotiations with the enemy could be helpful. There is too many walking wounded, and the family has suffered enough. Could she put this all behind her? What if a second stroke happened or the toxin levels couldn't be corrected? Better to bring on the conflict while she had reinforcements.

CHAPTER FORTY-ONE

Hope's stomach churned like a cement mixer. To her, the temperature within the hospital room fluctuated between hot and cold. She feared her emotions would turn to concrete and harden her path if she waited much longer to talk to Janie.

Hope tried to lean around the curtain far enough to see the room clock with no success. What was taking so long? Had Janie decided to leave? Hope drummed the fingers of her right hand on the bedsheet. Were they trying to convince Janie to stay? She tapped her hand on the bed.

When Janie had been Hope's personal assistant they never seemed to be on the same page. Their discussions always appeared forced. Would this be the same stilted conversation as in the past? She shifted her bottom, then repositioned herself again.

The angle of her body and her view felt off as she glanced toward the entrance. "Mayve a different outhlook would work." With the bed controls, she tried to get comfortable by raising the head of the bed but ended up going too far causing the pillow to slide down behind her shoulders. Hope lowered the bed partially and the pillow bunched behind her causing her to hunch forward. "Oh great! Thath's all I need. Ith's going to annoy and disthract me."

She struggled to reach behind her. After several tries, she gave up. "Thupid wireth and tuubth." Hope closed her eyes as frustration built. Once again, her hiding place evaded her. Had it become a self-imposed neurosis? Was she losing her mind? "Come on Hofe, get a grif."

The wetness forming on her cheeks gave way to her pity party. "No! Why are you doing thith now?" Panic spread. She looked up to the ceiling and pleaded. "I need to get thith under control."

No, you don't. Let Me help you get through this. This is who I am. Let Me carry you through this.

Where did that come from? The shaking began as it had when she and Josh mended their fences.

But Janie stole her husband.

Have you considered that you stole her boyfriend? Did you ever have the feelings for Kenny that you now have for Steve? Or, was your marriage a convenient access to Kenny's leadership skills you saw early in life?

Could she be so desperate to be free of it all that she concocted God's words deep in the recesses of her mind?

Defeated, Hope's shoulders drooped.

Hope heard the door open and looked up to watch Susan step around the curtain and into the room closely followed by Steve.

Hope searched for her sister.

Steve turned back to the door and whispered, "It's all right." He reached back.

The near mirror image of herself peeked around the corner. Janie now had strawberry-blond hair with brown streaks. Her eyes were a bit darker brown than Hope's caramel.

Janie's red-rimmed gaze locked onto hers and Hope heard her whimper. Her own waterfall battle began.

In a burst of speed Janie approached Hope. "Let me get that for you. That pillow must have dropped down. You look so uncomfortable."

The scent of jasmine perfume wafted across Hope's nostrils. It was Janie's scent. Neither of them could control their pronounced shaking.

"Janie!" Hope's right arm clutched onto her sister for dear life.

"I was so afraid," Janie blubbered. "So, scared I'd lose you without saying how sorry I am."

"I felth the same way."

"How are you? I mean, really, are you going to be okay?" Janie pulled back and put her hands on both of Hope's cheeks. "Will you fully recover? This isn't like you to not be going a hundred miles an hour like your hair's on fire."

Hope watched Janie's eyes dart back and forth. Real fear radiated from them. This same look had shown up when she was a junior in high school while dating Kenny when she thought herself pregnant. Her anxiety had been overpowering then. Janie's chin quivered like that now.

Hope carefully pulled her sister back into as tight a hug as her right arm could without crimping the wires and tubes. She took a quick glance toward Susan.

Susan wiped her own cheeks as fast as she could.

A blurry vision of Steve floated by. Hope squeezed her lids closed, then tried to refocus on him as he dropped to one knee and bowed his head. He seemed to do that a lot.

She watched him raise his hands and look heavenward. It could be worse. He could have been a half-conscious drunk.

Hope stared up to where Steve gazed, expecting to see a long-haired man with a beard. The glare off the lights intensified. She squinted, and for a second or two, wondered if it were possible that God and the lights were connected.

With keeping the universe from tilting, God didn't have time for small potatoes like her. Did He? He wouldn't want her anyway. Would He? She was a screwup, and God surely wouldn't want to waste His time. But she didn't have time to deal with those thoughts now. The Janie situation needed to be fixed.

The hug they shared lasted for almost a full minute.

Though nice, the embrace needed to end and the hard part had to begin. She gave a look to Susan to let her know now was the time.

"Janie, why don't you sit?" Susan lowered into the seat assigned to her as before. "Pastor, could you grab that other chair from the hallway and set it over there?" She pointed to the opposite side of the bed near Hope's knees.

Hope felt the reluctant release as Janie pulled back.

Janie's pale face looked as though she had just washed it. No makeup left to hide any blemishes.

Hope reached to the bed tray to grab some tissues. Her right hand stretched as far as possible without entanglement, and she offered the tissues to Janie.

Instead of drying her own face, Janie brushed Hope's cheeks which had been given their own recent bath.

What's going on? Not since childhood had they ever shown a closeness like this. A warmth flowed with the questions. Why was Janie being like this? The better question, why was *she*? They both broached a new territory.

Steve returned and she watched the man sit down, then Janie did the same.

He raised his brows and silently mouthed, "It's okay to love her." He extended his hand to the tissue box and extracted several. He pressed them into Hope's hand.

Without hesitation, she wiped off Janie's wet cheeks which caused Janie's tears to start again.

Once more, Steve delivered the tissues.

Again, Hope dabbed. "Please sit." She gestured to the chair.

As Janie sat, her eyes dropped to the floor. "I know it's time to face my responsibility. I'm ready. How do we do this?"

Hope raised her eyebrows. Did she really want to repair our relationship? How would they proceed? Or could they?

CHAPTER FORTY-TWO

A sour taste rose in Hope's mouth and the taste's dryness became difficult to swallow. The face to face with Janie grew more uncomfortable.

Janie continued to apologize for her past actions, then finally stopped and lowered her head.

Still several questions needed to be addressed and Hope dreaded it. She watched Susan touch Janie's shoulder.

"Hope tires easily and is struggling to speak. I'm going to try to communicate to you Hope's words as best I can. I'm glad to be part of this long-overdue conversation."

Janie lifted her head and looked at Hope, then gave a quick glance at Pastor Steve and blew out a heavy breath.

"Hope, I believe Janie wants to clear the air as much as possible." Steve patted Hope's forearm. The contact reassured her that she was not alone. "I told you both that I would not disclose to anyone what has been told to me in confidence, but I encourage the two of you to reveal what you are thinking. Honestly and kindly."

Hope nodded. She placed her hand over the tingling in her chest. Was the medical issue returning? *Can we get through this before I fall back into a coma or worse—die? I didn't want to go there. Maybe I should have jumped on board the Christian train when I had the chance.* Hope closed her eyes, took a deep breath, and released the tension. The tingling ceased and relief flooded her mind.

"I agree." Janie looked at the tissue box and its dwindling contents.

"Before this is over, I'll need another crate of those." Her lower lip trembled.

Hope smiled at Janie's attempted humor. "Me too," was all Hope could push out. She looked to Steve and to the box.

"I'm on it." Steve jumped to his feet and headed to the door. He called over his shoulder, "I'll be right back."

Susan rearranged herself in her seat. "We'll discuss the method of our communication and your agreed involvement."

Janie smiled and glanced to Susan, then back to Hope. "I don't know if that's fair. You two have that secret language you share."

Hope frowned the best she could in mock displeasure. Her chest tightened when Janie's brows furrowed and her eyelids lifted.

Janie's eyes widened. "Oh! I…I didn't mean anything by that. I just remember how I could never understand you even though a few times I tried to decipher your methods." Her chuckle sounded strained. "I thought I had it once. It suddenly changed."

"Yeah. About that." Susan crinkled her nose and clenched her teeth. "We had two different methods. We changed it every couple of weeks."

"You know, you both took Spanish and I wouldn't have understood that." Janie slid back farther in her chair. "I took French and was still at a disadvantage since smarty pants over here learned French quicker than I did and she didn't take the class."

Pastor Steve reentered the room and placed a new tissue box on the table. "What did I miss?"

"Pastor Steve, we were discussing the methods these two used to deceive everyone with their special language." Janie responded.

He laughed. "They gave me a demonstration earlier. I can see the disadvantage, but I think it's cool, too." He glanced over to Hope. "It's like the special language a Christian has with the Lord through His Holy Spirit. It comes from a special relationship similar to how you and Susan are linked together. But the believer and Jesus are bonded even closer.

It's a blood security. His blood and his love."

The poster near the church's bowling alley flashed on Hope's mind. What does Jesus want from you? Nothing but a relationship full of love, forgiveness, and friendship.

"Shall we start before we tire you out?" Janie settled into her seat.

Hope nodded.

"Hope, I'm sorry for—"

Hope's right hand shot up to halt Janie.

Janie gasped.

"You neffer sthof luffing him, did you?" Hope pointed to Susan and moved her hand in short quick signs.

Susan seemed to focus on every movement Hope made, then interpreted it without giving her opinion. "Did you ever stop loving Kenny? Did you start dating other boys to make him jealous?"

Hope pulled her hand up, swept her fingers across her brow, and past her ear. The gesture carried their distinctive sign for Kenny. Her finger and thumb went from wide to narrow.

"Or were you afraid you were getting too close to Kenny?" Susan continued.

"Yes, the possibility of living my entire life with him terrified me. We were too young." Janie bounced a curled knuckle against her mouth. "After the close call our junior year, I got scared and broke up with him. But I never stopped loving him. I wish I could have. You didn't deserve what we did." Once again, she reached for the tissues and dabbed her face.

Hope closed her eyes briefly. She pointed at herself, hiccuped, and with two fingers motioned to Janie, then to Janie's heart.

"Was Hope just a hiccup in your and Kenny's love?" Susan's interpretation spot on.

"We thought we were over each other when I came to work for you. But, being around him stirred the old feelings of love. Not just for me, either. Then you assigned projects and we were thrown together while you traveled on business." Janie closed her eyes and dropped her head. "We couldn't take it anymore. We knew it wasn't right. I mean you were still married. But we let it get out of hand and once we kissed again, we knew it wouldn't stop."

Hope clenched her teeth.

Beep-beep-beep-beep

Hope saw the immediate alarm on Janie's face.

Steve's head jerked up to view the screen. His hand drifted over and stroked Hope's forearm.

Beep-beep…beep-beep…beep-beep.

Hope shot a look to Steve and glanced heavenward. "Thankou." She turned back to Susan and nodded.

"Continue Janie."

"We planned to have him start small fights with you and have them escalate until you finally had enough and divorced him. But you caught us." Janie's full-throated whimper boiled out. "We didn't want your marriage to end that way. After you divorced him, we planned to wait a while and start dating publicly again." She brought her hands up to cover her face. "Dad always said, 'Beware your sins will find you out,' and they did."

Hope gave a few more gestures to Susan.

"Hope understands that she and Kenny were never a close couple. She focused more on the business than on him." Susan paused and scrunched her face.

Hope made a few sharp hand movements.

"She also sensed that he didn't have a great commitment to the marriage. They were more business partners than a couple. Her anger came more out of the betrayal, which put the company at risk, than a loss of love for him."

Hope pointed at Janie. "You're my sisther. I want you happy. I forgif him and you. We go slow. Mavee ith take time."

Janie took in a shuddering breath. "It's time to mend. You are my sister, and I want you happy, too. Thank you for forgiving me." She reached for Hope's limp hand. "Yes. Slow. It will take time." She raised Hope's hand and kissed it. "As long as it takes. But let's focus on getting you well first. That's the priority." She gave a quick glance at Susan. "Let me know when and where and I'll drop everything to help."

"I am tired. I neeth sleef." Hope turned to Steve. "Fleaze stay for a little while." She turned to Janie and extended her right arm. "Hug?"

"Sissy, I want desperately for this to work." Janie had not used the family nickname for Hope since she had joined Janie's eighth-grade class. "We should have done things differently." She rose from her seat and hugged Hope.

Hope watched her sister step forward to leave with Susan.

Janie turned back to face Hope and her knuckle tapped lips again as though she were thinking about something. "You may not believe it, but I missed you all these years. It's in God's hands, now." She aimed her finger toward the heavens. "I need to fix me. I have to get right with Jesus." She turned on her heel and left.

Hope looked up to where Janie pointed. Once again, the florescent lights flickered. Hope flinched. The lights freaked her out. The last two times the Dream Stranger showed up to challenge her the difficult questions were companied by a bright light. She didn't want to answer, and she hadn't wanted to engage in conversation with this…whatever or whoever He was. Yet, even in the confusion, He comforted her.

She still needed some alone time with Steve to talk about what they discussed at the church bowling lanes. But the emotions all drained her.

Exhausted, she gave a sideways glance to Steve. A yawn started and she did her best to hide it behind her hand. A wide-open mouth in her state worried her, and she didn't want Steve to see that. Even though the weight of the day pulled her quickly toward slumber she tried to fight it.

Steve's fingertips touched her hand. "You need to rest. It's been a busy day for you, and I need to check in at the church. I'll be back tomorrow evening."

Hope's eyelids drooped as he left the room. *Do they match my sagging face? Will I always be like this?*

It had been nice to have Susan and Steve help with Janie. Maybe their relationship would be better now. Could she put the past aside? A dull, hollow ache pulled at her soul and pulled her down further as Hope's eyes drifted shut.

Hope wanted the family struggle to be over. Something told her she couldn't let it go. Her personal pride now became the issue. The dishonesty and disrespect within Kenny's and her marriage needed to be dealt with. She reached up and rubbed her throbbing temples.

CHAPTER FORTY-THREE

The light merged into the darkness of her dreams as Hope's eyes eased open. She stretched her right arm and looked around. A lush meadow with a spectacular display of yellow mustard-seed flowers spread out before her. The sunlight warmed her and she pushed down the blanket to her waist.

Hope's eyes widened. "Wait! How did I get here? Who pushed my bed outside?" Stunned, she gulped in the warm air. "Where did the snow go?"

Hope, it's odd when things aren't as expected, and life goes contrary to the rational.

Behind her, the soft gentle voice startled her and she tensed. She shifted to turn her head toward the voice, but fear gripped her firmly and held her in place.

Don't look back. Don't worry, I won't harm you, but it is best you don't turn around. I took you out of your current circumstances and placed you into a comfortable location so you won't be distracted as we talk.

"You're that person I heard before while I was still in the coma." Who was he? What did he want from her? Terror struck and her body shook.

Relax. Don't be afraid, Hope. I'm more than that voice. I'm the One who put all this together. A hand waved over her head and in front of her and pointed to the beautiful landscape. *Think of me as an equation that you have yet to understand. I have watched you your entire life. I saw you as a child before science, mathematics, and your business model became your focus. You set me aside and ignored me. You only listened to the world's view. I did this*, the hand swept around her again, *to get your attention.*

"No! this can't be happening." She shook her head. "I believe you're nothing more than my imagination gone rogue. This is a random memory in my subconscious."

Okay. If that's what you want to think. Let's look at some facts. He continued speaking with a voice calm and soothing. *Are you willing to accept the possibilities if the facts hold up?*

"Yes. I want the facts." She took a deep breath to slow her thumping heart, then released it.

To answer that question forming right now within you, no, I don't normally do things this way. Only in special situations. I usually send one of My special messengers. But you needed some personal attention.

"That's only a lucky guess. In this situation, anyone would have questions." Could it be Him? Her heartbeat rose. Her breath quickened. Scary didn't begin to describe it.

Let's look at what we know. You're in the hospital because of toxic build up from excessive drinking. Your life crashed. The direction you've been going can't be continued. Now, you face a decision. It's time to make a choice between a life with Me or the direction your life has been headed. A life of peace or one of strife and conflict?

"So, I need to conjure up a make-believe god to fix things?"

No, what you need are some real solutions like everyone else. Your health depends on it. But, first, just sit here and talk with Me.

She shook her head to clear it. This isn't real. I'm not actually outside.

You're right. It couldn't be real. Or is it? Relax and we'll talk for a while.

How did that happen? Was he a mind reader? He's known what I thought twice now. Her stomach tightened at the uncertainty. The hair on the back of her neck rose causing a prickling sensation up her scalp. Could the sensations be from the affected nerves due to the stroke?

She took another cleansing breath to make her body relax. How does one debate…? Hope rubbed her hand across the knot forming in her stomach. Is it possible? Could I talk to Him and survive? A holy God? Why would He be bothered in my current state?

You're beginning to see the difficulties, aren't you?

"You're scaring me."

I can see that. Hope let's get back to our discussion. I'll let you answer some of your own questions.

Doubt crept in again. "How would you know what my questions would be? I don't know you and…" She looked out across at the meadow which reminded her of the field across from her parents' house. "you don't know me."

Oh, really?

"No, no, no. I'm not falling for that." She rubbed her forehead. Could she wipe out the possibilities and regain some semblance of control? She hoped so. "You're playing mind games." None of it made sense and she needed something to pull it back into perspective. "Oh, wait a second. Of course, You would know because You're in my head. This is a hallucinatory episode from the medication. I'm still asleep." Hope sighed. "Yes, that's what's going on."

Are you? What does your analytic mind tell you? If you were dreaming, would you dream that you were dreaming?

"You're confusing me. My thinking is off due to my illness."

Maybe ponder this. Since you were young, you have been unsure of Me. And yet, you won't research the Bible since you're afraid to find out it doesn't contradict science. Am I real? If I'm not, why have you been talking to Me lately like right now?

"Perhaps, I'm losing my mind. So, you're saying that you are Him?" She snickered. "Listen to me. I'm acting like this is really God. This defies science and logic."

He chuckled. *You know believing in Me doesn't mean you have to reject science and mathematics.*

His remark slashed at her doubts.

Of course, mankind usually thinks three dimensionally. Humans forget about time. But I defy time. You have only thought about Me as a figure in history and not in the present or the future of your life. But I would never ask you to be anything other than who I made you to be. Why can't you be independent, and yet dependent on Me?

"I don't know. I'm not thinking in a logical manner right now." His feet shuffled behind her. She rubbed her hand over the tingling goosebumps. How do you debate someone and not look them in the eye? "You don't seem concerned about me challenging You."

Who do you think gave you the ability to do what you accomplish? Who gifted your intellect? Who gave you the hiding place to lighten your strife?

His inquiries spilled over and inundated her mind. She trembled at its plausibility of a higher being and intellect. "I guess I never thought about it that way."

Deep down you have always thought Janie and Josh could connect with others and everyday life more than you. This caused your insecurities. You never feel you're enough, which is why you are self-destructive and sometimes insensitive. As you know, you are an alcoholic and always will be. It will continue to be a thorn in your side, and yet it will eventually be a blessing to others as they watch your struggle and learn from it.

Hope shifted her backside on the sheets. "Perhaps, the alcohol is causing delusions now. I'm probably desperate and need to fabricate someone superior to me like AA suggests."

Hope, would you fall for that? Think of the questions which have always plagued you with science. There are still many unanswered questions that require a larger leap of faith than believing that I am who I say I am.

"If You are who You say You are, why waste Your time with me? I have rejected God all these years. Why me?"

Why anyone, Hope? Why everyone? Remember what I told you when you were at the bowling alley? What I wanted from you?

"I wondered why I couldn't get that poster out of my head." The fears and the emotions of the last few months rushed in. "Wait. How do You know my private thoughts from that night?" She cringed and rested her head back onto the pillow. "So, You really want a one-on-one relationship with me? But why?" A tingle ran up her spine, *He—God— is so near to me. Could I be this close to God and not be crazy? Could I talk with Him like this every day? But why me?*

Because I love you, Hope. I desire to be a closer friend to you than Susan or Steve could ever be.

Could anyone be closer to her than Susan? Could anybody touch her heart more than Steve?

Hope, I need you to look at yourself by considering who I am and not comparing yourself to others. If you choose righteousness and seek Me in everything—business and personal life every day, all day—we can walk through life together. He paused. *I have come that you may have life, and that you may have it more abundantly.*

I've always thought others could do better with some effort like I did, but then I go out and create a mess of my own life. "I don't think You want someone like me. I've committed some pretty bad sins. I'm a mess."

Hope, you're not listening. His voice came across stern but gentle. *If you claim to be without sin, you deceive yourself and the truth is not in you. But if, as you say, you are full of sin, like you just did. I will be faithful and just to forgive your sin and to cleanse you from all unrighteousness. That's what I had the Apostle John write.*

"To have this kind of relationship with You, how do I fix my life?"

Do you believe that I am the Christ who will forgive all your sin? If you do, you are born of God and you will confess Me.

"The arguments are compelling." Her body shook again as her mind and heart engaged. "I want to believe. I think I always have but was afraid to admit it. You seem to know what I need to talk about. You're easy to talk to. I believe I could use You in my life."

You and I can do many wonderful things together if you'll walk with Me. But you have to start trusting Me if you want to be happy in Me.

Exhaustion swept over her and tears cascaded down her face as she brought her hand to her chest. "So, I get another chance?"

Shall we hold hands and bond in our walk together through life? His voice soft. *Hope, I did it for you. But I won't force you. If you will reach out and take My hand, I'm offering you a life full of love, forgiveness, and a friendship that will never fail.* He extended His hand past her immobile arm.

Her eyes widened. She reached out and touched the scars. A tingling ran throughout and her chest tightened.

CHAPTER FORTY-FOUR

Stifled murmurings drew Hope back from the One who would salvage her life. The dream—so real that she reached to grasp His hand.

Their talking ceased. A gasp escaped from Mom. "Look!"

Somewhere in the distance, Hope heard Susan's whispered cry, "Oh, my. She's moving her left arm."

Hope threw her eyelids open and she cried out, "Forgive me, Lord." The loss of His presence filled her and brought a crushing blow to her spirit as she stretched back for His touch deep within her dream. A jolt of energy surged through her when His and her fingertips made contact. The filth of her sins flushed away as a single drop of His blood splashed on her. Then, He was gone.

Nothing else mattered as she cried out, "I'm yours and will be forever." Hope looked to heaven and the smile formed with no tingling in her face.

After another examination, the doctor eased into the chair beside Hope's bed. He tilted his head forward to look over the rims of his glasses. His brows rose crinkling his forehead.

The nurse's eyes darted over at Hope as she fiddled with the IV.

They had investigated her ears, looked up her nose, and down her throat. Both poked and prodded with a continual line of questions.

They must have thought they were viewing an air-pocket which once held her brain when she answered all questions with one word, "Jesus." Her vision blurred with the constant shining of the flashlight. It annoyed her, but she didn't balk.

"Hey! That hurt."

"That's good." The neurologist turned to the doctor as he withdrew the pin that connected Hope to a machine in his own battery of tests. "The machine is working correctly. I'm confused. The results aren't agreeing with all the previous readings." He scratched his head and walked out pushing the machine ahead of him.

"I don't understand." Dr. Singh shook his head. "It shouldn't happen this way. Usually a finger will twitch or there will be a tickle on the toes from the blanket." He snatched his spectacles off his nose and jabbed them at her. "But never has one of my patients recovered so quickly and so completely."

Hope grabbed the brush from the bedside table and brushed with short strokes to untangle the mess her hair had become. She missed this simple self-sufficient deed over the last few days. After a flip of the covers off her feet, she reached for the IV pole, and proceeded to get out of bed.

The nurse stopped her mid-move. "No, young lady. You're not ready for that."

"I wanted to look in the mirror to make sure."

"We'll know the test results in about an hour." Dr. Singh rose to help lower Hope back into the bed. "Take it easy for a few more days. We need to be sure."

"I am sure. Jesus is with me now. Even if anything comes back, nothing will change."

"Are you going to be a difficult patient?" Nurse Betty raised her brows.

"No, I'll be good." Hope dropped back onto her pillow.

Nurse Betty's hand slipped into her scrub's pocket and withdrew a compact mirror.

"Thanks." Hope didn't want to linger and seem vain, but the need to reassure herself was overpowering, still she was awed by what Jesus did.

Hope sat Indian style on the hospital bed gazing out the frosty window. This winter had altered the direction of her life. The pressure on her bicep was one of the two reminders of her hospital stay. The other was the constant beeping sound which had drifted into background noise. For the first time she could remember, thoughts of work didn't crowd her life.

When all the medical tasks were completed, her family invaded the room.

The latest afternoon shift nurse came on duty and warned the growing group to make their visit short.

When everyone gathered around her bed, Hope turned to her brother. "Josh, could I make a request of you?"

"Sure Sissy. What can I get for you? Burgers and fries and a large cherry-coke?" His normal playful banter brought comfort.

"As tempting as that sounds, could you call Pastor Steve and ask him if he's available for a conference tomorrow morning?"

Susan moved to stand beside her husband. "He's said he'd be here tonight right after he took care of some things at the church."

Hope sighed and stared at Josh. "As much as I want to see him, let him know there is no rush and that I need some time alone with family. He'll understand."

She smiled over to Mom and Daddy, then to Janie.

"Janie? Is Kenny at home in Farmington?"

"Yes, he's at work right now. Why?" Janie winced as she glanced over to their parents.

"Do you think he could drive over here for a talk?" Hope scooted to the edge of the bed and leaned forward. "I need to speak with him."

"Yeah, I'll call, but he might not get here until late." Janie tapped her lip with her knuckle. "Are you sure?"

"Do you want to have that conversation in your delicate state?" Daddy's strong, unyielding voice rolled across the room as he stepped to her bedside.

"Daddy, I'm fine. This needs to be done for the healing to be complete. It's been the uncomfortable proverbial elephant for too long and must be confronted. It wasn't easy with Janie, but that happened before the change. I won't be alone." Hope looked up to the ceiling as a sense of calm eased her inner turmoil. "We'll deal with it."

"Punkin, I'll hand it to you, you've got moxie." He patted Hope's hand, glanced at Janie, and shook his head. "You two are going to be the death of me." He slid his other arm around his wife. "Margie, remind me again why we had girls." He laughed.

"Charles, you know God gave them to us to give us patience." Mom pulled Janie against her chest and stroked her back.

Josh turned to Susan and laughed. "See, I told you I was their favorite."

Groans crossed the room.

"Janie, Josh. Please, go take care of those things." Hope shooed them on their way, once again in control of everyone's life. Before Janie was out the door, Hope called out, "Oh, Janie, before I forget. Make sure you come in with him."

The results of her tests came in late afternoon. With a slow motion, Dr. Singh scratched his cheek as he scanned the findings. "I'm still puzzled." Hope snickered as the doctor plopped into the chair.

"This can't be right." He frowned. "According to this, there is no sign of a stroke." The doctor raised the iPad into view. "Your toxin levels are back to normal. That shouldn't happen for weeks. We'll do them again in the morning, and once you are released, we'll want to do regular checks on those levels. This is quite unusual."

Hope grinned at him. "I guess when God fixes a person, He does a complete job."

The doctor rose from his seat and looked down at Hope. "If this was any other circumstance, I would send you home. Nevertheless, due to the severity of your trauma when you came in, I still want you to stay for a couple more days for observation."

"Can I walk around the hospital and do a little work?"

"Yes, but don't overtax yourself. I'll have the nurse remove the IV and disconnect you from the heart monitor for your walks. Only short walks around the room at first to regain your strength. Later today, you can go for longer ones down the corridor." He paused by the door. "If for any reason you feel any unusual symptoms let the nurses know immediately."

"I will, doctor, and thank you for your care."

An hour later, Josh pulled out a file from his briefcase. "Hope, Parnell Industries wanted to ensure the order they made would arrive on time despite your illness."

Hope held up her hand to stop him. "Not now. Let's just enjoy each other's company. Work can wait for a little while." She smiled. "Josh, I love my work, but I'm not going to let the job consume my life like in the past. Don't get me wrong, we need to work and go forward. But I don't want it to control my life in the same way anymore."

About four-thirty, Kelsey dropped by to visit. Hope had not seen Kelsey since Hope collapsed in the office. Since Kelsey had started working for Hope, she had not seen her without her daily planner.

"How's the coffee shop going? Is Georgia doing okay? Is all this," Hope gestured around the room, "creating a problem for the café?"

"Actually, things have gone so well that we made a change. Dougie had to quit because school has become more demanding. We were able to move Cindy in as shift manager for Wednesday through Saturday. She has been such a blessing." They continued their conversation for another half hour.

After Kelsey left, Janie came in.

"Did you get hold of Kenny? Is he able to come?" For the first time in a couple of years, Hope's chest didn't constrict when she said his name.

"Yes, he was able to get off early and took tomorrow off. He will be here in a couple of hours." Janie's knuckle was at her lip again.

"Let me know when he gets here, please. Look, I know this won't be comfortable for any of us, but it needs to be dealt with." Hope's tentative smile meant to encourage, but Janie continued to tap her lip.

"Are you sure? He didn't sound like he's feeling well."

"Yes, I understand what he's going through. I'm not very excited about it either. Make sure you come in with him." Mixed emotions filled Hope. At first, she wanted him to feel bad, but hearing that he was ill didn't satisfy the long-held desire to burn him to the ground. As she inhaled a deep breath and blew it out, her anger subsided.

She wondered if the angst of an upcoming conflict with her had caused Kenny's upheaval. Her own internal alarms rang in her ears. She had to trust that quiet Voice coming from within her heart.

The rest of the family had returned and Hope looked around at them as they stared wide-eyed.

Daddy's mouth dropped open. A glare crept to his eyes.

Mom wrung her hands, shredding the tissues she held.

Hope stood up by the bed and pulled her mom under her arm and reached for daddy's hand. "I know everyone is apprehensive and a bundle of nerves, but could you leave the three of us alone when Kenny arrives? I don't know how long our talk will take. Why don't you all head home and get some rest? Play with Ginny and Heather."

Susan stepped close and whispered, "Are you sure you don't want backup?"

"I have backup in the Lord. I trust Him to get me through this." Hope patted Susan's cheek and reached to squeeze Josh's hand. "I won't belabor my talk with Kenny." She laughed. "I need to get some beauty sleep. Steve's coming by in the morning. And I want to speak to him alone." Hope winked at Susan.

CHAPTER FORTY-FIVE

Hope reclined back against her pillow and watched the family file out after the call came to let Janie know Kenny arrived. Janie followed the rest of the group in order to retrieve him.

For the first time since their breakup, Hope didn't have an upset stomach or a sour taste in her mouth due to the coming encounter. Even thoughts of running away to avoid the confrontation weren't prevalent. *Is this what the peace that believers have talked about feels like? Could Christ be the new secret hiding place?* The past battles seemed a foreign presence across the seas beyond and they couldn't touch her with Jesus now in the skirmish.

Awestruck as to how this peace came so soon after she submitted herself to the Lord, Hope looked toward the ceiling. "Though there will likely be clashes in the future, I believe You and I can handle those now that my war with You has ended."

She drew her knees up and hugged them to her chest, then stared at the opposite wall. "Lord, if Steve and I go forward, it's okay. But if not, I can live with that now. But I can't go forward without releasing this albatross that hovers over my life. Kenny and Janie need the pressure off them as well. The family needs relief and only You, Jesus, can give it."

While one hand held her knees, with the other, Hope reached for her water cup.

The door swooshed open and the sound of shuffling shoes rushed at her.

Janie peeked around the curtain. "Are you ready?"

"Yes." Hope had never paid much attention to how similar she and her sister were. Their looks and many of their mannerisms were so alike. She watched Janie suck her lip under her teeth, a trait Hope used in a state of extreme consternation.

"Sissy, do you really want me here for this?"

"Yes, absolutely. All three of us are in it, and that's the only way to get it resolved. Together."

Janie extended her hand back around the curtain and dragged a pale Kenny into the room.

His focus remained on the linoleum.

Hope understood his hesitation. He had experienced Hope's wrath even before his infidelity. Her past outbursts provided evidence of a life that showed no mercy. She hoped to change that and whispered a silent prayer, "Lord, let me show some grace and compassion for these two." Amazed at what had transpired in the previous twenty-four hours, Hope's hand covered her mouth to control her chuckle as she shook her head slowly.

Janie's eyes widened. "Ahh, we can come back later, if it would be better." Janie extended her lower lip—there was the trepidation again—but she shoved Kenny back toward the door.

"Oh no, don't go!" Hope released her knees, set the cup on the table, and dropped her legs flat onto the bed. "I was just laughing about the change that has taken place in me over the last few days. What I now feel inside astounds me." She motioned to the two chairs. "Janie, pull those even please, and both of you sit before you fall down. I'm sure you're as nervous as I am."

Janie slid over and plunked down. She glanced up to Kenny.

He sagged into the chair.

Why would he slouch? That wasn't his style. Was he so ill? Maybe she should reschedule. Another possibility hit her. She had seen him fight depression before. He went through it when they lost a big account with a large company. He fought hard for that contract but lost it over a slight technicality.

She grabbed a second drinking cup and poured water into it. She extended it to him. "You need this."

His eyes drifted up to the offering. "Thanks."

When he grasped it, their fingers touched for the first time since before the evening of discovery two years prior. Hope felt him tense. She glanced to Janie and watched her sister close her eyes and grimace.

Were they as worried about the unknown as she was? Would Kenny realize she didn't pull back? She gave him a slight smile hoping he might relax. How long had he been struggling with this burden? Was it since the restaurant incident? Was he remorseful for the betrayal or relieved to be rid of her?

Hope tucked her right foot under her other thigh and pulled her knee up to rest her chin on it. They stared across the battlefield. Would there be a conflict, an armistice, or total surrender?

Beep, beep, beep, beep.

The sound of the heart monitor's beat scolded her. The prior inner peace faded as her stomach moved to a stream of nausea. She choked it down. Hope reached for her own cup and took another sip of water. "So, here we are, and I know it's awkward. Don't worry, I'm not going to yell and scream, so, you can relax." She looked down at the call button lying beside her.

Who sighed louder, Kenny or Janie? Hard to tell.

"Kenny, as you know, Janie and I resolved some of our issues. What you don't know is that my life has taken a drastic turn. A near death experience can do that to a person. When you come close to the end, you tend to re-evaluate life."

Kenny's mouth hung open as he batted his eyes like a bullfrog in a hail-storm. Had he been living in fear, like she had?

"I…I hope you're doing better." His head dropped to his chest.

"Hope, I'm sorry for what I did to you. I wanted to explain, but you wouldn't talk to me."

"And we're not going there now." She took a quick look to Janie and tried to smile.

Janie arched a questioning brow.

Hope leaned forward to readjust her balance and continued, "I know, I would normally ask questions as to why you did it, and if you ever loved me. I have my own reasons for not chasing after that information."

Kenny jumped up and ran to the room's lavatory.

Both, Hope and Janie, wrinkled their noses and clenched their teeth as they heard him expel what had been in his stomach.

After about five minutes, he re-entered with a sheepish grin. "Sorry. This whole thing since we saw you in Rolla, and your illness, has wreaked havoc on my system." As he sat down, he brought his hands to his face. "Oh man, I'm whining about me after all you went through, and all I put you through."

For so long, she wanted to destroy them. Here they sat broken. Now, she understood Jesus' compassion for her sins and wrongdoings.

Hope watched as Kenny readjusted his chair, then his lips went into a straight line and his eyes narrowed.

She glanced to Janie and saw her eyes widen as her hand shot out and grabbed Kenny's arm. "Now's not the time, Kenny." Janie tugged on his sleeve. "Let's not do this."

"What?" Confused, Hope sucked in a sharp breath.

The beeping of the machine increased its rhythm.

Her hackles rose as she prepared for the upcoming fight.

"Do what?" Her mind's laser bored into her ex.

Sparks flickered. Could an all-out battle explode so soon after the short-lived fragile peace she had experienced and now craved?

CHAPTER FORTY-SIX

The tension in the hospital room drew as taut as a bowstring. Hope's eyes threw daggers at her ex-husband, Kenny.

Janie pulled at his shirtsleeve in desperation.

His attention jumped to Janie. "Janie, if I don't do it now, I'll never do it. Even you don't know the whole story."

"Kenny, why don't we just forget the past and go forward?" Hope glanced over to the wood-grain veneer cabinets, then to the bathroom door. Her old nature wanted to lash out despite her desire to just drop the entire untidy past. A strong need for a drink swept over her. Something to calm her. The air around her sucked away all the serenity from earlier.

Like a volcano, the magmatic anger increased and built pressure. It could blow any second. The destruction she saw coming looked destined to destroy any hope for peace in the future.

Beep-beep-beep.

Hope listened to her own ragged breath.

"No. This needs to be said." He rubbed his forehead with his fingertips. He blinked and sighed. "Hope, you and I said a lot of horrible things to each other. For that, I am sorry. You didn't deserve my remarks about you being heartless. But you must admit, you didn't make life easy. I won't get into the details because that isn't what this is about." He stood and walked to the end of the bed and placed both hands on the end rail. "It's time for me to be honest about why I married you."

Hope's muscles tighten. The lioness from her past crouched and focused on her prey ready to pounce when an opening became available. She licked her lips. Kill or be killed? Perhaps maim and disfigure.

Peace swiped away at his words. She fought the desire to vent.

She challenged. "Okay, why?"

Janie scrunched her eyes closed.

Everything needed to be out in the open. "What's wrong, Janie, don't you want to see the carnage that is about to happen?" She knew the sharpness of her remarks cut deeply and she immediately regretted it. Was she losing the inner peace the Lord had given her? She took a deep breath. "I'm sorry. I shouldn't have said that."

Janie's hands covered her ears. She clamped her mouth shut.

Kenny's voice drew Hope back. "I loved…love Janie." His tone held full emotion. "When she thought she was pregnant back in high school, we both panicked. She told me that she feared we were getting too serious. It crushed me when she handed me back her promise ring. I got angry. It didn't take long for me to start dating again."

Hope battled to control her temper. "I can see that. Girls were envious of Janie."

"As soon as I got out of the way, the guys started hitting on Janie. It wasn't long before *she* was dating again as well. Too soon as far as I was concerned." He ran his hand through his cinnamon-colored hair. "That frustrated me. I still loved her."

"Why didn't you get back together back then?"

Janie dropped her hands and threw in, "It became complicated."

"Yeah. Then it was too late. I got bitter and wouldn't even look at her. I hurt so much. I avoided her." He cleared his throat. "I managed to block her out of my life throughout our senior year. But I continued to ache for her."

Hope struggled to remember the details of the time. She had already enrolled in college courses along with completing her final high school work. As usual, too busy to pay attention to others' lives or pain.

Kenny continued. "Once at the University of Missouri, I centered my attention on my studies. Then I saw you coming across campus and decided to pursue you. Hope, this is where the story gets sticky. The day I first saw you there, you reminded me of Janie. I knew if I could date you, I would get to be near her again and perhaps fix things."

Hope's skin crawled.

"The next thing I knew you and I were married and starting SSL. My excitement for the business and what your plans entailed helped me justify the marriage. Both of us were busy with the company. We traveled for the job so much, I don't think our marriage ever settled. And then, you hired Janie." Kenny's hands gripped the railing of the bed so hard his knuckles turned white. "You threw us together on special projects while you traveled. Janie and I began talking about what happened between us."

The venom of hatred seeped out and tried to poison Hope. "So, you are blaming me?"

Beep-beep-beep-beep.

"No. I'm just letting you know how it progressed. I'm sorry."

"I see." Hope swung her legs over the edge of the bed.

The nurse swept into the room, her wide eyes darted to Hope, then to the heart machine, and back to Hope. "Are you all right?" She glanced between Janie and Kenny.

"Yes, I'm fine. I got a little excited and restless. Thank you for checking on me."

"Do you need anything?"

"Actually, I'd like to take a walk. Could you disconnect me from the heart monitor?"

"Are you sure you're okay?"

Hope nodded.

"Okay. Only a short walk. As soon as you return, we'll hook you back up." Once disconnected, the nurse left.

"Janie, could you toss me those blue slippers, and would the two of you give me a few minutes?" Hope jiggled one slipper onto her foot, shuffled into her other shoe, and grabbed her robe as she stepped out the doorway.

Hope passed the nurse's station and nodded to a pair of scrub-clad women behind the counter. Her mind scampered from one detail to the other. She made two laps around the pale green corridors before gathering enough courage to tackle the issue, all the while talking and praying with all her strength to this new Counselor in her life.

Back outside her room, she leaned against the wall beside the doorjamb to amass the grit for the possible upcoming scrimmage.

"Lord, I don't know what to do or say. I'm flabbergasted by what Kenny revealed. So, I was right to assume he carried her heart all along?"

Serenity encompassed her as though hugged in a large comforter. She muttered her reply to the empty space. "Just let them go? You're right. I'll be free of the weight, and You'll carry the burden of it all, right?" The heavy anvil pressing down on her shoulders seemed to grow wings and flew away.

She lingered for another minute, hesitant to leave the contentment. "Oh, yeah Lord, from now on, we're gonna talk a lot."

Hope pushed away from the wall and squared her shoulders. "Here we go."

Back in the room, Hope fluffed her pillow and climbed onto her bed, then leaned back. She glanced at Janie and Kenny.

"Is everything okay now?" Janie steepled her hands together, pressed them to her lips, and looked at Hope.

"Yeah, much better." Hope tested a smile. "Kenny, when I re-evaluated our whole relationship, I must confess that you fit my doctrinal business model. A model that first developed back before I entered high school. Josh and Tommy, along with Susan also fit into my hypothesis. The timing of your and Janie's breakup became a convenient vehicle to accomplish my goals."

"You mean, you used me?" From the chair beside Janie where he now sat, he straightened his back and placed his hands on his knees.

"Yes, and no." Hope twiddled her open hand. "I guess kind of like you used me."

The time to reveal her own short-comings had arrived. "I didn't understand romance. I thought I loved you because you were what I wanted and needed to go forward with my life's plan."

Kenny frowned.

"When I let you go, I lost a lot. You did your job well—until you didn't. I didn't love you romantically. I liked and needed you. It's one of the many reasons I kept your name on the company doors—and as my own. It was good for business and not romantic. I'm still a bit confused about love, but I'm sure about Jesus."

"So, your conversion to the Lord is true?" Janie leaned forward with widened eyes.

Hope nodded. "I hope I'm not too much of a disappointment to Him."

A shadow crossed Kenny's face.

"Here's the deal. I forgive you for what you did behind my back. I'm not going to interfere in it any longer. I accept your relationship as true love." Hope raised and lowered her shoulders. "If I didn't, I don't believe I could ever find true love myself. Jesus forgave me of my sins through His unmitigated love. Am I better than Him? No. So I will do the same."

"Thank you, Hope. Can we be friends again." Color flowed across Kenny's cheeks. "That's all I really want. I took advantage of the job situation, and I'm sorry."

"We both did, Kenny." The burden shifted and sloughed off. "Go make a life together. The rest," she motioned between them and herself, "will work out in time."

Janie bounded out of her chair and threw herself into Hope's arms.

"Thank you, Sissy." She pulled back and stared at her. "Is it true what the family's saying about Pastor Steve?"

Hope sucked in her lower lip and shrugged. "We're meeting in the morning to discuss things. It's a delicate situation. But my love for Christ is here to stay no matter how Steve and I proceed." She smiled. "And yes, as I'm beginning to understand love, with as much as I know, I believe I'm hopelessly in love with the man."

She turned away to grab her cup of water wishing it was doctored with something. The struggle still real. Her smile faded.

Why couldn't this desire just disappear? But with the acknowledgement of her weakness, the urge drifted away. Would Steve think she converted to please him? Could she live without him? Could she still be his friend? The next morning would be the test.

CHAPTER FORTY-SEVEN

Awake and restless since too early, Hope searched the dark corners of her room for some answers. A nurse came in and offered her something for sleep.

"No, thank you, but would it be possible to be disconnected again from the machine so I could take a walk for a bit?" Perhaps walking would help bring clarity to the jumbled mess in her mind.

The nurse did as Hope asked.

What are my options if things with Steve don't go the way I desire? Could I deal with the loss of his friendship … if not more?

A soft sigh broke through and chided her.

"How quickly I forget." She glanced around as she rounded the corner of the corridor and chuckled. "I should have been discussing this with You, Jesus."

Midway down the hall, Hope stopped and leaned back placing her hands against the smooth handrail behind her.

"I'm new to talking to You." What she saw Steve do and what her mother told her about showing reverence to God was more reasonable now. Her position with a holy God and His cleansing of her sin made so much more sense. "How do I do the reverent part and not make a spectacle of myself?"

"The draw for more from You has become personal. Am I selfish to desire You to a greater degree, or could it just be my own intellectual cravings? What do I do now? Do I have to kneel down? Bow my head? Close my eyes to show how great You are?" Her lower lip sucked in under her teeth while her eyes darted to each end of the hallway. "You told me I could be myself. I could be independent, and You would help me."

The quiet voice in her head whispered and she responded to it.

"That's a good question. Do I respect my parents? Of course. How would I speak with them? There are things I don't share with them. At those times I go to Susan. Oh yeah, I forgot to tell You, I love You." The worry deserted her.

She pushed off the wall and continued down the passageway. As she passed the nurses' station, she spotted the wall clock—Four-ten a.m.

"Okay, where do we go from here? I want to get to know You better. I want to know who You really are."

Hope cupped her hand over her mouth to stifle the laughter that escaped. "I think Steve was right when he said that in any relationship to get to know someone better, you need to understand who that person is and what is expected within that relationship. Man is he going to be surprised that I actually listened to him. But, how do I do that with You?" She blew out a breath and continued down the hall. "I guess the way to get to know You is to first talk to You and to others that know You. Do I start at the beginning in Genesis? I tried that before and didn't get very far.

"Right now, I need a mentor more than a boyfriend and husband. Thank you for that insight."

She paused beside the entrance of her room with the urge to get some work done. "Okay. Nice talking to You, Jesus. I feel weird carrying on this casual discussion with You. I mean You are holy and I'm not. I have issues, like the drinking and the arrogance of always thinking I'm the smartest in the room. I need help to overcome these concerns. I feel —hopeless.

"What happens if I fail again? Will I be able to hear You anymore? If You don't speak to me inside my head, how will I know what to do?"

Frustrated, she leaned her forehead against the doorjamb and let the tears cascade. But the inner dialogue with the Lord didn't continue.

"Ms. Sparks? Are you okay?" A gentle hand landed on Hope's back.

Hope tensed at the soft touch, and yet the words of concern warmed her.

The middle-aged nurse with the New England accent intruded into her private world. "Do you need me to help you back to your bed?"

Hope turned to face her. "No, no, I'm fine. I was talking to someone." She looked to the ceiling. Relief passed over Hope as the words left her mouth. Other than her one-word answers to the doctor and nurse, it was the first time she admitted her new-found faith to someone outside of family. It felt good to let it out.

The nurse nodded

"I was talking to Jesus. I'm a new Christian and new to praying." She looked down at the nurse's cute, pixie face and petite frame. Hope's wet cheeks flushed.

A smile crossed the woman's face. "Then, you're okay physically?"

"Yeah."

"You're the miracle lady. That's what we call you on this floor." The nurse reached into her scrub's pocket and withdrew a tissue and offered it to Hope. "My name is Barbara." The name sounded more like Bobb-raw. "But my friends call me Bobbie."

Though they had just met, a familiarity washed over Hope as though she knew the woman in a deeper sense. A similar feeling came the day before while interacting with Mom and Daddy. Something more profound than family bonds. That same awareness embedded itself.

"Excuse me for my rudeness. Did you say Barbie or Bobbie?"

"Yes, that's what I said." Bobbie's smile rolled over her face and she winked.

"Which?"

"Does it matter? I answer to both. It's a New Hampshire thing." Her accent made the state sound like Hampchur instead.

Hope sputtered out her laughter. "I'm happy to meet you, Bobbie. I'm Hope."

Bobbie grinned, then turned serious. "Hope, regarding you speaking to someone. I talk to Him all the time." She pointed up. "I've been a Christian since I was a teenager. The Bible tells us to pray without ceasing. My husband and I recently came back from the mission field in South Korea. He's a surgeon working here at the hospital. We've depended on our conversations with the Lord."

"Can I ask you a question?"

"Sure, anything to help. Would you like to step back into your room?"

Hope nodded.

As she settled back against the headboard, she watched Bobbie adjust herself into the chair beside the window. "Don't you have patients that need you?"

"Is that the question?" She gave Hope a wink and a grin. "Yes, I have patients. Thankfully for the moment they are all sleeping, and I haven't had a break all night. Haven't even had time to grab a bite to eat."

Hope relaxed. "I don't want to hold you up."

"No problem. Someone is covering for me. I usually meet with my husband for breakfast when I get off. I needed to sit down. My feet were killing me." Bobbie pulled her foot up and rubbed her toes. "Now, what was the real question you had?"

"Like I said, I'm a new Christian. What if I slip up and fail Him?" *Should I tell her everything? I don't know her. Still, there seems to be a closeness to her. Could I open myself up to a stranger like this?* "I don't want to lose what I have with the Lord."

Hope pulled her knees up to her chest and dropped her forehead down. Then, she raised her eyes to meet Bobbie's face. "I'm an alcoholic. As you may know, I'm here because my toxin levels got out of whack. I fear I might fall back into my old life and fail to hear Him anymore. If I stop hearing Him, how do I get back the connection?"

"So, what you are asking is, what happens when you fall into sin again? Did you notice I said sin and not just drinking?" Bobbie's eyebrows arched. "All sin, not only our greatest weaknesses, separates us from His holiness. When we sin and don't immediately repent, we move farther from holiness and the close relationship with God. It becomes easier to take another step back into the old sinful pattern until we make excuses for our behavior and give in to our old self and that lifestyle."

"I didn't think about that. I guess when I get frustrated with how things go at the office and let it fester, I get angry and disappointed, then I want a drink."

"Sometimes it comes when we anticipate a certain result and misunderstand or are misinformed. The result—we jump to a wrong conclusion. We can run with our assumptions until we are weakened and in our exhausted sinful state, we give up and fall further into our old nature. We need a way to get back. That's where God's word, the Bible, can help bring us back to a right standing with God. It can also aid in not stepping into sin in the first place."

"So, the Bible is where I get the answers?" Hope stood up from the bed and walked over to the window. She pulled open the curtain and looked out into the darkness. "Where do I start?"

"After I received Christ as my Savior, I needed to get to know Him. My youth pastor told me I should start reading in the Gospel of John. I would also suggest reading some of the Psalms and Proverbs as well. They will comfort you and give you wisdom. The Apostle Peter says in 1 Peter 2:2-3, 'As newborn babes, desire the pure milk of the word, that you may grow thereby, if indeed you have tasted that the Lord is gracious.'"

"So, I should get to know Him more directly and ask God to help me understand what He means in the Bible." Hope scrunched her brows and pressed her back against the wall. "Where have I heard that before? Steve."

"Steve? I don't understand."

"Steve, my friend. He never left my bedside while I was in a coma and prayed for me."

"Oh, Pastor Steve Burrow. I never saw him except when he entered or left your room." Bobbie's mouth dropped open. "Wait, you're his friend the prayer request was about at church. He hasn't been at the church that long since he moved here from Kansas City. My husband met him, but I have only seen him from down the hall. Where did you meet him?"

"It's a long story." Hope walked back to the bed and crawled in. Her eyes burned, and she stifled a yawn. A nap would be beneficial before Steve arrived. "Steve said that in order to know anyone well in any relationship, we needed to learn as much as we could about that person. He is a true friend and stood by me despite my self-destructive path. Maybe, he will help teach me how to know Jesus better."

Bobbie rose from her chair. "Has your doctor decided when you'll be released?"

"I hope today. They'll probably hold me until tomorrow to be sure. We're waiting for more test results."

"You look tired. Perhaps a nap will help. I need to do my rounds. My shift will be over soon." Bobbie's tiny hand patted Hope's leg. "If you ever have any questions, feel free to stop by and ask," she smiled, "especially, if you can't sleep."

"I don't think that is going to be a problem right now. I want to be fresh for when Steve comes."

CHAPTER FORTY-EIGHT

With tired eyes, Hope watched Bobbie bounce out of the room. The hospital's morning regimen usually bored Hope. And this day appeared no different except for meeting Bobbie. Why did everyone here seem to have a wait-and-see attitude toward healthcare.

Life needed to move forward, especially in business. Still, she didn't want to cause problems. The hospital staff treated her like a delicate flower that might break. When they coddled her, she smiled and thanked them for their care, while she gritted her teeth.

Hope glanced at the clock after Bobbie left. Four-forty-five. In spite of her eyes burning, she had a pressing need that couldn't wait. It called her from the bedside drawer, and she couldn't ignore it. The intensity built to the point that it rivaled her desire to build a thriving company.

She slid the drawer open and withdrew the Bible Mom loaned her. Jesus had been the mystery man in the dreams while she slept. Now she wanted—no needed—to know who He was. Bobbie might be right when she said the answers could be found in this book, but where?

Bobbie had mentioned the Gospel of John. Wasn't that located in the New Testament and the New Testament was in the second half of the Bible? She flipped to the back and worked forward.

Hope read the first words that she saw from the book of James. "Therefore lay aside all filthiness and overflow of wickedness, and receive with meekness the implanted word, which is able to save your souls. But be doers of the word, and not hearers only, deceiving yourselves.

For if anyone is a hearer of the word and not a doer, he is like a man observing his natural face in a mirror; for he observes himself, goes away, and immediately forgets what kind of man he was."

Hope had always been a practical person. Serviceable information is what she wanted. The writer looked to be a rational person. Could she work with a practical God? Yes, she could. She would keep this book of James handy. Continuing to turn the pages, she found the Gospel of John.

The contrast of light and darkness the writer of John spoke of in the first chapter, intrigued Hope. Though she wanted to stay awake and learn more, her body wouldn't comply. Her eyelids drooped and she resigned herself to get some rest. She fluffed her pillow. The limited noise in the hallway helped welcome the quiet as she contemplated the Light of the world.

Her time in the hospital shed light on the darkness her life had become. Her drinking created the chaos that had been her world. God had spotlighted her behavior and directed her to see it for what it was—sin.

Still five hours until Steve returned, the day's strain caught up to her. She rolled to her side and closed her eyes.

Clatter, tink.

Hope jerked awake as her heart leaped from her chest.

"Good morning, sleepyhead," the cheerful assistant chirped while rearranging the breakfast plate on the bed table.

"Morning." Hope clutched the front of her pajamas and attempted to slow down her racing heart. *Deep breath. And again.*

"Did I startle you, hon?"

"A little. I must have dozed off. What time is it?"

"It's eight o'clock."

"Uh oh. I better hurry and eat. I have to shower and get ready for my friend that's coming."

An hour and a half later Hope scrambled back onto her freshly made bed to wait for Steve and the doctor. Anxiety grew with every passing moment. She shifted her position. Her legs trembled. Restless legs? Now? The desire to get up and pace built. Calm didn't seem an option as she shuffled and bounced her calves on the bed's surface.

Hope glanced at the curtain on the entrance side of the room for a third time. Its distraction irritated her. She couldn't contain it anymore, she jumped up and dragged the offending drapery open. With quick movements, she climbed back into position on the bed. "I can't wait to see his face and to tell him of my dream and of Jesus. He'll be so shocked."

She punched her pillows to get the right consistency and leaned back. Maybe a talk with the Lord would help.

After draping her right arm across her forehead and eyes, she started her prayer. A couple of minutes into it, footsteps sounded nearby.

"Hope? Are you awake?" His voice—music to her ears.

"Uh huh." She kept her face cloaked beneath her arm to hide her grin.

"How are you doing this morning? How was yesterday?"

Chair legs scraped across the floor and she peeked over her forearm.

His forehead creased with worry. He scrunched his nose and his eyelids dropped halfway over his magnificent blue eyes.

Why toy with him like this? But the thrill of it spurred her on. She watched him glance around the room and determined not to make him suffer any longer. When he glanced toward the door, Hope dropped her masquerade.

Steve turned back to face her. The puzzled expression on his face lasted several seconds like he needed to replace some missing pieces.

Hope fought a giggle.

He batted his baby-blues like the shutters of a camera would adjust his focus—the longer stare—the open mouth—but no sound came out.

"I hope you weren't getting used to the new look. Someone didn't like it on me and chose to return me to my former self. Is that okay with you?"

"Oh, my goodness! Praise God!" He leaped out of his seat, threw both hands over his ears, and quickly paced the room. He stopped, stared, and wiped at his eyes and face.

Hope could hear his labored breathing. She laughed.

He sounded like a slow-moving steam locomotive straining to leave the platform. He huffed and puffed and paced, then repeated the cycle.

"Whoa. Praise the Lord." He sat back into the chair. His eyes bulged as he continued to stare. Up again to march more. His arms shot straight up, and his hands waved. "My Father's so good. My Father's so good. Praise His holy name."

Hope jumped out of bed to join him in a joyful dance. She couldn't help but unite in the revelry with her own shouts of praise. "My Father's so good. My Father's so good." With her arms raised high, she hip-bumped Steve.

It didn't take long for the nurses to rush in.

After establishing her welfare, the two nurses laughed and clapped to the dance Hope and Steve shared in.

In the middle of their jubilation, Hope spun around and spotted her doctor whose smile spread across his face.

All the excitement winded Hope, but Steve did a jig and pumped his arms like a prize-fighter. Her heart pounded. She sat on the edge of the bed exhausted and fanned herself with both hands.

"Doctor, I'm out of shape and out of breath. What should I do to remedy that?" She smiled as large as her mouth would allow. Hope glanced back over to Steve and felt herself flush again, then her attention moved toward the doctor once more.

"Well, my prognosis is for you to rest one more night. In the morning, gather your things and go home to recuperate. Don't be in too much of a hurry, but work to build up your stamina and don't rush back into the office. Ease in. Call my office and set up an appointment for two weeks. Also call my office if you have any, and I mean any issues." Dr. Singh smiled and pulled his stethoscope from around his neck. "The test results were all negative which is what we want. Let's do a quick check just to make sure everything is good after your little performance."

Hope tried to force her rapid breathing to subside. Though difficult, she needed to pull her focus off Steve and onto the doctor, otherwise, her heart rate would never slow down. She looked at Dr. Singh before she spoke to Steve. "Hear that, Steve? I get to go home. Do you think I can catch a ride with you tomorrow?"

Hope laughed at the stunned, fish-out-of-water look on Steve's face. Her memory's album now had a lifetime portrait embedded in it she would cherish. "We have to talk about what happened since I last saw you. A lot has changed, my friend."

CHAPTER FORTY-NINE

After their audience left, Hope leaned back on her pillow. "Steve, please come sit. I have an exciting story to tell you." She pointed to a chair close to the bed. Her new life in Christ and His goodness filled her with wonder. Better than good, tremendous had to be the operative word for what flooded her. And she wanted to share it with the man she loved.

"This whole situation is exciting. I've never actually witnessed a miracle before, and I wish I had been here when it took place. Were you by yourself when it happened?"

"No, my mom, dad, Susan, and Janie had just come into the room. I was asleep and having the dream. You'll have to get their perspective of what they saw."

A bewildered look crossed Steve's face. "The dream?" He adjusted himself in the chair. His intense stare a look of concentration and his mouth gaped open. "What dream? Tell me what happened."

Hope leaned forward and grabbed both his hands. "Yes, the Dream with a capital D." She wiggled her backside to get comfortable, then shivered.

"Well?" Steve's eyes widened even more.

Hope chuckled. Apparently, excitement about Jesus was contagious.

"If you remember the other night, though sleep was taking over, I watched you walk out. I don't know how long I slept. I was amazed that I woke up feeling so refreshed. Now, here's the odd thing." She reached over and squeezed his fingers. The softness of his palms contrasted with the calluses on his fingertips. "I didn't wake up in the hospital."

"Excuse me?" Steve leaned back, looked at her with a tilted head, pursed lips, and a wrinkled brow.

"I know you think I've lost it. I would ask you to guess where I ended up, but there is no way you could." The pressure on her cheeks from the wide smile hurt. She rubbed her face. "I was looking out at a meadow with beautiful springtime flowers. I couldn't believe it." The gravity of what she wanted to say struck her and goose bumps popped up on her arms.

"Steve, it was like someone touched my shoulders and held me in place. A voice told me not to look at Him."

"Who touched you? You mean, in your dream?"

"That's just it, Steve. I don't know if it was a dream or if it was real."

Steve nodded. "I think I understand. The Bible tells of the Apostle Paul having a vision of going to the third heaven? He had an experience and said he didn't know if it was a dream or if he died. He knew what he went through and still didn't know how it took place."

"Steve, I felt things. Physical and emotional things like never before in a dream or nightmare." She pulled her hand free of him and clasped them to her chest. "I sensed a peace when He spoke, and yet, He challenged my intellect like I've never been tested before. Not high-end mathematical equations, even though He spoke of those. He debated common sense things that always bothered me. He knew exactly what to ask."

Steve closed his eyes and sighed. "Hope, since I first trusted in Jesus, I hoped to have a close experience with Him like you're describing." He opened his eyes and his stare grew intense. "How long did He speak with you?"

"It seemed all day long, but I don't know for sure. His final test came when He extended His hand to my left immobile hand and invited me to reach out and take it. My need to respond to Him overpowered me. I just reached out for Him. I needed to feel His touch."

Steve sighed and his body shuddered as tears trickled down his face. He stood and moved toward Hope.

He had been right all along. The bond solidified their relationship beyond the physical desire. They shared a different kind of hug than before—easy and innocent.

Could the rest of their relationship be set aside? Would this be all they had? Had God put them together at the mission those months ago for this purpose alone?

Hope pulled herself away from Steve. "I know that Susan and I followed our friends as children when we were baptized. I didn't understand. Susan got rebaptized when she made a personal decision for Christ a couple of years ago. Now that I am a new believer, in this relationship with God, I need to be baptized again. I have a request, if you are willing."

"What's that, Hope?"

"Could you mentor me? With all my education, I'm a dunce when it comes to the Bible. You were right, I need to get to know Jesus and everything I can about God." She reached up and touched his cheek. "Thank you for everything you have done. You went beyond the call of duty. You have shown me the love of the Lord through your actions. I will be eternally grateful."

Over the next two hours they discussed her talk with Kenny and Janie, her meeting Bobbie, the nurse-missionary, and various other minor things including an agenda for a discipleship program. Right before lunch came, Steve let her know that he needed to return to the church and call the director of Victory mission.

"So, Steve, are you going to start helping out there like you did in Kansas City?" She lightly finger-tapped him on the chest. "There are a lot of Gus's out there who need your heart of compassion."

"I'm thinking seriously about it. They don't have anyone but a handful of men to get it done. The director says that he will be retiring soon, and they need to have someone with experience to step in to help organize things."

Steve fidgeted and looked away.

"What's going on? What's troubling you?"

He walked to the window and pulled back the drapes.

She waited. A longing stirred within.

When he turned, his eyes burned a hole into her.

"Now that you are a Christian, I would like to officially ask you out. But, if you want to wait until everything settles, I am willing. I don't want to hurry you. I have a pretty good idea of how I feel about you."

Hope's smile stretched across her face. "Yeah, about that. Susan told you that I heard some things while I was semi-conscious. I think I love you, too. Like you said, let's not rush into something. If the Lord wants it, it will happen."

After two weeks of working at home with Susan and Kelsey under Mom's constant supervision, Hope stepped into her office for her first full day back.

As she walked from the parking lot, the large, front shipping bay door rose. The entire employee family materialized in front of her. Thunderous applause rang out.

Hope tried to keep the welcome subdued. A chill ran up her spine while a contrasting warmth swept through her heart for these dedicated individuals. Could their welcome have more to do with job security, now that she was back running the company than any personal attachment to her? They were understandably, concerned about their job first, then money and their family's well-being. *Rational thinking says they are devoted to their employment and by extension, to me. I can understand and live with it as such. After all, I am the boss.* Another smile spread across her face.

Now back full-time, Hope stood with the office door wide open and stared. It looked different, and yet, comfortable—like home. She had already welcomed Loriann back from her injury.

Hope called over her shoulder, "Loriann, do I have any messages?"

"Yes, Ms. Sparks. Let me get them for you."

"Thank you." She turned and looked at her receptionist. "I want to tell you how much I appreciate what you do around here. How's the pregnancy coming along?"

Loriann scooped up Hope's messages as she pushed herself up from her chair. "Three more long months."

Hope couldn't imagine the discomfort the woman must be experiencing. Still, Loriann's face carried a glow.

"If it gets to be too much, let me know and you can take an occasional day off." *What am I thinking? In the past I would be irritated that she couldn't get the job done, and now I'm offering time off?* Hope shook her head, turned back, then noticed Loriann's slight limp from the ankle injury slowing her down.

"Thank you for the offer Ms. Sparks. As it stands now, I'm doing fine."

"Here, let me take those." She reached back to take the notes. "How's the ankle? You need to stay off it as much as possible." Hope's business intuition jumped to the forefront. "We don't need you to reinjure it, especially here on the job. We can't afford any workplace injuries. Go back to your desk. With that slowing you down, you won't be able to get to the phone quickly, and we don't want to lose any business calls." Hope smiled and winked.

Hope slid into her chair and glanced around her office. What had gotten into her with this attitude? This wasn't her usual mindset. Light dawned and she looked at the ceiling, then nodded. Jesus changes everything.

Not long after Hope's exit from the hospital, she joined a

discipleship program with Bobbie, her nurse. She felt like a whole new world opened up to her as she read God's words with understanding for the first time. Now, she saw most things in a different light.

During their dates, Steve took his time to explain anything she still did not understand.

There were times when Hope's thinking would run ahead because she wanted to absorb as much as she could.

Steve's gentle manner kept her centered and in check, not allowing her attention to run amuck.

The longer she spent around him, the more she appreciated his intelligence. She smiled across the table. "Steve, what was your G.P.A. in college?"

"I passed."

"Come on, I told you mine."

He shrugged. "I graduated with a three-point-four."

"Not bad. You made the honor roll." Hope opened the Bible to the passage he was attempting to explain to her. She paused as what he said sunk in. "Wait a minute. Your cumulative grade point average was what? I thought you flunked out when you first went to college. If that's the case then you got almost straight A's the whole time you were in seminary."

Steve shrugged.

Could there be more to this man than a loving soul and deep mesmerizing eyes? He never ceased to surprise her. The mystery of this man became her challenge. Hope loved a challenge.

CHAPTER FIFTY

Late April, Springfield

The week following Hope's return to work, she stood waist deep in the lukewarm baptismal waters beside Steve. She gave a quick glance out into the large audience of First Baptist Church—the entire third row filled with family and friends.

Steve's strong baritone voice quavered. "I almost can't believe I'm standing here with this young woman. I won't go into detail as to the path she traveled to make it to this point in her life. That is her story. I have had the honor of making part of the journey with her."

He placed his hand at the base of her neck and gave a tender squeeze.

She shivered at his touch.

"Hope Sparks, do you believe that Jesus has forgiven your sins? Do you desire to live your days following Jesus as your Lord?"

Hope straightened her shoulders. "Yes, I do."

"Based on that profession of faith, I baptize you, my sister, in the name of the Father, and the Son, and the Holy Spirit. Buried in the likeness of His death and raised in the likeness of His resurrection."

The water rushed over her face, and her spirit soared.

As she came out of the water, shouts erupted from the third row. Hope flushed.

Hope's phone rang and a tingle from the smile drifted across her

face when she saw the number on her screen. She lifted the mobile to
her ear.

"Hi. How's my girlfriend doing?" Steve's singsong greeting brought a
fullness to her.

Now pleasant thoughts lingered long after their last date and the
smoldering kiss at her front door.

"I like the sound of that. What's up?"

"I have been asked to go to Kansas City and preach next Sunday at
my previous church, Hope Harvest Community."

"Wow, that's weird." She twisted a strand of hair around her finger.

"How's that weird?"

"Next Friday, all our top management has been invited to a special
meeting at Scranton in Kansas City. Tommy's bringing Anne."

"It is odd. I thought I might go up Friday, then go down to the
mission on Saturday morning to help out with the breakfast."

"Steve, I have an idea." She bit the corner of her mouth. "How
about if I meet you down at the mission and we can help out together in
honor of Gus?"

"Would you have time with your schedule?"

"I'll make it work."

Disappointed with the meeting the day before at Scranton, Hope slid
into her Mercedes. Management in both companies seemed to be
enthusiastic about what had been discussed. But Hope saw it as nothing
more than rehashing old agendas.

As she started up Baby, a sigh escaped and she smiled. The weekend
wouldn't be a total loss as she'd at least get to spend time with Steve at
the mission and stay for church on Sunday.

Ten minutes later, she pulled up to the curb and watched the line
form at the front door of the place that changed her life. Her opinion of
the huddled masses had transformed since her first visit. She picked out

a few people to observe. Her mind went back to months prior and a scruffy old man named Gus in a dirty, navy blue peacoat jacket, coughing and hacking in spite of the springtime warmth.

A tear trickled down at the remembrance of those few short minutes of interaction with a man that helped redirect her life. Heat crossed her cheeks at the crafty, ole Gus's sneaky introduction to the good-looking preacher almost a year before. She reached for the door handle and chuckled. What a year.

Hope entered the building and wandered through the crowd scanning faces looking for Steve. With her focus on seeking him out, she hadn't paid much attention to individual faces she passed. She approached the serving table planning to step around to offer her services and almost bumped into the first attendant. When she dodged the man, she did a double take.

"Josh? What are you doing here?"

He grinned. "Doing the same as them." He pointed his tongs down the line.

Hope gazed down the multiple serving tables. Stunned, her mouth dropped open.

Susan, William, Gloria, Tommy, and Annie doled out entrées to the indigent crowd. She spotted two more helpers down the line. What? Mom and Daddy? What were they doing here?

"Have you seen Steve?"

"Over there, I think." Josh pointed to another table.

Hope followed the direction he pointed.

Janie pulled coffee cups out of plastic wrap and directed Kenny to place spoons close by.

Hope brought her hand up to her mouth as her eyes darted about the cafeteria. Why hadn't Steve told her when they spoke last night that everyone would be here? She spotted him behind Kenny and Janie coming out the door of the kitchen carrying another container.

Their eyes locked and the shock of his sky-blue eyes jolted her as they did the first day she looked into them almost a year before.

He smiled. "Where's your apron? Don't gawk," he winked at her, "get busy."

She wanted to get busy wrapping her arms around him and pressing her lips to his. She snickered.

As the breakfast wound down, Steve told all the help to grab a plate and settle in over at the tables near the side door while he took care of a few lingering obligations.

After Hope filled her plate, she waited for her daddy.

"Hope, Steve has a great heart for the homeless." Her dad placed his hand on Hope's back to guide her toward a table. "I admire that in a man. Not many have such compassion."

"Daddy, Steve is quite a servant of the Lord. If not for him, I wouldn't have Christ in my life and we wouldn't be having this conversation." Hope looked up at her father. "Did you and Mom come up here just to feed the homeless?"

"We heard he was preaching at the church here and wanted to see it and hear him."

Ten minutes later, a hand touched Hope's shoulder. She turned and stared into the deep pool of Steve's eyes and her breath caught. After she regained control, she stammered, "There was a huge crowd today."

"Yeah." He glanced around. "Hope, do you recognized where you are sitting?"

Hope did a quick scan. She looked over to the table behind her less than ten feet away.

"Gus sat right there when he introduced us that day." Steve pointed.

She brought her finger up to wipe the tear that dripped to her chin. When she turned back to Steve, her eyes widened.

Steve knelt on one knee before her chair with a small box open.

Speechless, she struggled to breathe as her head quickly bobbed.

<u>*Epilogue*</u>

Early May 2018, Springfield

Six years of continued hard work had paid off as Hope placed her hands on the podium and smiled while the applause died down. Her heart swelled with emotion as she looked down at her husband whose face glowed. Surrounded by family members, Steve smiled up at her. The Springfield Chamber of Commerce had gone the extra mile by putting this evening together.

Every year the Chamber offered the Small Business Award. But this year they combined it with another award.

The first presentation caused her to almost burst with pride. The citation sat on the table in front of Steve.

Her eyes could not leave his face as Steve laid his plaque alongside the large ornamental Key to the City given for his work as director of the mission and other satellite operations.

Hope had reason to be overjoyed. She worked hard and had coveted this recognition for years. Her part seemed minor and not what caused her delight tonight. Still, the reminder of her earlier stomach cramps while listening to Steve's speech rushed to the forefront and caused her to crumple her notes. If the throbbing heartbeat in her ears continued as it had before, the cramps would soon return.

Hope pointed to the man. "Please, another round of applause for the director of our local mission, my husband, Pastor Steve Burrow."

She stepped to the side away from the microphone to listen to the thunderous acclaim and whispered her plea to God. "Lord, let me get through this before it hits me again. The anticipation of this moment and my anxiety have collided. Let the other hold off until later."

As the clapping dwindled, she stepped back, smoothed out her wrinkled notes, and took a deep breath.

Her mind shot back to her high school Valedictorian and college Salutatorian speeches and the nerves that crested over her personal barriers—the same obstacles that tried to overwhelm her now. She forced a smile and looked across the faces of the crowd.

Her hands fidgeted with her papers. "I want to thank the Chamber of Commerce for the opportunity to share the story of Sparks System Logistics.

"I know that you all want to hear the boring details of how it started and its long rise to what it is today." She chuckled as the butterflies fluttered inside. The crowd laughed with her. "But, tonight, I'm going to let you in on a secret. Success is measured in how you recover from your failures and adjust to the changes that must take place. My story of success began when my life bottomed out. It takes us back to our previous award winner, Pastor Steve Burrow. I occasionally give speeches at some local venues and tonight I want to start with my opening remarks like I always do."

Hope squared her shoulders and glanced around the room.

"Hello, my name is Hope Hart Sparks Burrow. I am an alcoholic. I have not had a drink for six years, five months, and thirteen days. I first met Pastor Steve Burrow the morning after I hit rock bottom." She reached for the cup of water provided for her and took a sip. "While celebrating a wonderful success with my dear friend, William Scranton of Scranton Corp," she gestured toward William and Gloria. "I drank myself into an incognizant state. Dressed in my party dress and heels, I crashed a morning breakfast at a mission in Kansas City. There I met the man who God would use to change my life. A man who had compassion for this prideful, arrogant woman. He introduced me to his best friend, Jesus. At that point, the battle began for the success of my business and the mastery of my life."

Pain clutched Hope's abdomen, and she scrunched her eyes closed. She raised her pointer finger to request a moment while she rode out the wave. Many seconds later, Hope caught her breath. Her eyes opened as she resumed despite the continued discomfort.

"I heard once that all business owners must expect change. They must have a contingency plan in case things don't run smoothly. Tonight, my original speech is not going according to plan." She bit down on her inner lower lip to avoid the keening wail wanting to escape. With shaky fingers, she crumpled her notes. "I must ask my dear husband if he can go retrieve our car. We have a pressing engagement."

Hope raised her brows and tilted her head at Steve's perplexed look. She loved this man's usual intuitive mind. This time, he appeared to be lagging behind the curve. As she watched his eyebrows raise, she smiled. Another spasm washed over her and she leaned over.

Steve scooped up his plaque and ornamental key.

The scrambling whispers spread to the next table where Susan and Josh sat with Mom and Daddy.

She scanned the crowded auditorium. "These awards are so appreciated. But Steve and I are about to receive two greater rewards as my body is trying to let me know I better leave soon." An embarrassed chuckle came out. She groaned in relief as the contraction ebbed. "My assistant, Kelsey, can take over from her."

She glanced to her brother and brother-in-law. "Josh? Kenny? While Steve gets the car, could I request some assistance getting off this platform?"

Hope smiled to the cheers of the crowd. "Our son, Billy, is about to welcome his twin siblings." She raised her award high as she waddled toward the edge of the stage.

Success! Such a different meaning hangs on that word now. As Kenny and Josh helped Hope down the stairs, emotions wrapped around her. Who knew having a sound mind in Christ would have brought such change? The business thrived, and she could now deal with her developing company. With Christ at the center of life, a wonderful husband and her growing family, forgiveness had reframed any and every goal.

About the Author

James Burgess lives in Northern California with Beverly, his loving wife of forty-seven years, and his grandson, Reese. *A New Hope* is his first fiction novel. He is currently writing his second novel, *Devastatingly in Love*. James is published in three Inspire Press Anthologies: *Inspire Love, Inspire Kindness,* and *Inspire Grace*.

If you enjoyed *A New Hope* please review it on your favorite site.

You can connect with Jim on:
www.JamesBurgessAuthor.com
www.booksJamesBurgess.com